DEATH ROW BOY

NASRIN SADRIAN

Copyright © 2024 Nasrin Sadrian

All rights reserved.

ISBN: 9798884546509

To my grandchildren, Liam and Sophia.

May you and all the children of the world find safe harbor in the storm.

PART I
April 1982

CHAPTER 1

The village road was mainly free from snow, but it was in sorry condition. Last winter, the violent storms had given its surface a good beating, eroding the weak sections, leaving large, muddy puddles all along the path.

Mahmood pedaled his bicycle full throttle, trying to avoid the obstacles in his way. His friend, Ali, with him as usual, was sitting side saddle on the middle bar, jostling about.

The two young men were on a quest to steal chickens today.

Even though they were both capable and bright, neither Mahmood nor Ali had ever held a permanent job or worked in the family fields. They often loitered around the village, gambling and wrestling with the younger crowds. When they fell short on money and only if their moods agreed, the pair would go to town and work at construction sites. Stealing from the villagers, however, was always far more appealing to them than doing any physical labor.

آرش

Nervous and jittery, they rode along the lane. They passed several tiny shacks where children of all ages were scattered about – thin-legged boys running after soccer balls, giggling girls chasing each other around.

"What's with all the kids everywhere?" Mahmood complained.

"School is…out…today," Ali answered in spurts between bumps in the road.

"What for?"

"Some imam's birthday."

"Whose?"

"I do not know. We…have hundreds…of them."

"With so many damn imams, we may never get to eat chicken again!" an amused Mahmood chuckled, pedaling faster.

They steadily moved on.

Farther up, at the outskirts of the village, the road was in much better shape, almost intact. Now with an easier ride and no more children in sight, the young men were more relaxed, even able to enjoy their surroundings.

On that early spring day, the village was exceptionally beautiful. Dozens of streams were running high and low, harboring patches of melting snow. Young and old trees stood in a boundless expanse – some covered with blossoms, others gracefully unfolding their leaf buds. The wildflowers and vegetation were also vivacious, as if they had not been buried in snow just weeks ago.

The scenery had a calming effect on Ali, especially the colorful flowers amidst the vast green landscape. He wished they could afford to walk among them for a while.

A sharp turn was up ahead. To gain more traction, Mahmood extended his outside leg, pushing heavily into the pedal. As he swept through the curve, an elderly man emerged from behind the bend. He was very thin, skeletal. His tiny, weathered face resembled a forgotten plum, left out for days.

"Watch this," Mahmood spat out, swerving his bike toward the traveler.

Ali began to laugh but, stifled it quickly when he saw the fear in the old man's eyes. Associating with Mahmood always brought about moments like these that conflicted with Ali's good nature.

———— آرش ————

The space between the houses started to grow and soon only a lone farmhouse stood in view. Mahmood exited the main road and made a beeline for the shoddy structure.

About a hundred yards from the loot, a large dog appeared in their path, growling.

A quick U-turn of the bike did not stop the angry dog. She hurtled toward them, rapidly narrowing the gap.

Ali fished some rocks out of his pocket. He threw one at the snarling animal before he realized he could not hold on to the bike with only one hand. "Go faster, Mahmood! Go faster!" he shouted, frantic.

Focused on the road, avoiding the rocks and broken branches, Mahmood pedaled with full force. He did not slow down or look back until he reached the main road.

The dog ceased its chase after only a short run and stood its ground, barking triumphantly.

"Go faster, my ass! Is that how you help?" Mahmood scoffed. "I should have pushed you off the bike, you idiot."

Ali, seething inside, chose to be silent. He knew he had to relent when Mahmood was irritated. His arrogant friend, however, continued shouting and insulting him as they moved forward.

———— آرش ————

After a long stretch, a new target was located – a shack enclosed by a mud wall. A mature alder tree stood nearby, its branches reaching all the way to the wall.

how his domineering friend would react. He struggled to surmount his racing mind for a while, knowing all along that he would eventually stay put: *I just need to keep my distance from him. Maybe I'll collect some flowers for my mom!*

With a vast array of floral options, Ali soon had a lovely arrangement in hand, each blossom vibrant and beautiful. He tied their stems together with a long blade of grass and made his way back to the bike.

"Is that bouquet for me?" Mahmood shouted from a distance.

"It is for my mother, asshole!"

Brushing off the insult, Mahmood rinsed his bloody knife in the stream and wiped it on the grass. Giving Ali an unfriendly, lingering look he said, "Nobody is to know about the chickens."

آرش

Ali made his way down to the widest part of the stream, where a large, smooth rock looked inviting. He removed his shoes and immersed his feet in the icy water allowing his mind to float on a cloud of memories. Soon he drifted back to when he was a thin, eleven-year-old boy.

Three days a week, an old minibus would take Ali, Mahmood and other village kids to a school in town. Ali was not friends with any of these children, as his house was at the other end of the village, the poor side. Mahmood, on the other hand, knew all the boys well. He had already picked a fight with every single one and had established his superiority among them.

The boys, adapting to the hierarchy that Mahmood had set, always tiptoed around him. They voluntarily shared their snacks and let him copy their homework. Yet, regardless of this deference, none of them was immune to his occasional outburst.

Strangely, Mahmood had always been popular. He had a special charisma, a stance, an indescribable lure which pulled toward him the same bruised kids time and time again.

Ali would shuffle to the bus station in the mornings, carrying the crushing weight of his shame and worthlessness. He was determined to be invisible, not to make any friends or enemies. When the bus arrived, he would creep onto it like a shadow, avoiding eye contact. He would sit alone, in the back, a location that would give him partial protection from the aggressive kids. Still, he suffered the occasional shove by Mahmood and others.

One day at school, Mahmood snatched a younger boy's lunch sack and pushed him into a mud puddle. The boy soon returned with his older brother, about thirteen, to claim his food. Mahmood, cool and relaxed, continued eating as the two brothers approached him. He let them get very close. And then without saying a word, he leapt up and pounced on the older boy, beating him severely.
Word quickly spread at school that Mahmood had had a rock hidden in his fist during the assault.

On the way home from school that day, the atmosphere on the bus was unsettling, saturated with a violent energy. The abused brothers sat next to each other, the older one with a black eye and bloodied lips. Other boys were mostly out of their seats, moving back and forth and talking among themselves, all the while, excluding Mahmood.
Mahmood was unusually quiet the entire ride. He busied himself cutting away at the back of a seat with a sharpened piece of wood.

It was a minimum day and Ali was excited to get home. He wanted to play with his sisters without feeling ashamed or harassed. Much to his dismay, he had to stay behind to search for his coat; some kid had hidden it under a pile of papers in a corner of the bus.
Finding his jacket at last, Ali began to walk toward his house. Shortly, he spotted something shiny on the ground reflecting the sun's

rays. It was a broken bracelet. Hoping his newfound treasure was made of gold, he picked it up and hid it in his fist. A broad smile appeared on his face – this could be a good gift to his mother!

Approaching a huge almond tree, his marker for the halfway point to his house, Ali heard some commotion coming from the lower grounds. Without making a sound, he hid behind the mighty tree and eavesdropped. The voices were familiar; they belonged to the kids from the bus.

He peered around the tree.

Mahmood was encircled by a few boys; they were daring him to fight.

Being a cunning fighter, Mahmood knew he could easily take down one or two of these kids at a time. But he was intelligent enough to foresee the outcome of this battle – once he started rumbling with one, they would all attack. So, he stood there calmly, staring at the ring of faces while twirling the sharpened piece of wood in his hand. He declared that he chooses when he fights and that he would jam his stick into the eyes of the first one to try him.

Having suffered repeatedly from his bullying, Ali had never liked Mahmood. Yet watching him trapped and treated so unfairly, he couldn't help but feel sorry for him.

He waited for a while, expecting the boy to give up. But Mahmood just stood there. He did not beg, nor did he apologize; he even managed to be intimidating, brandishing his stick.

Mahmood's composure was heroic and worthy of admiration, but it was clear that the crowd would eventually break him and rob him of his well-guarded pride.

Ali started to run. He knew where the boy in trouble lived.

In no time, Mahmood's mother reached the kids surrounding her son.

Sakineh, a capable-looking, young woman, who could fight as ruthlessly as her son, was ferocious. Cursing and screaming, she swung a big stick at the boys, hitting each one with full force. The youngsters attempted to scatter, screeching and wailing in pain.

As Sakineh effectively terrified the children, Ali thought of his own repressed mother and her tiny body: Would she be able to save me if I was in the same predicament?

Mahmood never acknowledged Ali for the rescue, but he did stop picking on him.

For another three years, Ali continued to sit alone at the back of the bus until one snowy morning when Mahmood plopped down next to him. It was the day Ali had returned to school, after a week at home mourning his murdered father.

Reliving his childhood experiences, Ali, was at once overcome by an avalanche of pain, now having an even stronger desire to leave.

———————— آرش ————————

"Hey man, aren't you hungry?" Mahmood said, standing right above Ali.

"I can wait till we get home."

"That might be a while, Ali. There are still a couple of hours of daylight left. We cannot afford to be seen with this bloody box."

Mahmood, in a playful mood, dangled his slingshot in front of Ali's face, moving it side to side. He then pointed at a series of birds roosting on a nearby tree. "Take your pick before I push you in the water," he said.

"Alright, alright. Just surprise me."

Mahmood turned on his heels, stretched the elastic of his slingshot and instantly pegged a fat dove. He picked up the fallen bird and twisted its head in one rapid motion.

"Go gather some berries, Ali. I'll make a fire."

CHAPTER 3

The chosen spot for brawling was by the main road; the wrestling mat was a large, old *kilim*.* There were not many rules to the game. As long as their bodies remained on the *kilim*, the players could use any technique or trick to pin their opponent's shoulders to the ground.

Ali and Namat were the first pair to compete.

Namat, a newcomer to the village, was a tense individual with a large head and small elephant eyes. His body was bulky, but he could move with surprising agility. Ali was smaller but he had a lean body and plenty of wrestling experience.

Brimming with confidence, Namat stood in the middle of the ring. He stared intently at each in the band of unknown spectators before coming to rest on Ali. His fear-inducing manner made many gamblers uneasy. Even Mahmood, aware of Ali's abilities, was for the first time nervous to bet on his friend.

Ali casually dismissed his opponent's stare. He was a crafty wrestler with numerous winning matches under his belt; he could not be easily intimidated.

The contest started by the challengers pawing at each other for a long while. Namat was clearly shooting for Ali's lower body, but no one had a clue about Ali's plan.

After a couple of failed attempts, Namat finally got a hold of Ali's right leg. To flatten him out and loosen the grip, Ali kept driving his hips down, lower and lower. His strong rival, however, remained in control,

---

* *a flat woven tapestry*

pulling the leg, knocking him off balance.

Ali was taken to the ground.

───────────── آرش ─────────────

In a nearby tree, a set of twin boys, about four years old, were climbing happily. One noticed the wriggling bodies on the kilim and climbed down quickly. "A fight! A fight!" he shouted running toward the bystanders. The second twin who could see better higher up, yelled back, "It is not a fight, they are wrestling. Wait for me! Waaaaaait!"

The twins came closer to observe the match. One of them squeezed his way past the spectators and stood next to Mahmood. Mahmood put his hand on the boy's head and affectionately ruffled his hair. The boy looked up at him and smiled.

Ali was in a precarious position. Namat had fully mounted him now, dominating the match.

The nervous gamblers stood still, their eyes fixed on the two wrestlers on the mat. The silence was so potent it was as if no one was breathing.

Suddenly, a wailing pierced the air, "Let go of Ali! Don't hurt him!" one of the twins screamed, clutching Mahmood's leg.

Not beaten yet, Ali focused on reversing the situation by using a special maneuver. He grabbed Namat's wrist and yanked it across his own waist. Using his other hand, he then reached out and secured the newcomer's arm above the elbow. He turned his body with skill, pulling tight on the arm.

Not knowing how to undo the trick, Namat landed next to Ali, flat on his back.

Ali deftly mounted him.

The crowd had become energized as the end of the match drew near.

"Finish him, Ali! He is no match for you!"

"His shoulders are almost touching! Go for it!"

"Damn it, Namat! Get up! Push him off of you!"

At that critical moment of the match, Mahmood suddenly noticed his sister, Neloo in the distance. She was moving hurriedly, scurrying from bush to bush, before disappearing behind a row of houses.

Mahmood was enraged; he knew his sister was off to see Ahrash again.

With a final burst of strength, Ali flattened Namat's shoulders to the ground.

Cheering erupted. The twins, with tear-stained faces, high-fived each other, jumping up and down.

"I got him, Mahmood! Look, I got him!" Ali shouted, sitting atop Namat, urgently seeking attention.

Before Mahmood could return his eyes back to the mat, the defeated Namat wriggled and shook Ali off of him. Both wrestlers then stood up with their hair and clothes in disarray.

Mahmood started collecting the bets.

CHAPTER 4

Thirteen years ago, on a beautiful, spring day in the northern Iranian village of Kultappa, a boy and a girl entered the world. The newborns' families were neighbors, their houses on either side of a narrow dirt road, both with the views of an immense lava rock, known as the Village Boulder.

The girl was named Neloo, meaning waterlily and the boy who was born five hours later, was named Ahrash, after a mythical legend.

Neloo's mother, Sakineh, already had a six-year-old son who was the center of her world. She worshipped the boy so intensely that she had pledged to never share her love with another child. She had even terminated a couple of pregnancies on the sly, using local plant extracts and by lifting heavy objects.

Neloo, however, was a stubborn fetus. She fought for her fledgling life, tenaciously clinging to the womb until her father learned of her existence. Sakineh, then, had no choice but to go through with the pregnancy.

When Neloo was only three months old, the unhappy Sakineh decided to leave her under someone else's care and work in the field alongside her husband.

She approached their neighbor, Aziz, a religious and kindhearted woman.

Aziz had two sons of her own, a seven-year-old named Issa and the new baby who had been born on the same day as Neloo. She would have had three children upon Ahrash's arrival, but, tragically, she had lost her five-month-old daughter two years prior.

———— آرش ————

Neloo and Ahrash grew up together like a pair of twins in Aziz's house. They were fed and put to sleep at the same time and in the same bed, often cooing, babbling, or crying simultaneously. They started crawling within a few days of one another and took their first stumbling steps, grasping each other's tiny hands. Aziz had always claimed that the children's first words were each other's names.

Their toddler phase was absolutely memorable. Never a dull moment, Neloo and Ahrash played all day, making the best use of the few toys they owned. In nice weather, they would mainly stay out in the yard, feeding the chickens, gathering berries, and running after the birds and butterflies. When it rained, they would walk around and rescue stranded worms. Winter often afforded them the opportunity to make snowmen and to crawl through icy tunnels.

If storms attacked the village, Aziz would keep them inside, warm and safe. She would bring out her *daff** and play exciting music, the two toddlers and Issa dancing all the while.

———— آرش ————

The children started school at the age of six. Three days a week, a minibus picked them up early in the morning and took them to school in the nearest town. They usually returned late, being the last to be shuttled home. Never minding the long trip however, the two friends sat next to each other and chatted endlessly.

On the days there was no school, Ahrash and Neloo studied together, sharing what they had learned with Ahrash's older brother, who had never been to school.

As they grew older, their families became closer. They visited each

---

* a frame drum musical instrument

other more often, exchanged gifts over the holidays and picnicked in good weather.

The children enjoyed all the family gatherings but, the most favorite group activity was, by far, the midnight trips to The Hill.

The Hill was a high ground in the middle of the village atop an ancient burial site.

The children would be awoken at three o'clock in the morning. Half asleep, they hurriedly left the house with their parents to join the other families at the Village Boulder. When the assembly was complete, the caravan moved toward The Hill, many lanterns brightening their path.

The climb took about a half an hour.

Once at the plateau, the adults spread their blankets on the soft dirt and each family nestled together. The kids fell back to sleep right away; the parents talked intimately under the star-cramped sky.

With the first dim light of dawn, the women got busy preparing breakfast. They were all lacking sleep yet were energized by the adventure of being high on The Hill, closer to the vast sky.

The men and children were woken to a fiesta of boiled eggs, handpicked fruit, fresh bread, goat cheese, goat's milk and of course, tasty, sweet tea.

After the morning meal, the gathering became filled with uncontrolled excitement. Men in pajamas played backgammon, shaking and rolling the dice boldly, against the wooden board. Women joked and laughed as they cleaned up and prepared hookahs to go around. Young mothers nursed or soothed their babies in their arms, while children ran around flying kites, or sword fighting with wooden sticks or newly discovered bones.

The chaos after breakfast often provided young Mahmood the opportunity to control and manipulate the other kids. He ordered them around, confiscated their toys and shot pebbles at them, all the while threatening to push them off the edge if they breathed a word to their parents.

Ahrash never joined the other children when they were on the top of The Hill. He only played with his older brother while enjoying the spectacular panoramic view of the village and the fields below.

He and Issa often dug in the dirt searching for treasures and bones; Neloo invariably accompanied them on their archeological adventures.

Something interesting was always found. Once they dug a perfect human femur which Neloo's cousin confiscated from them to take to his science teacher.

——————— آرش ———————

As the kids grew older, the trips to The Hill happened less often for Ahrash's family and they finally ceased altogether. Mahmood's increasingly aggressive behavior made Aziz nervous for the safety of her boys.

CHAPTER 5

Neloo cleared the dirt road and stopped behind a house out of her brother's sight. Her mind was filled with both elation and fear. The anticipation of being with Ahrash had given her a euphoric rush. Her excitement however was tainted by the dread that Mahmood had spotted her crossing the open pathway.

She decided to stay hidden, not leaving her cover until her brother started collecting bets for the next round of the match.

The love between Neloo and Ahrash was not some ordinary teenage crush. It was an immeasurable affinity, an unalloyed affection between two beings who truly believed they were placed in this world to be together.

For almost ten years, these children grew up side by side. They fed on the same **sofreh**,*** *heard the same stories, and learned the same set of ethics and principles. Now that they were older, by protocol of their culture, they were not to spend any time together.*

This required separation conveniently coincided with the birth of Neloo's twin brothers. Sakineh stopped working in the field and decided that there was no more need for Aziz's services.

A few minutes of brisk walking brought Neloo to a small blossoming meadow, dotted with grazing sheep. She immediately started running in the direction of the scattered herd.

At the other edge of the meadow, her soulmate, Ahrash, sat on a rock with his German shepherd, Jolfa, at his feet. He was a thin boy, and

---

* a cloth spread on the ground for serving food

definitely small for his age. His face was simple and ordinary, except for a pair of very large brown eyes.

Jolfa's ears perked up. She gave a short growl and started tearing through the meadow. The dog's action brought a smile to her master's face; Ahrash knew right away who was approaching. He rose to his feet, his heart drumming faster and faster as Neloo's body grew closer.

———— آرش ————

The path to their usual hiding spot was covered with fragrant flowers. Neloo squatted down and breathed in the strong smell of tuberoses. She cut one flower from the cluster and placed it in the buttonhole of her dress. "Our flowers!" she turned toward Ahrash, wanting him to smell.

When they were four years old, on a cold and overcast winter day, Ahrash and Neloo had planted many tuberose bulbs by the stream.

Aziz had removed the bulbs from the front of her house where her in-laws had planted them decades ago. The bulbs had multiplied over the years and every spring when they resurfaced, they would block the pathway to the house.

After uprooting most of the bulbs, Aziz placed them in a basket and carried them through the meadow with Ahrash and Neloo marching in front of her. She then helped the toddlers settle the bulbs into their new home by the stream.

Now, nine years later, the bulbs had exploded in number, dominating the wildflowers around the watercourse.

The sweet and strong scent of these flowers always reminded Ahrash and Neloo of their childhood, a time they could openly and happily be together.

———— آرش ————

Hiding behind a willow tree, they perched on a rock like a pair of doves. Their heads were touching, their bare feet dangling in the gurgling stream.

Neloo gazed at the crystal water running between her toes, enjoying its cool sting. The sunlight danced on her face as the willow branches swayed in the breeze.

Ahrash was hypnotized, not being able to take his eyes off her soft peachy skin and perfectly designed face.

In spite of the deep affection for each other, the two teenagers had only kissed once. They had elected to forgo any further desires of the flesh, any temptations that might sway their future plans – plans that they had set meticulously. Their path included completing high school with honors and attending college on scholarships. After graduating, the pair would marry and start a family. They wanted at least four children and pledged to have Ahrash's brother live with them forever.

Neloo unwrapped a bundle on her lap and handed Ahrash some klucheh.*

"It is warm!" Ahrash said as he took in a whiff of the bread.

"I baked it right before I left the house. I think it is exactly how your mom makes it."

At the edge of the stream, not too far from them, a pair of ducks lazed on the warm land. The female duck had one wing spread open, sweeping the ground with it over and over.

"I think that duck has a broken wing," Ahrash pointed at the bird.

"Oh no! How will she migrate when the time comes?" Neloo sighed.

"Maybe her body will repair itself by then, of course, only if she stops moving it so much."

A brief silence overtook the teens. Jolfa, however, ran in and out of the water, seeking attention.

The duck continued to flap her single wing until, suddenly, a little

---

a sweet bread

yellow duckling squeezed itself out from under her and darted toward the stream. The mother duck quickly followed the unruly offspring, revealing four more tiny ducklings under her wing.

In no time, the entire family was drifting along the gentle current.

At the sight of the ducklings, the teens looked at each other and burst out laughing. Neloo, slapped the water forcefully with her feet, spraying Ahrash. Ahrash did the same to her and they played like the children that they were.

"How nice would it be if we could get married today and be together without any fear?" Neloo sighed.

"Children cannot get married, Neloo," Ahrash said with a boyish charm. "Let's start reading our poetry now instead of thinking about the impossible."

"I have something to show you first," Neloo interrupted Ahrash, pulling out a small, faded book from her bag.

"A new book?"

"Yes and no. I just got the book, but it was printed about thirty years ago. It's a collection of Forough Farrokhzad poems," she murmured.

Ahrash had never heard of the poet as no teachers were allowed to mention her name and no bookstores could carry her books anymore.

"She is an amazing poet, a pioneer woman. She describes her feelings and desires in the way no female has ever been able to do in this country," Neloo said and paused, tearing at the grass angrily. "The stupid mullahs call her a whore now, not a poet."

"Where did you get the book?"

"My cousin gave it to me. You can borrow it if you want. I have already read it twice."

Ahrash skimmed through a few pages and placed the small book neatly into his sack.

"I will read it with Issa," he said. "Let's read *Shahryar* now. I marked where we had left off."

آرش

Her head on his shoulder, Neloo listened to Ahrash reading aloud. She was confident that Jolfa was guarding them devotedly. After a good period of time, however, she became nervous, wondering how long a wrestling match could possibly last.

"I had better go before Mahmood comes after me. I'll come tomorrow when they are wrestling again."

"Great, Issa will be here too. But are you sure they will be wrestling tomorrow?" Ahrash asked, following Neloo out of their hiding spot.

"I am sure. Ali and Mahmood were discussing it at dinner last night."

"Ali sure is spending a lot of time at your house. Are your parents going to adopt him?

Neloo gave a loud, silly laugh. "Sakineh? Maybe. She'll do anything to please Mahmood, even adopt his friend."

"Why do you always call your mother by her first name?"

"I don't know. Maybe because I was raised by your mother and not by her."

CHAPTER 6

Aziz was tall and thin with an immeasurable natural beauty. She was a woman of strong faith and unwavering devotion. She prayed three times a day, fasted during Ramadan, and paid her tithes without exception. Even after her first son had been born impaired and she had lost her infant daughter, she was still a loyal servant of God.

———— آرش ————

Her baby girl was whole and healthy before her sudden demise. She slept well, had a good appetite, and hardly ever fussed. And then one morning, she was just gone, found in her bed not breathing.

Aziz mourned her gravely, beating herself and screaming like a mad woman.

Elders in the village gathered around her, trying to calm her nerves with brewed local plants and gentle words.

Holy men visited her at home, praying that God grant her peace and restore happiness in the family.

Sadly, all the efforts had been in vain, for nothing seemed to ease this wounded mother's pain.

Aziz continued to grieve for months and then suddenly it all came to a halt. Having accepted her destiny, she appeared quiet, drifting around the house, soundlessly performing her daily routine.

Her silence and placid facade however failed to conceal the uproar in Aziz's mind. Khalil, her loyal husband, was perfectly aware of the underlying depression that was systematically destroying his wife. He tried beyond his ability to help the woman he loved but repeatedly failed in his quest.

The birth of Ahrash came to the rescue at last. It caused a big shift in Aziz's psyche, making her more optimistic and excited about life.

———— آرش ————

When Aziz was asked to take care of Neloo, she was hesitant to accept. She, herself, was the mother of a newborn and had a son who needed special care. The second Neloo was placed in her arms however, all her doubt and uncertainty dissipated. She felt a warmth in her heart, an indescribable sense of closeness to the baby. It was as if she was holding her own daughter. *Maybe this is God's way of telling me to stop grieving.*

She accepted the offer.

———— آرش ————

Every day Aziz fed and cleaned the baby girl, sang her lullabies and rocked her to sleep just as she did with Ahrash. Taking care of two babies, in addition to watching over Issa, was exhausting. Nevertheless, with her strong parental instincts, she was able to enjoy looking after all of the children.

She continued to care for her neighbor's infant, in good faith, for months. Then there came a day when Neloo was sick with a fever, refusing her bottle and crying in pain. Aziz tried everything to calm the restless baby. She unbundled her, rubbed her tummy, and carried her for hours at a time. Exhausted, she finally sat down in a corner and secured a pillow between herself and the wall. Humming a tune softly, she cradled Neloo in her arms.

Fatigue took over and she dozed off.

When she opened her eyes, Neloo was asleep, calmly suckling at her breast.

An unearthly ecstasy took over the young mother, a feeling that she never knew existed even after nursing three babies. She placed a kiss on Neloo's forehead and held her tighter in her arms.

Neloo's fussing persisted in the days that followed and Aziz continued to nurse her without pause.

With the appearance of two tiny white wedges in her lower gums, Neloo finally calmed down. Aziz's desire to nurse her however, remained strong. Each day, as dawn approached, she became fidgety and overzealous in anticipation of receiving her. And at the end of the day, she felt whole and complete, mothering two sons and a daughter.

Despite the superficial happiness, a pang of guilt gradually began to consume the religious Aziz. A sense of betrayal to Sakineh and Neloo, made her feel unworthy and impure.

The depression that had never fully left her mind, now flourished, making her new problem seem much bigger than it actually was. Unable to resolve her difficulty, torturous questions formed in her head and circled in a never-ending cycle: *What is the force that is pushing me away from my faith? Am I cursed? Am I harboring a demon inside me?*

Bit by bit, paranoia blanketed Aziz. She could not sleep at night and her break-of-day excitement was replaced with sad wailing.

Utterly concerned about his wife's emotional state, Khalil offered to take her to the mosque for Friday's mass prayer.

———————— آرش ————————

The men's praying session finished first.

Waiting for his wife, Khalil stood under a lone tree outside the mosque. Several pigeons were pecking at the seeds that had been scattered by the precants.

As he thoughtlessly watched the birds, a murder of crows passed over the tree and swooped down on the pigeons. Their movement sent the barely clinging leaves floating down the tree's half naked branches. Khalil brushed the leaves from his coat, wondering if autumn had come early to his already withered life.

There was a time when Khalil considered himself the luckiest man in the village. He owned his home and had fertile land. His family was well fed year-round and bundled and warm in the wintertime. Above all, he was blessed with an angelic wife, a content, calm, and loving woman with whom he shared a deep bond.

Then tragedy arrived. Their daughter's death struck like a hurricane and in the blink of an eye, crushed all their happiness.

———— آرش ————

In the mosque, Aziz sat crouched in a corner, clasping the Koran to her chest. The women finished their prayers and left one by one. Aziz studied the passing faces intensely, wondering if they too were possessed.

Shortly, the mosque had emptied out.

Awash in guilt, Aziz recited the *Surat At-Tawbah** as penance, rocking back and forth, pressing the Koran to her heart. She wept bitter tears, repeatedly asking God for forgiveness.

The mosque custodian, a grumpy middle-aged man, closed the windows, and started tidying up the rugs on the floor. He appeared annoyed.

Aziz, unaffected by the man's presence, said the same prayer a couple more times. She then stood solidly and left the mosque a calm woman.

Catching sight of his wife, Khalil quickly strode toward her. He reached her and their eyes met. Aziz began to cry softly. He wiped her tears, pulled her in and clutched her in his arms.

A new set of tears appeared on Aziz's face. This time, she wiped them herself. "I am alright, Khalil. I have made my peace with God."

---

* *a verse of penitence*

CHAPTER 7

Ahrash had never told anyone, even Neloo, about his fear of being alone in the meadow. Danger seemingly lurked everywhere, beneath bushes, behind trees, at the bend of the stream, all so formidable that even Jolfa could not protect him.

Today however, with Issa beside him, the meadow was safe.

──────────── آرش ────────────

Lungs filled with the crisp morning air, Ahrash and Issa led the sheep to the grassy pastures, a loitering moon following them with conviction.

They were silent during their walk and remained as such once they reached the stream.

Like a pair of monks in their quiet monastery, the two brothers sat at the edge of the meadow, mutely welcoming the rising sun.

After a long meditative period, Issa took his *ney*[*] out of his pocket and began to play.

Gloomy as usual, the melody inflated Ahrash's worries, illuminating the harshness of the lives around him. He thought of Neloo and her family's disapproval of him; he dwelled on his weary father and forever bereaved mother, all the while agonizing about Issa's blindness.

A tiny butterfly came to rest on his sleeve. He examined its delicate wings and curved antennae intensely. "What is this butterfly thinking? Is she recalling the darkness of the cocoon," Ahrash wondered as he raised his gaze over the little creature to his brother.

Issa was sitting solidly like a steep rock face at the edge of a wild

---
[*] *a wooden flute*

sea. His sleek, shiny, chestnut hair was parted in the middle and tucked behind his ears; his manly, jutting forehead was curved high above his large eyes and lashes, lashes that were twice as long and twice as full as his brother's.

"Issa, so dignified and beautiful, will forever be in his own dark cocoon," Ahrash lamented.

Their mother often talked about the day that Issa was born. "He had a full head of hair, the biggest and most beautiful eyes and glowing skin," she would say. "When the midwife first placed him in my arms, an image appeared to me, a picture that I had seen at an Armenian friend's house: the image of Jesus on the cross. I decided to name my boy Issa."

Issa was keenly intelligent. For a blind man, never having been to school, he was well informed and impressively knowledgeable. He knew by heart hundreds of poems by Hafez, Rumi, Khayyam, and his favorite, Shahryar. He could recite page after page of literature flawlessly and occasionally even delivered some of his own works.

In spite of his disability, he worked every day alongside his father, digging, planting and harvesting in the field. With his broad shoulders, vast upper body, and shorter legs, he effortlessly carried heavy loads and did other work Khalil was no longer able to do.

"Who taught you to play the *ney*?" Ahrash asked.

"I do not remember, maybe the grandpa that you never met? All I know is that I was not quite five when I began to play," Issa answered, slipping the instrument into his shirt pocket

"Aren't you going to play another song?"

"I'll play later. We have a long day ahead of us. Let us have breakfast now."

─────────── آرش ───────────

After their morning meal, the brothers began to walk along the stream. Ahrash devoured his surroundings with avidity as he had never ventured far into the meadow when he was alone.

They soon reached a wider section of the stream where countless floating lilies were congregating all along the edges, dancing delicately with the soft flow of water. As the two approached, some floras were even unfolding their petals.

Ahrash was overwhelmed by all the beauty around him. The pasture with its sparkling grass and the stream embroidered with white lilies dazzled the young boy.

Absorbing nature's grandeur now filled him with a unique melancholy; he questioned why Issa must be cheated out of all this exquisiteness.

آرش

At midday, the brothers sought refuge under the domed roof of a willow tree. They poured over a variety of books before lunch and then again after. Every break they took, Issa played his *ney*.

The day went by fast.

The last note of Issa's song hung in the air as the sun slowly faded from the sky. It was now time to pack up and take the sheep back.

They gathered their animals, herding them leisurely while enjoying the slap of the cool breeze on their skin. Jolfa, fully aware of the surroundings, walked along her masters at the same speed.

Halfway back to the house, Ahrash tugged on Issa's arm. "Stop, Issa. Ripe plums."

Today was their lucky day. They had always passed by this tree but never had seen any ripe fruit left unmolested by the birds.

Issa crouched down under the fruited branch. Ahrash climbed onto his shoulders, reaching out to grab two perfectly ripe plums.

Enjoying the tasty fruit, they continued to walk. There was only one small hill to climb before they arrived home.

Once at the top of the hill, Ahrash froze at the sight of Mahmood, Ali, and Namat. The men were by the boulder, rolling a single sheep vertebrate around on the ground. Ahrash quickly put the leash on Jolfa and handed it to his brother.

"Is he there?" Issa asked quietly.

"Yes. Him and his disciples."

The brothers sped up as they ventured into enemy territory. Issa strode alongside Ahrash, keeping the seventy-pound Jolfa at his command.

They got beyond the men safely; relieved that Mahmood was too involved in his gambling to bother with them.

Seconds later, Mahmood stood up. He put out his half-smoked cigarette, lodged a rock in his slingshot and took aim.

Issa was jolted by a sudden pain in his neck.

Deducing what had likely occurred, Ahrash swiftly turned around and marched toward the boulder. His fear totally forgotten, he stopped before Mahmood and pushed him with all his might. "Stop messing with us!" he shouted.

Hardly affected by the shove, Mahmood grabbed Ahrash's wrist. "And what will happen if I don't? Is your blind brother or your fuckin' old man going to stop me?"

"Let go of my hand, you stupid drunk!" Ahrash yelled, wriggling to free himself. Unable to escape the tight grip, he then began to kick.

Mahmood kept him at a distance, twisting his wrist ever so slowly. "I swear, one of these days, I will come to the meadow and fuck you over and over!" he said in a furious, hushed voice.

With every tweak to the boy's wrist, Ali's insides clenched. He took a few steps toward them but could not find the courage to get involved.

Jolfa barked nonstop, wanting to go to his master's aid but Issa held her in place, firmly commanding her to stay.

A few yards away, a man on a rusty bike approached the boulder. A big wooden box was attached to the back of his bicycle with a toddler girl perched on top. The man slowed down and with great difficulty stopped just a few yards past the boulder.

"Let go of the boy, Mahmood. Pick on someone your own size!" he yelled.

Mahmood glanced at the man but ignored him.

"Let him go or I'll tell your father. He is not even half your size!"

"This asshole is not half my size, alright, but he had the nerve to push me!" Mahmood grumbled.

"Still. Let the boy free for God's sake."

Mahmood released Ahrash reluctantly, but not before pulling him in closer and quietly spitting out one more threat, "I'll see you in the meadow soon."

Ahrash retreated backwards a couple of steps but hesitated to leave.

Raising his head, Issa detected faint sounds which steadily grew clearer. He sniffed the air intently and then called to Ahrash in his deep, manly voice, "The village herds are coming back. We had better bring our sheep in."

Glaring at Mahmood, Ahrash walked toward Issa with his head half turned back. He was still very angry.

The villager on the bicycle struggled to get back on the road but finally succeeded. The patient toddler gripped the man's waist and rested her head on his back as the bike moved away with a wrenching sound.

———————— آرش ————————

The air was suddenly filled with dust. From atop the hill, the village herd appeared with the shepherds trailing. The ground rumbled with the clatter of their hooves as they approached the dirt road, the very road that separated Neloo's and Ahrash's homes.

CHAPTER 8

As Neloo watched the sunset through the window, a man entered their yard. It took her few moments to recognize Khalil. She rushed to the door and threw it open, not even waiting for a knock.

"Hello *Amu** Khalil," she said excitedly.

"Hello Neloo *Jaan*.** Is your father home?"

Sharif, tall and hefty, appeared behind his daughter. "What a pleasant surprise to see you Khalil. Please come in," he greeted their guest with enthusiasm.

The two men hugged and kissed on both cheeks. Khalil removed his shoes and stepped inside into a large room.

The house was scarcely furnished, yet it was clean and welcoming. A few brightly colored, cylindrical pillows were propped up along one wall which complemented the two Persian rugs, covering the floor. The walls were bare, except for a mirror and a picture of Sakineh, holding two identical babies in her arms with Mahmood and Neloo standing on either side of her.

Khalil and Sharif had been neighbors and friends since they were toddlers. They were about the same age, but Khalil looked much older. The loss of a child, his wife's depression, and now arthritis had all taken their toll on him.

Guiding his guest to the back of the room, Sharif offered him a spot

---

* uncle
** dear

with a large pillow to lean against. He then turned to his daughter, "Neloo *Jaan*, bring some tea for *Amu* Khalil."

Neloo left the men and walked toward the kitchen by way of a narrow, short hallway.

"We have a guest. I am getting him tea," she told her mother as she entered the kitchen.

"I am aware," Sakineh stated coldly, standing by the stove, looking cross.

A wide pot, half full of water, was on a lit burner with a dead chicken lying inside. Sakineh dabbed the water with her finger a couple of times before turning off the stove. Allowing the pot to cool a bit, she began to pluck the bird.

Under her mother's scrutiny, Neloo poured tea into two clear glasses. She placed them on a small platter next to a bowl of sugar cubes and promptly disappeared.

Sakineh turned the carcass over inside the pot and continued plucking, cursing the bird whenever her hands touched the hot water.

When Neloo returned to the kitchen, she immediately started to help her.

Heads over the pot, the mother and daughter pulled feathers in unison, each eavesdropping on the conversation in the big room.

──────── آرش ────────

The men drank their tea without any words. Khalil looked uneasy, repeatedly parting his mustache from the center and sliding his fingers over his unshaven face.

Sharif lit a cigarette without offering one to his guest. He knew Khalil was among the few men in the village who had never smoked.

"I just saw the twins outside. I cannot believe how tall they've grown," Khalil bantered nervously. "I offered them some candies; I hope that was ok before dinner."

"Don't worry yourself. Nothing can spoil the twins' appetites. They play outside until they can no longer see each other. Once inside, they eat just about everything in sight," Sharif shared, laughing.

"Your boys were climbing the same walnut tree that we used to scramble up. Watching them reminded me of our crazy bull encounter."

"Yes, indeed," Sharif replied, recalling their childhood incident.

When they were about the same age as the twins are now, Sharif and Khalil had been playing outside. A wild and out of control bull, suddenly, appeared in the neighborhood, charging at everyone.

Sharif, the more nimble of the two, immediately scaled the walnut tree. His playmate, however, paralyzed by fear, could not climb up. Sharif stretched out his arm to help and, in doing so, broke the branch beneath him. He swung precariously by one arm for a bit but eventually managed to secure his position and pull Khalil up to safety.

Later, when the bull left to terrorize the other neighborhoods, the boys found themselves far above the ground. Evidently, in their panic, they had continued climbing higher and higher.

Stuck fifteen feet up on the tree, the boys cried out, wailing and screaming.

It took a long while before anybody noticed them and came to their rescue.

The two friends chatted a while longer, reminiscing about the old times. Khalil was still fidgety and nervous, and his discomfort was not lost on Sharif.

"You look stressed, Khalil. What is troubling you?" he asked.

Khalil hesitated to answer; he just stared at a tiny flower on the rug by his feet.

"Do you need to borrow some money?"

"No, *Shohkran-lel-Allah*,* we are doing fine."

"I hope your wife is not sick again."

---

* thank God

"Aziz is alright, but the boys are not. They are complaining that Mahmood is on their case all the time, harassing them without provocation. I wonder if my boys have crossed Mahmood somehow."

Sharif took the last drag of his cigarette and spoke resolutely. "I know our children well, Khalil. Yours are fine boys. It is my son Mahmood, the biggest disappointment of my life, who is corrupt. There is not a day that passes without a complaint about him. I do not know when or if he will ever act like a man. By the time I was his age, I was married and already a father."

Astounded by her father's remark, Neloo shuddered in the kitchen: *Isn't dad scared of Sakineh's wrath? How could he belittle Mahmood, knowing she could easily hear him?"*

Sakineh raised her eyebrows. She then gave her daughter a hostile look and without uttering a word, pushed her hand away from the pot. She continued plucking the bird herself with excessive force, slapping the carcass around in the pot. By the time she was through with the plucking, the bird's bare body resembled a Monet painting, blooming with purple bruises.

آرش

Khalil felt sorry about Sharif's disappointment yet was obliged to move on. "The other day, Mahmood shot Issa in the neck with a rock, leaving a big bruise. Our dog, Jolfa, was ready to attack him, but Issa did not allow her.

The thought of Mahmood hurting the helpless Issa, boiled Sharif's blood. A wave of anger traveled like hot lava through his veins, melting away his integrity and pride. He lowered his head but could not hide his crimson face.

After a moment of silence, he raised his head and looked directly at Khalil. "Mahmood is getting out of control and he must be stopped. Tell your boys that I will take care of this matter tonight," Sharif promised in a crisp and reassuring voice.

CHAPTER 9

Alone in the meadow, Ahrash poured over Forough Farohkzad's book. He loved her poetry, finding her style unique, somewhat different from traditional Persian poetry.

Oddly however, every single poem he read had a flavor of separation or death, powerful enough to make him feel spooked and unnerved.

Throughout the book, Forough, a master in weaving in sentiment with powerful metaphors, described her pain to such a sorrowful extent it was as if she was already mourning her approaching demise.

In one especially vivid piece that gripped Ahrash's imagination the most, the poet even aspired to plant her dismembered hands in a garden and watch them grow.

The poem disturbed Ahrash gravely. Knowing Forough had died decades ago gave the sensitive boy an eerie feeling of her potential surprise reappearance amongst the new growth.

He could not read another single line. All day, he sat motionless, jumpy at every little noise or movement. Even the sound of a bird regaining its balance on a tree branch sent a shiver straight through him.

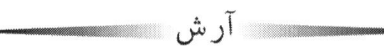

آرش

When Ahrash returned home, Issa was sitting on the bench in the yard, patiently waiting for him. The brothers had had a plan to read from their newly discovered poet that evening.

"I'll go wash up," he told Issa with a muffled voice.

Inside the house, Ahrash dawdled around, cleaning up and talking to his parents. After all he had experienced that morning, the notion of reading the same type of poems made him feel sick with apprehension.

آرش

"Sorry to keep you waiting, Issa. For some reason, I am oddly tired today," Ahrash said when he finally returned to the yard.

"Don't worry, there is joy in anticipation. And if you are tired, I do not mind extending the suspense through to tomorrow."

"No, we should read. Mom said that dinner will be late. She only just began cooking."

Ahrash plunked himself down next to his brother and started reciting. He managed to deliver several pages composed until a sudden shift in feeling, caused his voice to waver:

"'And I will plant my hands in a small garden
And I will grow green
I know I will, I know I will
And in the hollow curves of my blue fingers,
The swallows will lay their eggs'"

Distraught anew, Ahrash abruptly stopped reading. The poem had been a heavy burden on his mind all day; repeating the same verses now made him even more aware of the absurdity of life.

"Issa, do you think dead people grow green?" he asked.

"We bury our dead too deep. But you don't need to worry yourself with those sorts of thoughts."

More frightened now, Ahrash, inched closer to Issa. "It must be scary down below in the ground. Why do we not put our dead in boxes like Christians do?" he asked with a quivery voice.

"I honestly don't know. I heard a mullah once say that the souls of Christians get trapped in the box and never reach heaven," Issa snickered.

Finding Ahrash so disturbed by Forough's poetry, Issa felt guilty imposing this sort of imagery on his young brother. He was fully aware that despite his great maturity and intelligence, Ahrash was still a boy and fragile.

"Maybe we should give the poetry a rest for now and collect some berries; nighttime is quickly approaching."

He grabbed a folded mesh fabric on the bench and walked toward a large mulberry tree in the middle of the yard.

Unduly relieved, Ahrash followed him with a small pail in hand.

Minutes later the cloth was laid flat underneath the tree, and Issa, ready for action, was sitting on top of a limb.

With only one shake of the fruited branch, dozens of berries softly landed in the netting. A few chickens scurried over immediately to steal some of the raining fruit; a couple of finches joined in on the pilfering.

Ahrash began gathering the berries while still thinking of the Muslim burial method.

"Listen, Issa. When I die, I want them to put me in a box. I do not care if my soul is trapped or not; my body must not touch the dirt. And you are my witness," Ahrash demanded, adjusting the fabric and waving away the invaders.

"I promise to take care of the box situation if you promise to stop with these nonsense thoughts," Issa answered, still sitting on top of the limb.

———— آرش ————

By the time they left the berry tree, Ahrash's fear was slightly allayed. He suggested that they should continue reading until they are called to dinner.

His brother disagreed. "Maybe we should read Forough in a different season of our lives. I believe neither of us is quite ready for this type of poetry," Issa countered in a convincing voice. "Life sometimes inflicts forcible pain on us that we have no choice but to endure; we might as well protect ourselves from voluntarily suffering."

———— آرش ————

A pail of white berries was nestled between the brothers on the bench. They ate the tasty fruit by the handful, occasionally tossing a few to the birds.

Not too far from them a rooster had pinned a chicken by her feet and tried to perch on her back. She noisily protested.

Dashing toward the bench, Jolfa first stopped to interrupt the mating attempt. She then trotted over and sat by Issa's feet, enjoying the stroke of his hand on her head.

CHAPTER 10

A burly man pushed through the crowd and cleared a path to lead his camel forward. He reached the front door of a modest home and directed the animal to sit. The obedient camel lowered his massive body and right away started to gnaw on the apple in his owner's hand.

Nearly all of the villagers had gathered in front of *Hajji's** house. Even Jafar, the local gendarme, was there leaning on his small army jeep.

Before long, a taxi arrived and forced the crowd to fan out. A middle-aged man with a hook nose rushed out from the front seat and opened the rear door. Hajji stepped out of the car. He was dressed in a white shirt and slightly creased brown suit, his thick grey hair completely brushed back from his face.

Hajji was a slight man with a minor limp from a childhood bout with polio. He was the wealthiest person in the village yet always humble and unassuming. His good heart and ample generosity had garnered him respect even beyond the boundaries of the Kultappa village.

Everyone was excited by the sight of Hajji, the sole person in their village to make the blessed journey to Mecca. They wholeheartedly accepted that he was a new man now, holy and complete, maybe even no longer limping.

---

* *a person who has made the pilgrimage to Mecca; henceforth, this person is often addressed as Hajji as in the case of this village elder*

Making his way through the group, Hajji first met his family warmly, hugging and kissing his two grown sons and their children. A tiny baby then was placed in his arms; he visibly marveled at her with the broadest smile.

Clutching tightly at the baby, he climbed four steps to the entrance of the house and started to speak. "God bless you all for joining my family in this celebration. By the mercy of God, I am born again, free of all sin," he said and paused, dabbing his welling eyes with a white handkerchief. "I wish you all the same privilege of making the pilgrimage to *Kaaba**, the house of Allah."

Overwhelmed with a raw emotion, Hajji was unable to continue his speech. He stepped down from the stairs and handed the baby back to her father.

The hook-nosed man immediately took his place. "If you have children with you, Hajji wishes that you take them home before the sacrifice. Do not forget to give your name to Assad before leaving though," he said, pointing to a teenage boy holding a pad of paper. "We promise to put aside enough meat for the absent families."

───── آرش ─────

Hand in hand, Neloo and Ahrash walked by the gurgling stream. They were relaxed and without worry. It was no secret that most of the villagers had been waiting since dawn for Hajji's arrival and that they would remain there until they each received a portion of the slaughtered camel.

"Mahmood is helping the butchers today," Neloo said casually.

"Interesting. Is Ali helping too?"

"No way! Ali is too sensitive for that kind of job. He is probably hiding at home, not even joining the crowd."

Ahrash squeezed Neloo's hand. "I would have done the same thing."

The two friends continued strolling by the water, listening to its soft,

---

* a stone structure at the center of the holiest mosque in Mecca

gentle sound. Once they reached the part of the stream with floating lily pads, Ahrash suddenly paused mid stride. Seemingly battling a black thought, he turned to Neloo. "Do you know that I am really scared of your brother?" he said in a quiet voice. "He is an angry and unpredictable man."

"I thought Mahmood had stopped bothering you guys," Neloo responded.

"Yes, he has stopped. But I still feel his eyes on me," Ahrash breathed deeply. "Can you believe that Issa feels sorry for him?"

"For Mahmood?"

"Yes. He thinks there is something tormenting your brother on the inside which will destroy him one day. He compares him to a mountain cherry tree that often bears blossoms but loses them all on the same day."

"What does he mean by this comparison?"

"I asked Issa the same question. He believes that once you put yourself in a volatile situation, you cannot expect to survive long. So, just like a lone cherry tree on a stormy mountain hill, you will be vulnerable, infertile, and eventually uprooted."

"Wow. Issa is wise. Danger has always held an allure for Mahmood. Once he called me and the twins into the closet and showed us stitches along his abdomen. He said he and Ali got into a fight with a few guys in town."

"Mahmood's draw to trouble may be self-destructive, but I am in more imminent danger than him. Issa will not admit it, but I know he is concerned about my safety as well."

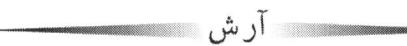

——————— آرش ———————

At the edge of the stream, Neloo sat on a rock in a patch of shade thrown by their willow tree. She lifted her skirt loosely over her knees and dipped her feet in the cold water. Ahrash landed next to her. The innocent touch of their arms warmed Neloo's heart with joy.

"Let's eat our *klucheh* now." She excitedly flipped open a

handkerchief on her lap.

Ahrash sniffed the bread with delight but did not touch it. "Can we share our bread with *Koor** Akbar?" he asked, folding the linen back over before receiving an answer.

Koor *Akbar was a blind man who lived in a tiny brick shack where the meadow met the woods. A few years ago, a benevolent villager had built this place for him on land that belongs to Hajji.*

The blind man used to venture out onto the village road and beg for food. But the merciless kids would tease him, poke him with sticks, and throw rocks at him. They even tricked him by putting dirt and bugs in his food.

Ahrash remembered as far back as when he was only five, desperately trying to remove the debris from the helpless man's food.

Ever since his hut had been built, Koor *Akbar decided to stay away from civilization and those villainous kids. The good and compassionate village people however, did not forget about him; they continued to bring him food, clothes, and medicine.*

The man's secluded life disturbed young Ahrash on a very deep level. He often stopped by his shack and started conversations with him. He even tried to read to him poetry, but Koor Akbar did not enjoy it.

———— آرش ————

Neloo peeked inside the hut through a tiny window. Scanning the disheveled room briefly, her eyes then rested on Koor Akbar. The man was buried under a haphazard pile of frayed blankets with only his bushy head and two thin arms poking through.

"Who gets him water?" she asked Ahrash.

"Hajji sends fresh water and food once a week. I have seen other people bring him food as well."

---

* blind

Ahrash knocked at the door. "Koor Akbar, we have some k*lucheh* for you," he shouted.

"Leave it outside," a frail voice answered.

"No, I can't. The bugs will attack it in no time."

The door to the hut opened and Koor Akbar appeared in its frame. He was gaunt and toothless, his face awash of blood. Without uttering a word, he stretched out his hand for the treat.

His papery thin skin wrenched at Neloo's heart.

Koor Akbar's life would have made a fantastic book. It was so bizarre that parents in Kultappa often used it as a cautionary tale for their children.

Decades ago, a young man named Jamal married his cousin Layla, the most beautiful girl in the village.

Jamal worked very hard at his job of transferring food and materials to and from the neighboring communities. Every day at dawn, he would put the bulky sacks on his horse, kiss his wife and leave the village. He would always return before dark.

One snowy evening, Layla had readied dinner on the sofreh *and waited for her husband's return. But Jamal did not show up, even after the last light faded from the sky.*

Layla's in-laws tried to convince her that the weather had forced their son to stay overnight in another village. But she could not be swayed, knowing her husband had come home to her in much heavier snow.

The next day and many more days passed without any news from Jamal. Family members and friends began looking for him, searching his entire route. Unfortunately, they could not find any sign of him or his horse. They had both simply vanished.

A four-month pregnant Layla sobbed day and night, all along, holding on to a glimmer of hope that her husband would return. After the birth of their son, however, she knew in her heart that Jamal was gone forever.

In memory of Jamal, Layla named their boy Akbar, her husband's middle name.

Once the year of mourning had passed, Layla's in-laws gave her their blessing to remarry. There were many men in the village who were willing suitors, but Layla rejected them all. She had decided to remain with Jamal's parents and raise Akbar with them.

Knowing how to sew, she purchased a sewing machine and started making clothes for the villagers. She was very talented and soon became a well-known seamstress in Kultappa and the outlying areas.

Layla raised her son well, sent him to school and watched him grow into a fine young man.

Sadly, once Akbar reached puberty, he began to lose his sight due to a degenerative disease. By the time he was sixteen, he was completely blind.

The catastrophe hit the family hard, yet the mother and son managed to have a decent life for many years together. Akbar's grandparents had left them their house and Layla had a decent income from her sewing jobs.

As Layla grew older, she became more and more concerned about her son, wondering who would take care of him when she was gone. She tried to find a wife for him, but no girls in their village were willing to marry a blind man.

A friend suggested an orphaned teenage girl from the Naansa village whose face was severely scarred from a case of smallpox.

The young girl, Goli, accepted the marriage proposal to Akbar, who was now in his forties.

Goli was not pretty, but she was smart and energetic. In no time, she learned how to cook, sew, and help around the house. She cared well for Akbar during the day and at night she was lustful and pleasing.

Akbar was madly in love with her. The mere sound of her footsteps around the house would send him into reveries of the moment when he could touch her soft legs in bed. And when she spoke, her voice made him feel as though he had an angel for a wife.

After some time, Goli's brother came to live with the three of them. Like his sister, he was upbeat, sociable and smart. He chipped in for the cost of the food and helped around the house when needed. Once, he even took the entire family on a pilgrimage to Mashhad in his employer's truck.

Goli's announcement of her pregnancy brought about an indescribable joy for Akbar and Layla. The mother and son had never been so happy before; life was prosperous, and their family was growing.

Shortly after this good news, Goli's brother told the family that his boss was retiring and that his truck was for sale. He expressed how much he wished to buy the truck and that he had only a portion of the necessary amount saved.

Goli approached Akbar for help. She suggested that he pay for the truck and become a business partner with her brother. Akbar, hesitant at first, was eventually convinced to sell his house and pay for the truck. They would buy a smaller home in the Naansa village, where properties were cheaper, and use the rest of money to start the business.

Everything happened quickly and smoothly. The house was sold and the truck and new home in Naansa were purchased.

Goli and her brother stacked all the family belongings onto the truck and drove to their new place to unload them. They were scheduled to return the following day for Akbar and his mother.

The next day however came and went without any sign of either sibling or the truck.

The villagers started looking for them. While asking around Naansa, they found that the two had never arrived. Like Jamal and his horse, the brother, sister, and truck had disappeared without a trace.

Before long, Akbar and Layla uncovered disturbing information. Goli, in fact, did not have a brother; the man was an imposter and likely her lover. All the papers that Akbar signed were false and no house or truck had been purchased in his name.

After losing their home and all their belongings, the mother and son had to live with a relative. Hajji bought a used sewing machine for Layla so that she could have some way to earn a living.
Seven years later, Layla died of a heart attack.
Akbar, blind and without an income, moved from relative to relative until he was not welcome anywhere anymore.

Saying goodbye to Koor Akbar, Neloo and Ahrash walked back to the stream and sat on a shady rock. Neloo's mind immediately went back to the camel, imagining the horrific images of the animal being slaughtered. She recalled her own family sacrificing a sheep in their yard upon the birth of the twins. The gruesome savagery of that day could never be erased from her mind. "Do you think the camel is already dead?" she asked.

"I am certain of it," Ahrash responded dully.

"That poor creature."

———— آرش ————

Mahmood and the two butchers were bent over the camel's massive body. Covered in blood they carved and sliced the carcass without any emotion. Hajji was standing by them, handing meat to the villagers. A few yards away, the camel's head, severed at the bottom of its long neck, lied on the ground in a river of blood – unattended.

Hassan, a disabled man dressed in layers of tattered rags, was next in line. The butcher handed over a good size portion, but before Hajji was able to give it to him, Mahmood snatched the meat away. "His wife already got some," he snarled curtly.

"But I have a big family to feed," the man protested.

"Hassan is right son, he has a large family," Hajji interfered. He was taken aback by Mahmood's lack of sympathy. Everyone in the village knew that Hassan could not find a job with his condition and that his family barely survived through the charity of others.

"Hang back, my friend. I am sure we will have extra at the end," Hajji consoled the crippled man with his usual kind voice.

CHAPTER 11

Ahrash Kamangir, the Arrow Thrower, is a highly admired hero in Persian folklore.

According to the ancient stories, King Manuchehr of Iran and King Afrasiab of Turan, had been engaged in a bitter war over their disputed border. After eight years without either side gaining an advantage, the two combatant rulers decided to make peace.

They agreed to have an Iranian archer stand atop Mount Damavand, in the Alborz Range and shoot an arrow to the east. The land that fell within the range of his bow's shot would belong to Iran and the rest would be Turan's.

King Manuchehr chose Ahrash Kamangir, known for his swift arrow, to undertake this monumental mission.

Mindful of the enormity of his task come morning, Ahrash Kamangir stayed awake all night. He meditated at the peak of the mountain, cleansing his mind and soul under a blanket of stars. By the time dawn had crept over the land, Ahrash was ready to defend his country's territorial integrity.

He picked up his bow and arrow and prayed one last time to Ahura Mazda, beseeching his Zoroastrian God for courage and strength. Putting all his power into the effort, he then strained his bow like never before and released his arrow.

The arrow traveled a thousand leagues, a distance equal to a forty day walk. As the arrow finally landed to mark the border, the brave archer too fell to the ground – his heart completely spent – and died instantly.

آرش

Ahrash Kamangir is one of the heroes in the epic *Shahnameh*, penned by the Persian literary giant, Ferdowsi.

Shahnameh brings to life the mythical and historical past of the Persian Empire. It covers the reign of fifty kings, telling stories of war, heroism, love, and betrayal. The poetry in the book is written in simple words, but the characters have complex personas. The most robust individual would sometimes show their weaknesses or flaws, while the villains would surprise the reader with moments of compassion and humanity.

Ahrash started reciting *Shahnameh* when he was about ten years old. At first, he only read it to Issa, but the verses and stories were so captivating, that his parents joined the brothers in no time.

Every evening, after dinner, the family gathered around the young Ahrash and he proudly walked them through the glorious era of the Persian Empire.

At that tender age, Ahrash was utterly fascinated by the book's characters, especially the warriors and heroes. When night arrived and he closed his eyes to sleep, scenes from the splendorous Persian army came to life before him. He saw the king on his magnificent white horse with a shimmering mane leading his cavalry toward the battlefield. He could smell the dirt scattered in the air and felt the warmth of the misting air swirling out of the horse's flared nostrils.

Among all the individuals in the book, Ahrash Kamangir was the one that particularly affected the young reader. Ahrash felt a kinship with the hero who shared his name and wished he had the power and ability to do extraordinary deeds like his idol.

When Ahrash shared his thoughts with Issa, his wise brother gave him a long and effective lecture. "Heroes in books are often symbolic, a way by which the writer can personify good traits in a human being. Heroism does not always have a tangible or an immediate result and heroes are not always known for one decisive act. There are many heroes among us. Think of Hajji, a down to earth man, who uses his wealth and power to help others instead of being self-indulgent. Look at Dad, who works all day in the field with his arthritic hands to provide for his family. And what about you, Ahrash? How many kids your age would give up their summers, get up at dawn and stay in the meadow all day alone, so that their parents could save a shepherd's salary? You, Dad and Hajji are real life examples of selfless heroes."

Issa held Ahrash's small hand between his own and after a long pause, he added, "You should know that you are your brother's greatest hero. You brighten his dark world each and every day."

CHAPTER 12

A towel on her shoulder, Neloo walked toward a small brick structure behind the house. She was in a great mood and, as always, grateful that she could wash up in privacy, unlike most villagers who had to use public baths.

She perfectly remembered when her father had started building the family's bath house; it had been in the middle of an especially hot and humid summer week.

Despite the brutal temperatures, Neloo insisted on staying in the yard to keep her father company.

Sharif, not being able to change his stubborn girl's mind, rolled a big log toward a nearby cherry tree and brought it to rest in the partial shade. "Sit here so we can talk while I am working."

A man of a few words, Sharif somehow found his loquacious side on those days. He entertained Neloo with stories of his childhood, his teenage life, his falling in love and getting married. He talked of his parents, letting his daughter know how much she resembled her grandmother.

Occasionally, Sakineh, eight months pregnant with the twins, brought lemonade in a large tumbler. Sharif sat by Neloo on the log, his long and massive body totally eclipsing the sun. He offered his daughter the first sip but Neloo was only interested in wiping the sweat beads from his forehead.

The breaks from work were short but each time ended with Neloo on her father's shoulders, grasping for the ripe cherries high above them.

It took four days for Sharif to install a furnace, run water lines from the well and build two interlocking stalls. Neloo, unwavering, stayed with him the entire time.

———————— آرش ————————

Her body was shimmering under the water as if she was carved from the marble. Slender and tall, with delicate breasts, a curvy waist, and a flat stomach, Neloo owned a beautiful figure and she was well aware of it.

She finished washing off but remained under shower, longing for Ahrash to be there to admire her beauty. She wished to be in his arms, the warmth of his breath amidst her hair, his hands caressing her neck sliding down to her breasts. The emotions expanded inside Neloo strongly. Her breath quickened, her lips swelled, and her nipples stood erect.

From deep in her reverie, she suddenly remembered that she needed to leave plenty of hot water for the twins. It was always a challenge to convince the boys to get into the shower but once in there, they never wanted to leave. They had somehow invented many interesting games to play in that small place.

———————— آرش ————————

Leaving the first stall, Neloo reached for her towel. The door to the outside was slightly ajar. She panicked: *I closed the door when I entered the shower. Someone has been here.*

The towel was hardly around her when the door was thrown open, slamming against the wall. Mahmood entered the stall and immediately put his hand over Neloo's mouth.

"Mom is at Auntie's and the twins are out in the street. It is just me and you," he said with a wide grin on his face.

Neloo was frozen with fear.

"Do not be worried, Sis. I am not going to hurt you," Mahmood slowly removed his hand from Neloo's mouth. "I just want to see you naked, that's all," he added in an unhurried voice, his revolting alcoholic breath invading the air between them.

"I just want to see you naked. Is that clear?" he said it again, this time, with grave authority.

Neloo frantically searched for an escape, but she came up blank. Her muscles seized and her words were trapped in her throat. She could only manage to clutch her protective towel more securely against her shivering body.

"I just want to look at you, Sis. What are you so worried about? Pretend I am Ahrash."

"Get out! Get out!" Neloo screamed, finding her voice at last. "I will tell dad and he will kill you!"

Mahmood covered Neloo's mouth again and put a knife to her throat. His piercing eyes were bloodshot, glaring at her with the empty savagery of a beast about to pounce on his prey.

"You won't tell dad. And if you do, I will kill all of you in your sleep."

Neloo inched her body closer to the door, hoping to run away if she got the chance. Mahmood quickly blocked her way and deepened the position of his knife.

"Let go of the damn towel!" he shouted.

A streak of watery pink blood ran from Neloo's neck and collected in a small pool in the hollow of her right collarbone.

"Listen my slutty sister. I could cut your throat now and run out, waving my bloody knife with honor. Do you understand?" He pushed the knife harder in place, releasing more blood, bright red now.

Neloo clung more desperately to her towel.

His patience waning, Mahmood brought his head forward, his face almost flush with Neloo's. "And do not think for a moment that I am not tempted to do it," he muttered, his lips barely moving.

The color drained from Neloo's face.

"Drop the towel now!" Mahmood demanded again and right away, reverted to speaking calmly again. "I just want to look at you, Sis. I promise I will leave after that."

A sliver of hope entered Neloo's heart with that promise.

She let go of her towel.

Mahmood withdrew his knife and stepped back, staring at his sister's quivering body with lust.

"Turn around now, very slowly," he commanded.

Neloo started rotating. Like a figurine affixed to a windup toy, she was completely at the mercy of a petulant child.

When the turn was completed, she quickly grabbed her towel only to have Mahmood snatch it away from her.

"Not so fast, Sis!" he said, running his knife around the curve of her breast, "I am not through with your body yet."

Blood ran from Neloo's breast and searched for an easy pathway to travel. She felt a warmth between her legs as urine started dripping down to her knees. Not knowing what would happen next, she just prayed for a miracle, someone, even one of the twins, to appear and save her.

Mahmood, unaware of her agony, continued to feast upon his sister's shuddering body.

An eternity seemed to pass before he finally backed out and left.

آرش

With her first step out of the stall, a creeping itch attacked Neloo. The sensation started at her scalp and quickly spread all over. It was as though thousands of bugs had emerged from their sacs and began crawling under her skin.

She started clawing at herself.

Unable to stop the itch, she scurried to the well, pumped water and poured it over her head. The water only gave her temporary relief and, in no time, the itching returned with a vengeance.

She dumped a few more buckets of water on herself and hurriedly left the yard.

The twins playing outside, trotted after their sister, calling her name.

Not getting an answer, they retreated and resumed their games.

———— آرش ————

At the edge of the meadow, Neloo sat on a fallen tree, where wild mint had shot up all around.

A finch was cooling off in a small puddle nearby. Undisturbed by the girl's presence, she only paused briefly and then continued flapping her wings in the water.

Neloo sat there for a while, reliving her horrid ordeal over and over. She thought herself filthy, and everything around her, sinister and soiled; even the tiny finch in the puddle was offensive to her.

She knew she was in desperate need of solace: *I must go to Ahrash.*

She rose to her feet and started walking up the hill. Traveling only a few yards, she saw Koor Akbar in not too far distance. He was standing perfectly still by his shack, resembling an old statue of a peasant. The blind man's presence gave the miserable girl a jolt, sharpening her ache of helplessness and surrender: *I am as alone as he is. No one is able to help either of us, not even Ahrash.*

Neloo turned around and walked back, relieved that she did not burden her soulmate with her suffering.

She sat on the same trunk and began to cry.

The finch ended her bath and flew away. A few other tiny birds used the same puddle in sequence.

When there were no more tears left to shed, the broken Neloo left the meadow. This time, she decided to go to Ali's house instead of seeing Ahrash.

CHAPTER 13

Ali's house stood atop a sloped lot with no fence or well-defined boundary. Neloo could easily see his sisters in the yard from a distance. Shereen was hanging clothes on a laundry line; Hanna was loitering in the vegetable garden.

The yard was unkempt and pitiful. Bushes were either overgrown or dead while broken limbs hung from most trees. Rusty tools, chicken wire and various wood planks were strewn about as though the place had been forsaken for years.

Approaching the house, Neloo tried to calm herself by taking small steps and deep breaths. She was determined to hide her pain and to not reveal her shameful encounter with Mahmood.

When she appeared on the patio, Shereen rushed toward her and immediately felt a jolt. "What in the world had happened to you, Neloo? Why do you have so many scratches on your face?" she asked, shepherding her friend toward a bench.

They sat down and the family cat joined them, kneading Shereen's lap, purring. "You have been crying. Is it your mom again? Are you and Ahrash in trouble?"

Without answering, Neloo plunged her face into her hands and began to cry.

Shereen was a close and trusted confidante. Neloo had shared with her many personal thoughts and secrets including her love for Ahrash and her suffocating relationship with her mother. Only three years older, savvy Shereen was always helpful, capable of bringing Neloo to a rational state in difficult situations.

"Hanna, go check on mom. See if she needs anything," Shereen called to her younger sister.

"I'll go when I am finished, there are still some ripe tomatoes on the vines."

"Go now. I think I heard her calling."

Hanna, with a bowl of tomatoes over her head, jumped out of the garden, spinning in the air. She put the bowl down at the edge of the garden and cartwheeled the rest of the way to the entrance of the house.

"I know something awful has happened to you, Neloo. If you tell me what is bothering you, I might be able to help," Shereen said once her sister could not hear them.

The pain was too much for Neloo to keep inside. Shereen was exactly the person she needed now, someone who would not judge her for Mahmood's crime.

She exhaled slowly and began to tell her saga.

"I am so sorry, Neloo. I am so sorry." Shereen held her shattered friend in her arms.

Neloo shed tears heavily like a squeezed raincloud.

When Hannah returned to the yard, she was as cross as ever. "Mom wasn't calling. She was asleep. Now that you made me wake her up, you should take her to the bathroom," she said and disappeared in a flash.

Shereen left to help her mother but her mind was on Neloo, entangled with negative and scary thoughts. She had heard stories about incest and how its dark power had destroyed many families, causing ruin, suicide and even murder. Neloo was in danger and worryingly alone. Sakineh was not a supportive mother to her and oddly worshiped her eldest son: *Who would protect this girl now?*

——————— آرش ———————

Carrying a cup of hot tea with a mint leaf floating on top, Shereen smiled gently at her friend. "It will calm your nerves," she handed the tea to Neloo and sat next to her. "I believe you should tell your parents what Mahmood did today," she said quietly.

Neloo shook her head, "I cannot. It is too embarrassing."

"Your silence will embolden your brother. Remember, it is always easier to take a head-down lamb to the slaughterhouse than its feisty cousin," Shereen continued to persuade Neloo to be brave and proactive. She even shared the stories she knew about incest.

If Neloo had heard those tales a day earlier, she would have had a hard time believing them. Now, after her own horrid experience she understood how helpless and vulnerable young girls can be, even in the close net of family.

"I am terrified to go back home but the twins need to wash up before their mother returns," Neloo agonized.

"Maybe I should go with you, help with the twins and stay at your house until one of your parents arrives. I just need a few minutes to finish hanging the rest of the laundry."

Although it was her own suggestion to accompany Neloo, Shereen had some apprehension about leaving her ill mother with the ten-year-old Hannah. She thought: *If Ali was here, he could help with the situation.* Unfortunately, her brother never stayed home or even offered to watch over their sick mother. In the last couple of months, she and Hanna had been out of the village only once, and that was for their mother's treatment in town.

Shereen was irritated but could not stay angry with Ali for too long. Compared to the perverted Mahmood, her brother was a saint.

Almost done with the clothes, she glanced at Neloo over the laundry line. Her friend was sitting on the bench like a frozen river, shrouded in a haze. Her face was so pale, as if the misery that had descended on her was bleeding the life out of her.

"Poor girl, she has fallen hard and far from grace," Shereen murmured.

CHAPTER 14

The lone window in the room was wide open, yet the scant wind was not able to diminish the heat exuding from the walls and the thin roof.

Neloo sat by the *sofreh,* avoiding eye contact with her family. She tore off a small piece of bread and chewed it listlessly while her favorite dinner, *koofteh,* * remained untouched in a bowl before her.

"Neloo *Jaan*, why aren't you eating tonight? Are you sick?" Sharif inquired.

"I don't know, Dad. I am just not hungry."

"It is probably the heat. Maybe you should splash some water on your face."

Relieved, Neloo rose to her feet and scurried toward the kitchen. Her mother snatched her untouched food and placed it in front of Mahmood. "You should eat her share then," she said.

———— آرش ————

Evening, when the entire family relaxed together, used to be Neloo's favorite time of day. It was not the same today. She was unnerved, as if she was in an unknown place, among strangers.

"Tell us a story," the twins asked, competing for their sister's lap.

"Sorry boys, no story tonight. I have had a bad headache all day."

"What is that?" one twin fretted, pointing at the scrape on his sister's neck.

She has scratches everywhere!" the other twin screamed, discovering more marks.

---

* *an Iranian meatball originating from the Tabriz region*

The boys' commotion caused everyone in the room to turn toward Neloo.

"I fell into a thorny bush at Shereen's house; it gave me a bad itch."

Both twins folded their arms across their chests and scowled. "We will spit and pee on Shereen's plant tomorrow!" one twin announced and his brother supported the idea. "Yeah. We will kick and destroy all her bushes!"

An earnest discussion on their attack ensued right away. The boys were lethally serious and wanted to be well prepared in seeking their revenge.

Mahmood was delighted with the way boys were strategizing. "Let me know if you need some help," he said, bursting with laughter. He then switched gears and asked the boys to sit on his feet while he did his sit-up routine.

The twin enthusiastically accepted the offer, abandoning their war talk all at once.

Sitting on Mahmood's feet did not last long either, as the boys soon grew bored and started crawling all over their big brother. "Wrestle with us," they demanded.

"I am not done exercising. Do you want a wimp for a brother?" Mahmood said with a roar, scaring the boys with his pretend paws. "No, I didn't think so!"

The twins screamed and ran away but returned instantly for more excitement.

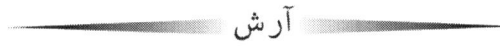

———— آرش ————

What happened in the bath house that morning had completely traumatized Neloo and, if it had not been for Shereen's support, she would have totally fallen apart. Shereen helped her retain a lucid mind, enough at least to ponder the situation and weigh her options: *I would never dare tell Sakineh and there is no chance to be alone with my father. If I am to voice my grievances, I should talk to dad tonight and in the presence of the entire family.*

She stole a glance at her father who was leaning on a large pillow at the front of the room. He was deep in thought. The cigarette at the corner of his mouth had developed a long ashy tip, threatening to crumble.

The massive presence of the family patriarch gave the broken girl a temporary sense of security. She inched closer to him, hoping he would notice her aching face and asked about it. But that was merely wishful thinking. Sharif had stopped looking directly at his daughter's face a while ago. He spoke to her now as if he was in the presence of a non-relative adult female, head down and without eye contact.

Gathering her courage, Neloo continued gravitating toward her father. At one point, she was sitting so close to him that she could even whisper her ordeal into his ear.

How on earth do I even bring up such a subject? Should I explain the event step by step, let him know that Mahmood was drunk and that he had a knife drawn on me? Should I say my brother threatened to cut my throat and that he forced me to disrobe and turn around in front of him? The thought sent painful spasms throughout Neloo's body: *Maybe I should waive all the details and just mention that Mahmood saw me without any clothes on in the bath house.*

Neloo breathed out deeply, recognizing at once that the shame would be colossal regardless of how she explains her nightmare.

Dismayed, she decided to seek refuge back in the kitchen.

There was a slight breeze coming through the window. She laid her arms on the windowsill and rested her chin on her hands. Closing her eyes, she tried to focus on her breathing, allowing her atrophied mind to gradually rebuild.

Shereen's voice echoed in her head: "What happened to you was beyond your control. You were a victim of crime and should not be ashamed or apologetic to anyone. Talk to your father, he is an intelligent man and capable of good judgment."

Shereen is right. Dad is the only person with the power to help me. I have to speak out despite the humiliation.

To avoid making a harried mistake, the logical Neloo started analyzing the situation one last time. *"What will happen after I reveal Mahmood's assault?"* She asked herself. *"Dad is a man intolerant of any indecency and Mahmood is like a rabid dog, on the ready to burst out with his aggressive power. What would be the outcome upon a confrontation between the two men? A horrible fight, maybe even bloodshed,"* she concluded.

Recalling how mercifully her father had handled the dilemma between Issa and Mahmood, Neloo also considered the possibility that he may only deliver an ultimatum to his son. *Would Mahmood then kill us all in sleep as he had threatened?*

No matter how outrageous her brother's claim was, Neloo couldn't put it past him. *I need more time to think, diving into a decision might end in disaster.*

─── آرش ───

Mahmood was standing in the middle of the room, nibbling at a bunch of grapes when Neloo returned from the kitchen.

"I want some," one twin demanded, darting from around the corner. Mahmood put his hand on his chest and softly pushed him a few feet away. "There! Stay right there and open your mouth," he ordered.

The other twin immediately joined them with a gaping maw.

As Neloo passed them, Mahmood rocked on his heels and sent her a sideways glance, flashing a smile. The proximity to her brazen brother in the room brought the miserable girl back to the untamed images of her entrapment, when she was in Mahmood's snare, powerless and fearing for her life.

A scream threatened to crawl from Neloo's throat and reveal her secret.

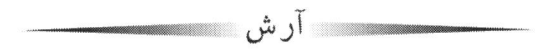

─── آرش ───

The painful, long evening was coming to an end. As with every other night, Neloo opened the closet door and retrieved the bedding. The twins immediately rushed at her, dragging out the blankets, tossing the pillows around. Soon they were wrestling on the piles of cushions and covers.

Pulling the blankets out from underneath the boys, Neloo suddenly felt an eeriness. Out of the corner of her eye, she noticed Mahmood was staring at her breasts.

She quickly bowed her back and pulled her clinging nightgown away from her chest.

---------- آرش ----------

Three beds were set in neat rows on the floor. Sharif's and Sakineh's were at one end, near the front door, the twin's and Neloo's were successively next. Mahmood's bed was a couple of feet away, perpendicular to others.

Mahmood took off his shirt and lied down. The twins immediately escaped from their spot and jumped on him. Rowdy and with full energy, they tried to push their big brother off his bed.

Involved in the game, Mahmood tickled the boy's ribs and the soles of their feet. "Go back to bed, you little devils!" he said, laughing uncontrollably.

Foreseeing a bitter night, Neloo sank deep into her bed and pulled the sheet high above her shoulders. She was weary and exhausted, yet too rattled to sleep. *What if Mahmood gets in my bed when everyone is asleep? Should I scream? What would happen if I did?*

Her mind muffled and clouded, Neloo closed her eyes. A high-pitched ringing started playing in her ears and the ground began to shake beneath her. Somewhere between a hallucinatory and rational state, she saw Mahmood standing above her dead parents with a bloody knife. She turned her head and found the twins lying next to her with their throats slit.

They cannot be dead − I can hear them giggling. Neloo tried to reason with herself, but confusion and horror had trumped her logical mind.

آرش

After sufficiently wearing out the twins, Mahmood held their hands between his own. The twins kicked him and escaped. He tried again, this time holding them tighter. "Now, what can you do?"

One twin wriggled free and tried to help the other screaming boy.

"Everybody, quit it! I have to go out to the field before sunrise," Sharif scolded his sons.

The twins quieted down but continued wrestling with Mahmood.

Gradually, the noise level rose again.

"Lights out now! And everybody in their own beds!" Sharif said, sternly.

The little boys scampered off to their beds. They carried on, snickering softly, while rubbing their heavy eyelids with their fists.

Mahmood rose to his knees and flicked the light switch on the wall above him.

CHAPTER 15

The room was filled with fresh air. The nighttime breeze had drawn in the sweet smell of wildflowers, fragrantly dusting their bedding. After the hot and muggy start to the night, the morning's cool and pleasant conditions allowed the family to remain asleep longer than usual.

When Neloo opened her eyes, bizarrely, it was to Sakineh's sleeping face. Confused for a moment, she then remembered switching places with the twins in the middle of the night.

Traces of Mahmood's features on her mother's face gave Neloo a jolt. She immediately squeezed her body like a spring to edge away from her.

I must have fallen asleep after dawn, she surmised, remembering still being awake when her father had left for the fields.

One twin immediately climbed over Neloo and nestled himself into her arms. The other twin, with his eyes half shut, joined them right away. He laid flat on his sister, his limp arms hanging over either side of her.

Neloo stroked the boys' hair gently, wondering if Sakineh might approve a permanent change to their sleeping arrangement.

"Tell us a story, Neloo," one twin asked.

"Yes, tell us a story. You promised last night," the other twin said, raising his head from Neloo's chest.

"You know that it is breakfast time, my dear brothers."

The boys nodded their heads and started showering Neloo with kisses. "Please," they begged. "Just one short story?"

Charmed by the twins' sweetness, Neloo couldn't help but oblige.

Long ago, in a faraway land, a genie gave a small bottle to a young girl. The bottle contained a sleeping potion, enough to put the entire town to sleep.

The girl hid the gift for many years until one stormy day on her thirteenth birthday. On that day, she wondered, "How does it feel to dance naked in the rain?"

She went to the community well before noon and poured in the entire potion. Hiding behind a tree, she then waited until all the families collected their daily water.

Soon everyone in town fell asleep.

The girl, confident that no one was around to see her, shed her clothes and danced, twirling for hours like a dervish.

"Is Koor Akbar a dervish?" one twin interrupted the story.

"No, he is not. A dervish can dance and twirl for a long time," Neloo explained.

"Now, listen to the rest of the story."

At home, the girl waited all day and all night, but her parents remained fast asleep. She ran to the neighbor for help, but they were not awake either. Fearful, she went from house to house only to find everyone in a deep sleep. Not knowing how to undo the curse, the girl went back out into the rain, removed her clothes yet again and twirled for all eternity.

"What is 'eternity'?" one of the boys asked.

"Forever and ever."

"We did not like that story. Tell us another one," the twins complained.

"It is time for breakfast now. I will tell you guys better stories tonight. I promise," Neloo vowed earnestly.

———— آرش ————

The twins finished their warm milk and bread quickly and ran out to the yard.

Neloo and her mother sat together for their meals. Neloo only drank some sweet tea. Sakineh did not ask any questions but looked at her with suspicion.

After breakfast, Sakineh walked to the window and grabbed a small jar off the ledge. She glanced inside the jar and instantly froze. "Bastard!" she hissed, landing a violent kick on the sleeping Mahmood. "You son of a bitch – you took money from the jar again!" she shouted.

With a groan, Mahmood sat up, half asleep, "What money? I did not touch any money."

"That was for our food, you bastard, not for your booze!" Sakineh continued kicking her son.

"Why is it that everything that goes wrong in this house is always my fault? Maybe Neloo took it and gave it to Ahrash," Mahmood snickered, looking at Neloo who was stacking the bedding in the closet.

Growing tired of kicking, Sakineh grabbed a large broom from the corner of the room. She attempted to whack Mahmood with its tightly wrapped fibrous handle. Mahmood dodged the first strike. He jumped up and ran around the room with Sakineh chasing him.

Isn't she afraid that Mahmood might hit her back? Neloo marveled at Sakineh's bravery, as she watched the mother and son scrambling about.

Mahmood sidestepped his mother and grabbed Neloo's shoulders, seeking refuge behind her. His contact made Neloo shudder.

"You useless piece of shit eating your father's food and stealing his money!" Sakineh snarled, still trying to get at Mahmood from around Neloo.

"I have never stolen anything in my life," Mahmood said, falsely solemn.

"Do you think that I do not know how you got that chicken? You dickhead bastard! You are the shame of this family!" Sakineh shouted, still struggling to hit her clever son.

With an unexpected jerk, Neloo freed herself from Mahmood,

lowered her body and snuck away.

Sakineh raised her weapon and hit her son so forcefully that the broom snapped in half.

Still not satisfied, the angry woman ran to the closest to fetch a new broom. When she returned, her son was gone. Inflamed, Sakineh grabbed Mahmood's clothes and threw them out into the yard.

"I hope a truck runs you over today, you traitorous thief!" she slammed the door and stomped off to the kitchen.

Neloo was incredulous. *How can a mother curse her son so spitefully, especially the son she appears to adore so much?*

──────── آرش ────────

The door to the house creaked open a minute later and Mahmood slinked in. Holding his forefinger to his lips, he invited Neloo to join in his duplicitous silence. He tiptoed toward the window sill and quietly snatched the fistful change left in the money jar. With a wink at his sister, he quickly disappeared.

CHAPTER 16

It had been three days since Neloo had been ambushed in the bath house. Her pain was still strong, indelibly etched on her face. She missed Ahrash badly but did not want him to see her so miserable.

───── آرش ─────

The gate to the house opened with a screech and Hanna entered the yard holding a bouquet of flowers. She skipped merrily the entire way, her ponytail swinging back and forth in the air. She reached the front door and pounded on it once. Hardly pausing, she knocked again, this time in a rhythmic tune.

Neloo heard the knock and stopped kneading her dough. She rinsed her hands and rushed to open the door.

Hanna continued playing her song with her knuckles even after the door was ajar.

"This is for you." She handed Neloo the colorful bouquet. "My sister picked them from the yard this morning."

"So pretty. Come on in, Hanna *Jaan*," Neloo said and left for the kitchen only to return quickly with a tall plastic vase.

"Can I have that one?" Hanna reached for a geranium cluster. "I like to put them on my cheeks."

Neloo gave the happy Hanna the geranium and placed the rest of the flowers in the vase.

Removing the petals from the flower, Hanna set each one neatly on the window ledge.

"Do you know my brother has a crush on you?" she casually asked, while still dissecting the flower head. "When he found out the bouquet was for you, he said, 'Neloo is certainly worthy of flowers.'"

"That was kind of Ali but it does not mean he has a crush on me."

"But he does. He always says you are the prettiest, smartest and the nicest girl he has ever known. I told him, 'Why don't you marry her then?' Do you know what his answer was?"

"No. What?"

"He said, 'Neloo deserves a much better man.'"

Hanna raised her head and gave Neloo a charming smile, "Can I tell him that you said hi?"

"No. That is not necessary, Hanna *Jaan*."

Hanna pouted. "Don't you like my brother?"

"Ali is a very nice man. But he is my brother's friend, not mine."

Not happy with the direction of the conversation, Hanna turned around in a huff and stood before a small mirror on the wall. She examined her face for a while, selected a petal, licked its back and carefully positioned it on her left cheek. Satisfied with the starting point, she continued adding more pieces. She was focused and had the steady hands of an artist.

In no time, the talented girl had created two perfect intertwining circles of petals on one side of her face.

Neloo stood behind her young guest, watching her in the mirror. Hanna's face had the vibrancy of spring flowers, her gazelle-like eyes shone with rebellious excitement. Looking at her, full of joy, so blissfully unaware of her fragile fate, freshened Neloo's wounds. "How many hungry wolves shadow this unwary child? When will her innocence be squashed?" she sighed.

"My sister told me I should stay with you and keep you company. Is that ok with you?" Hanna asked

"That sounds wonderful, Hanna Jaan, but I have to let you know that I need to wash the breakfast dishes and make some *klucheh*. I am also a little ill and will probably not be very good company. You might have more fun playing with the twins and the neighbor kids. It is your choice though."

"I saw the twins were playing with an older girl," Hannah said while inspecting her cheek closely in the mirror.

"Yes. Her name is Golpeera and she is very nice. I think she is six or seven years old. You should go and meet her."

It was an easy decision for Hanna to join the kids outside. "I will come and check on you," she declared, walking toward the door.

"Hannah *Jaan*, can you do me a favor before you start playing?"

"Of course, anything. As long as you let me tell Ali you said hi."

Neloo acknowledged Hanna's teasing only with a smile and added, "I promised Ahrash that I would read poetry with him today, but as I told you, I don't feel good."

"Do you want me to go to the meadow and tell him?" Hanna asked excitedly.

"No dear. I want you to go to Ahrash's house and tell his mother that I have a bad cold and cannot join Ahrash until I feel better."

"Do you really have a cold?"

"I feel sick. It might be a cold," Neloo said and paused briefly. "His mom's name is Aziz and she is super kind."

"I know Ahrash's mom. Once in the bath house, she told me that I am a smart and lovely girl. She compared me to you when you were my age," Hanna explained as she rushed to leave.

Back in the kitchen, Neloo stood by the window. She watched Hanna and the neighbor girl walking toward Ahrash's house. Strong gusts intermittently lifted their skirts. To beat the wind at its own game, the youngsters, fearlessly laughed and spun as they moved forward.

Neloo knew nobody had broken the girls' spirits yet.

CHAPTER 17

"I heated the bath this morning. Make sure to wash up before leaving the house," Sakineh reminded her son while serving him breakfast.

"Of course, Mother," Mahmood misleadingly agreed, knowing full well that he had already made plans to go to the river with Nader.

Nader worked in town but often visited his parents in the village. A few years older and mentally and physically solid, he was the only person that Mahmood admired growing up.

When Nader was around, he and Mahmood were joined at the hip. Together, they hiked unknown trails, swam and fished in the river, and shot down birds with stones. They also arranged sports matches and gambling events, engaging many of the village youth.

Today, the two friends swam in the river most of the afternoon. They then settled by the water and played backgammon, smoking and drinking. As the evening drew near, they decided to take up residence by the Village Boulder.

──────── آرش ────────

Leaning on the mountainous rock, Mahmood removed a small flask of vodka from his shirt pocket and held it toward Nader. Nader took a swig and returned the alcohol to him.

After a few minutes, Ali joined the men with a large piece of flatbread in hand. He outstretched his arm. "Have some. Fresh from Tandoor!"

Nader tore a piece off, but Mahmood rejected the offer. "I like my drink on an empty stomach," he muttered.

"It looks like we are going to have a storm tonight," Ali initiated the conversation, pointing at some dark clouds.

Nader nodded as he ripped off another piece of bread.

"How long did you guys swim today?" Ali asked.

"A couple of hours," Nader answered.

"How cold was the water?"

"Very cold, freezing."

A long silence followed next.

Feeling unwelcome, Ali sat on a rock and quietly nibbled on his bread. He stared at the massive clouds for a while, envisioning the rain dripping from their inky wings. When his gaze dropped to the horizon, he saw three figures in the distance.

"Is that Neloo talking with Ahrash and Issa?" he asked.

Nader and Mahmood looked in the direction he was pointing: Neloo was handing a piece of paper to Ahrash.

The silence returned amidst the men and grew more uneasy.

Mahmood guzzled the remaining vodka and proceeded to rub the neck of the empty flask, staring at it intensely. His quiet anger was alarming.

Suddenly the alcoholic vessel flew in the air. Ali dodged, narrowly avoiding the hit. "Fuck you, Ali," Mahmood grunted, leaping at his shocked friend. He grabbed Ali's shoulders and started shaking him violently. "You fucking dick! Do you always have to shove it down my throat that my sister is a whore?"

Ali was still processing the situation when he was let go and pushed back with a thick spit landing at his feet. "So much for being my friend, asshole."

The angry Mahmood turned and stomped away a few paces, his knife now drawn. He pivoted his head slightly toward Ali, "Should I kill her? Is that what you want?" he said with an eerily calm voice and bolted in the direction of his sister.

Nader ran after him. "For God's sake brother, relax and curse the devil! The man was just asking a question. Why are you making such a big deal about it?"

Without answering, Mahmood sped up. Nader, tugging at his arm, tried unsuccessfully to stop him.

The distance between the men grew quickly.

Ali witnessed Nadar's failed attempts, but he was unable to move, seemingly glued to the rock.

From atop the hill, the village herd appeared at once, sending dust clouds into the air.

Nader caught up to Mahmood, thankful that he had been thwarted by the herd. He curved an arm over his friend's shoulder and walked him back to the boulder.

Mahmood remained angry, cursing everyone's name – his sister, Ahrash, Issa, Ali, and even the herds.

"There must be a better solution, pal. Going on a killing spree is not the answer," Nader said with some apprehension. "Your sister grew up with Issa and Ahrash. They are like brothers to her. If you are not happy with their friendship, talk to your father, demand that he forbid Neloo from seeing them. There is no need for any bloodshed, man. Do not let the devil lure you in."

A cluster of veins swelled on his left temple as Mahmood paced in front of the boulder. He was still fuming. "I have had enough of this disgrace. I must kill them both at once!" he said and turned around, zeroing in on Neloo and the brothers yet again.

The herd was disappearing quickly.

Knowing Mahmood's view on the recent hike of honor killings in the country, Nader had no choice but to run over and position himself between his maniacal friend and the distant, unaware victims.

"I cannot let you go. You'll have to kill me first," he said, his arms stretched out wide, his chest welcoming an attack.

─────── آرش ───────

Coaxing the deranged Mahmood back to the boulder, Nader was relieved but seriously exhausted. The terrific reality of what could have just occurred left him dry-mouthed and sick to his stomach. Yet, he stayed vigilant: *I must keep him occupied until Neloo and the brothers go their separate ways.*

He grabbed the piece of bread that was left on the boulder and presented it to Mahmood. "You had better eat something – you must be hungry."

Ignoring the offer, Mahmood just stared at Ali with a pair of angry eyes.

"Do you believe this shit? He is not even–" he began to speak but was quickly stopped by Nader. "Please do not go there again. You know that Ali's intentions are always good."

"Good intentions, my ass. The bastard has no respect for me. He is just a mule, brainless and ignorant."

Ali was aflame. It was as if a bucket of molten lead had been poured over his head and down his throat. Even though he had contended with Mahmood oppressive temper for years, today was too much for him to handle. His friend had never insulted him in front of Nader before, at least not so maliciously.

He got up and walked away with a bruised ego and stooped shoulders.

─────── آرش ───────

Halfway home, at the big walnut tree, Ali sat down and drew his knees to his chest. He felt terribly sad. *Why do I stay under control of this psycho for so long, dragging my childhood humiliations into my adult life?* He abhorred himself for his servitude and blind devotion to a man with whom he carried no weight.

Besides the degradation he had just endured, Ali knew how close the very real danger had been for Neloo and Ahrash. He had always loved Neloo and had nothing against the brothers. *I should have helped Nader. I should have protected Neloo.*

As the thought ran through Ali's mind, he remembered the time when Ahrash stood up to Mahmood, defending his blind brother: *The scrawny boy could not accept the indignity without a fight. If I had the slightest semblance of self-respect, I would have confronted that bastard today. I am undeniably a pitiful, weak person not worthy of being called a man.*

Ali loathed himself even knowing full well the outcome of challenging Mahmood. He had seen the extent of his viciousness; they had been in many fights together, albeit on the same side. Breaking an arm or a leg no longer sufficed for Mahmood; he needed his rival to remember the defeat forever. "*Do not have mercy, Ali. Go for the spine, go for the head and neck, cripple him for life,*" Mahmood's words rang in his ear. He squeezed his temples with the palms of his hands until he could not handle the pressure any longer. A nearly suffocated voice inside him tried to scream out, "*For God's sake, stand up to him. Rip the skin off of this coward and send a real man out!*"

──────── آرش ────────

Mindful of the perilous trail before him, Ali trod back. He was like a ship in a violent sea, sails full of wind, speeding toward a most formidable cliff.

The sky was darker now. The clouds had amassed above, like a group of mourners, ready to spill.

He reached the big rock. The men were still standing there.

Determined to preserve his honor, Ali walked toward Mahmood glowering. He would confront him at once and demand an apology in front of Nader. Regardless of the aftermath of the scenario, he would then sever the unraveled cord of their friendship.

Before Ali could even open his mouth to speak, Mahmood held his cigarette box out to him, smiling widely. "Have a smoke, brother," he said, lacing an arm onto Ali's shoulder.

CHAPTER 18

Ahrash entered the baker's shop and put an order in for sesame bread. The store was small and the huge flaming *tandoor** in the center made it awfully hot. Still, Ahrash decided to wait inside; he would tolerate the fiery, humid air for the sweet aroma of the freshly baked bread. For some unknown reason, he had always paralleled the scent of bread to life and vitality.

The baker moved nimbly around the *tandoor*, maneuvering the bread deftly among the blazing fire. He resembled a tribal man, performing a ritual dance around a giant dragon with a wide flaming mouth.

From the corner of the shop, Ahrash watched the dancing baker. Every time a piece of bread exited the inferno, he envisioned a new soul entering the world.

———— آرش ————

Holding the sesame bread close to his chest, Ahrash scrambled up the dirt road. He was rushing to get home before the sky's dark clouds spilt.

As he ascended, the tip of the boulder popped into view and became more and more visible with each step he took.

Fixated on the giant rock seeming to grow before him, Ahrash was startled to find Mahmood and Ali standing there, next to the boulder. Mahmood had a cigarette dangling from his mouth and his fists were both shoved deep into his pants pockets. Ali, leaning on the rock, appeared smaller than usual.

---

* *a clay-lined pit in the ground used for making bread*

No one was around and the men and the boulder both looked peculiarly sinister.

Ahrash returned to the bakery and slumped down against the storefront.

Per usual, Neloo instantly materialized in his head. He remembered how she had appeared earlier that day. She did not look well. Her face was pale, almost white, and she had clearly lost weight. Besides, the entire time they spoke, she only said a few words and did not meet his eyes even once. *Whatever was troubling my girl must be serious.*

——————— آرش ———————

"Did mom forget to cut the onion?" Issa asked, sitting with his father by the *sofreh*.

Khalil slid a plate with a fully peeled onion toward him. "You had better cut it. She forgot again," he said, nudging his son's hand with the handle of a big knife.

The curtain in front of the kitchen drew back and Aziz appeared, carrying a big tray with bowls of rice, stew, and fresh herbs.

Once the food was on the *sofreh*, Khalil covered the rice and stew bowls with plates. "Let's keep it warm until Ahrash gets here," he said with a slightly anxious voice.

Issa rose to his feet. "He left a while ago, Dad. I should go and search for him."

"Maybe the baker is behind today. Just wait a few more minutes, son."

——————— آرش ———————

The patches of dark clouds were now mostly unified, hovering over the entire village. Ahrash worried that if he stayed any longer, he would return home with soggy bread. He heaved himself up and set off for home, praying that his enemy would be gone by now.

Going up the hill again, he found the boulder standing alone. He was partially relieved yet mindful; he strained his eyes and ears for the faintest stir.

Nearing the boulder, prey to a colossal threat, he sped up.

Suddenly a massive object hit his bony torso, causing him to fall flat on his face. The bread in his hand went flying and landed onto the muddy ground a few feet from him.

"Give me Neloo's love letter," Mahmood demanded, holding Ahrash against the giant rock.

Stiff with fright, Ahrash still managed to reply, "There is no love letter."

"Give me the letter, I said. I saw it myself," Mahmood snarled, kicking the rattled boy in the shins.

Ahrash tried to piece together what Mahmood might have seen. "Neloo wrote a poem. She gave it to me to read to Issa," he said, writhing in pain.

A whack landed on Ahrash's collarbone that tightened his throat. He gasped for air while trying to hold back his tears.

"Give me the poem then, asshole."

"But I have not read it to Issa yet."

"Do not fuck with me Ahrash!" His patience running thin, Mahmood pressed Ahrash's shoulders roughly against the boulder and commanded Ali to search his pocket.

Ali found the letter and handed it to Mahmood.

Letter in hand now, the angry Mahmood kneed Ahrash between the legs and thrust him away with a shove. "Talk to my sister one more time and I will kill you," he growled.

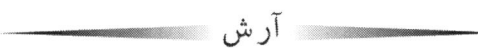

———— آرش ————

Aziz was standing by the window, quietly praying for her son's safe return, when the gate opened and Ahrash entered the yard.

A few seconds later, the distraught boy walked into the house and hastily closed the door behind himself. He leaned against the doorway and handed the soiled bread to his mother, "Mahmood pushed me and I dropped the bread," he muttered.

Khalil snatched the offending bread from Aziz. "Did Mahmood hurt you, son? Did he?" he asked.

A flood of uncontrolled tears started to run down Ahrash's cheeks.

"Did he hurt you?" Khalil asked again. He then abruptly left the house without waiting for an answer.

"Don't go, Khalil. The man is crazy. He will kill you," Aziz pleaded with her husband as she followed him barefoot into the yard.

Khalil continued walking, taking big strides.

Turning around to get her shoes, Aziz bumped into Issa. She tugged at his sleeve. "Where are *you* going now?"

"I have to go, mother," Issa drew his arm away.

"Wait for me then, let me get my shoes."

───── آرش ─────

Alone in the room, Ahrash walked to the window. He stood there with his face close to the pane, watching his family heading toward the boulder – his father significantly ahead of Issa and his mother.

He swallowed the lump in his throat and stepped back from the window. Not knowing what to do, he started fluttering around the room like a confused bee. His eyes then fell on the large knife beside the quartered onion. He picked it up and ran out of the house.

In the yard, he stood atop a mound by the gate, straining his neck for a better view.

Khalil was waving the bread in Mahmood's face when, in a flash, the two men started exchanging punches.

Ahrash opened the gate and darted toward the brawl. In no time, he passed up Issa and Aziz who had not yet reached the boulder. He stopped a few yards short of the big rock where Mahmood was sitting astride Khalil, beating him viciously.

With every blow, Ahrash closed his eyes and turned the handle of the knife in his hand. A couple of times, he took a couple of steps forward, but his shaky legs were not able to carry him further. He knew he could not stop that madman with his meager body and if Mahmood were to get a hold of his knife, he might use it against his father.

His eyes helplessly flitted to Ali, pleading.
Ali looked down and then away.

"I have had it with you and your fucking boys," Mahmood yelled slamming Khalil's head against the ground. He then put his large hands around the man's neck and began to squeeze.

A short piercing cry suddenly filled the air. Ahrash leapt toward Mahmood and stabbed him in the middle of the back, using every bit of his strength.

CHAPTER 19

The crowd was swelling at the boulder. Mahmood, in Ali's arms, was limp and unresponsive. His eyes were shut and his mouth hung open. The only sign of life was the foam, tinged with blood, bubbling at the edge of his lips.

"Someone get his father quickly! Someone get Sharif!" Ali cried repeatedly.

The news reached Sharif. He left the house instantly. Panic-stricken by the sight of the large crowd, he started running, almost sprinting; the pebbles of the road crunched under his bare feet.

Neloo, who was in the yard with the twins, also heard that Mahmood had been stabbed. She sent the boys back into the house and followed after her father with breakneck speed.

―――― آرش ――――

The seemingly lifeless Mahmood was now placed into Sharif's arms. Ali stood next to the devastated father and Neloo, trying incoherently to explain what had happened.

Neloo had only heard a part of the recount of the accident before she saw the twins. The boys were standing not too far from them, looking, in terror, at their brother.

"Oh dear! You should not be here. I had asked you to stay inside the house," she said, wiping the tears off her brothers' faces.

The boys continued crying, louder and louder.

"Mahmood will be fine. I promise. Dad will take him to the hospital and the doctors will fix him right away. We had better go home now," Neloo said, trying to direct her little brothers away from the horrific scene.

The wailing twins, however, refused to leave no matter how much she insisted.

Unable to convince them, Neloo eventually agreed to let the twins stay as long as they did not look at their big brother. She stretched her arms around the boys' shivering shoulders, turning them inward, toward herself.

The twins clutched at her legs and sank their heads into her skirt. Occasionally, one of them would steal a glimpse at the scene and then cling tighter to his sister.

From atop the hill, Hakim, the village medicine man darted down, rushing to the side of Sharif and his injured son. He removed his thick glasses and laid his head sideways on Mahmood's chest, blocking every one's view with his bearish body. He then pulled Mahmood's eyelids back and looked into his eyes.

"We must take him to the hospital right away. Someone, get the gendarme quickly!" Hakim shouted, his fingers on Mahmood's neck, monitoring his pulse.

A young man reached Sakineh at her sister's house. "Your son is hurt. He is at the boulder," he told her and quickly ran back to the scene.

Shortly after, Sakineh reached the throng of bystanders, screaming for her son. The crowd parted voluntarily to give her a clear path. She took a few steps toward Mahmood and glanced at him briefly. Unaware of the severity of the situation, she turned around and faced the spectators.

"Who has hurt Mahmood? Who?" she demanded.

An awed hush fell upon the villagers. They looked at one another, mouths agape.

Sakineh eased her scarf from its hold and started pacing back and forth, eyeing everyone with a grave hostility. She embodied a formidable lioness, ready to avenge her injured offspring.

"I want to know who hurt my son?" she asked again, more demanding.

Ali's memory stirred. Travelling back in time, he conjured up the image of a younger Sakineh, by the walnut tree, brandishing her stick at the kids who had been taunting her young boy.

Amid Ali's reverie, Sakineh's eyes lasered onto him. She made quick strides toward him and stopped in front of the distraught man. The angry Sakineh stared into his confounded face as if he were solely responsible for the crowd's disobedient silence. She knew Ali well. He was slow to rile, winding up his wires of anger before flying into a rage.

"Do you know who did this to Mahmood?" Sakineh asked in a controlled voice after having drawn in a long, labored breath.

Ali's gaze darted around the crowd and found Ahrash. His wrath renewed, he leaped toward the frightened boy, screaming, "He did it, that bastard son of a whore!"

Issa immediately moved to shield his brother, while a few men struggled to restrain Ali.

Sakineh shot Ahrash a chilling look and left for Mahmood's side. She crouched down next to him and allowed her fingers to tenderly travel over his closed eyes. Using her scarf's ends, she then gently dabbed the bloody foam around his mouth.

Suddenly, a thunderous shriek filled the air. "Oh God! Oh God!" Sakineh screeched, noticing the knife handle protruding out of her son's back.

"Pull the knife out of him!" she wailed, striking her face and head. "Pull it out Sharif!"

"No! Don't!" Hakim objected vehemently, "The doctors should do that at the hospital."

"I said, take the knife out of my son. It's hurting him!" Sakineh commanded again. "For God's sake, can't you see he is dying?"

Sharif hovered his shaking hand over the knife handle. He looked at Hakim over the edge of Sakineh's head, waiting for his approval. Hakim held his hands up, firmly urging him to stop.

Frustrated with her husband's hesitation, Sakineh grabbed the knife handle herself and with a swift jerk, pulled it out.

Blood wildly spurted from where the knife had been lodged.

An uncontrollable storm rushed through Sharif, ripping at all his organs along its way. "God have mercy on us!" he cried, pushing his palm against the erupting wound.

The jeep arrived. Its tires kicked up huge dust clouds as it screeched to a halt just inches away from the onlookers. Jafar, the young gendarme, hastily got out and made his way through the crowd. He glanced at Mahmood and turned to Ali, "Help me put him inside the jeep."

A fine, misty rain began to fall, scattering the smell of dirt in the air. Ahrash caught the whiff of death rising from the ground.

CHAPTER 20

A profound fatigue came over Neloo; carrying her little brother had never been so difficult before. She was out of breath, her chest burning so badly as if the air in Kultappa had lost most of its oxygen.

Struggling for solid footing, her steps gradually grew smaller, forcing Ali, who was carrying the other twin to slow down.

She needed to rest.

A large rock off the path looked accommodating. She stopped briefly, marshaled her energy with a couple of deep breaths, and aimed for the makeshift seat. As she trudged toward the rock, the boy's body on her shoulder went limp, his arms and legs dangling around uncontrollably. It was clear that he had fallen asleep.

The tired Neloo relinquished the rest and walked back toward the house: *This miserable child is better off staying asleep.*

Trailing behind Neloo, Ali was having a difficult time as well. The twin in his arms was inconsolable, wailing and screeching with a strong conviction.

He tried any way he could to soothe the boy. He sang, whistled, and talked about his wrestling matches, all to no avail.

The distraught twin continued crying until they reached home.

———— آرش ————

Inside the house, Neloo set the sleeping twin down on the rug. She brushed the tears off his face, unclenched his fist and placed a kiss on his forehead. The boy released a long, weary sigh.

The second twin reached for his sister from Ali's arms. He was still bawling; his face streaked with tears and residual blood from Ali's shirt.

Neloo carried the boy to the kitchen to clean him up.

Standing in the middle of the room, the dreadful day replayed in Ali's mind over and over. His memories were hazy and dreamlike. Yet, amidst the dimly cast events, the image of the injured Mahmood in Sharif's arms was in sharp focus. He wished he knew of his condition and was utterly disappointed in himself for not jumping into the jeep with Sharif and Sakineh.

The sleeping twin moaned a couple of times. His face crumbled into a frown and his little chin started quivering; he was on the verge of crying.

Ali sat next to the boy, held his hand and began to hum. When Neloo returned to the room, she found him tenderly rubbing the tiny cushion pads of her brother's fingertips.

"I set out a clean shirt by the sink, Ali. You can wash off and change before going home," she said.

In the kitchen, Ali removed his shirt and washed the blood off of himself. He could hear Neloo's lullaby coming from the living room. Her voice was soft, effectively soothing his inflated nerves. He lingered in the kitchen for a while until all the crying stopped.

When he returned to the big room the twin in Neloo's arms was entering dream land. His eyelids were shutting slowly as he twirled a strand of Neloo's hair around his finger.

Ali looked in the direction of the drowsy child and his gaze landed on Neloo. Instantly, he felt a flurry in his heart – in the dim light, the beautiful Neloo looked angelic.

The twins were in their beds now, sleeping next to each other. Neloo took a thin sheet out of the closet and covered the boys. She then sat beside them, running her fingers through their hair.

Watching the three siblings, Ali for the first time in his life, felt an intense appetite to have his own family.

"I can ask Shereen to stay with you tonight," he told Neloo, eyes down at his feet, not looking at her.

"That would be unnecessary trouble for her," Neloo refused. "My family should be back soon."

Ali headed to the door. "I will be sitting outside the house then, until they return."

"You better go home Ali, there will be a storm soon."

"No. I would rather stay. I'll be fine."

———————— آرش ————————

The measly awning attached to the house afforded Ali just enough protection from the rain to light a cigarette. He stood under the cover and took long drags, inhaling every molecule of smoke.

A new set of screams rose from inside the house, followed by woeful crying. He pressed an ear to the door panel, wondering which one of the twins was having the nightmare.

Fortunately, the crying did not last long.

Ali's focus shifted back to Mahmood and his injury again. It was not uncommon for men to be stabbed in the village. Only last month, he had witnessed a nasty fight among a group of farmers resulting in many injuries. One man was seriously hurt, almost completely disemboweled. Nobody expected him to live but he did indeed survive. *If that farmer could cling to life, Mahmood, younger and stronger, will certainly pull through.*

A calm came over Ali but it was short lived. He recalled that the surviving farmer was stabbed in the gut and not in the heart.

What if Mahmood dies?

He stared at Ahrash's meager house across the road, allowing vengeful thoughts to brew in his head with a wild energy: *It wouldn't be too difficult to take care of the boy and Khalil, even with Issa around.* He flattened his cigarette under his heel and tore through the yard. Once he reached the gate however, some strange feeling kept him in place. He had a perplexing emotion, it was as he was going to a loved one's funeral, subconsciously desiring to be late.

Hesitant to move forward, Ali stood by the gate, despondently rubbing at the watered-down blood stains on his pants.

The daylight was waning and the trees were already dark forms against the clear rain. Amidst his fervent scrubbing, a notion that he was being watched came over Ali. He raised his head and saw two huge eyes gazing at him through the branches; the same two pleading eyes, begging him earlier to save his father.

The fear embedded in those eyes shook Ali to his core. He envisioned Mahmood, as ferocious as a wild beast, sitting atop Khalil while Ahrash witnessed his father's skull being crushed, his throat collapsing.

What else could the helpless boy have done to save his father? Despite himself, Ali allowed a warm feeling to run through his heart for Ahrash.

The wind picked up, whipping the rain in all directions and at every object. Ali remained by the gate and continued to work on his trousers' blemishes until his hands were raw. By then the sky was completely dark and the rain had given way to a clattering hail.

"I should go back to the house and check on the siblings," he decided.

Neloo opened the door to a knock; Ali was standing in the frame, drenched in water.

"Please go home Ali. We are getting a lot of rain; it could easily flood the road," she pleaded.

This time, Ali agreed to go without any protest.

CHAPTER 21

As nighttime settles in, the village becomes quiet and dark, seemingly an empty place. Before dusk, the few existing shops roll down their corrugated doors and everyone leaves the bazaar. The animals are collected and ushered into their pens while children, one by one, disappear from the alleys. Normally, by 8pm, all the villagers are at home with their doors closed to visitors.

On this night, the village appeared darker than usual. The earlier patches of clouds had now conquered the entire sky, imprisoned the moon and blocked out the stars. Rain poured down in sheets and columns while a merciless wind stripped the trees of their blossoms.

At the bend in the road, two funnels of light appeared. They flickered through the rain and grew brighter as they zeroed in on the boulder. Minutes later, a jeep stopped by the side of the road, its headlights shining on the big rock. Jafar, the young village gendarme, clambered out, leaving the car running. He pulled the collar of his windbreaker up against the wild rain and raced toward Ahrash's house.

——————— آرش ———————

"Why tonight? Can't you wait until tomorrow?"

"I am sorry, Khalil, I have to take him now. It is an order."

"Let my boy stay home, Jafar. I promise I will bring him to the station early in the morning," Khalil pleaded again. "I do not understand the urgency."

Jafar took one step closer to Khalil and whispered into his ear, "Mahmood died on the way to the hospital."

A heavy stillness took over the room. Despite Jafar's hushed tone, they had all heard him.

Khalil's face turned white. He put his hand up against the wall of the house to steady himself.

"Officer, please come in and have some tea," Aziz broke the silence.

The young gendarme was taken aback at the formality with which Aziz addressed him.

Jafar's mother and Aziz were cousins whose families had lived in their mutual grandparent's house. The two cousins became best friends during their childhood and continued their closeness even after each had had her own family.

When Jafar was eight years old his mother became seriously ill with tuberculosis. He clearly remembered Aziz spending all day at their house, taking care of him and his two younger brothers. For over a year his aunt cooked, cleaned and looked after the kids while simultaneously nursing their mother back to health.

"Auntie, please call me Jafar."

"Alright dear but you have to stay a while longer and have something to drink."

Jafar shook his head, "Sorry, I cannot stay. I am on duty and have to return to the station soon. If you look outside, you'll see my jeep is still running."

Aziz was on the verge of crying. "As God is my witness, Ahrash is innocent, Jafar."

"Of course, Ahrash is innocent. Everyone knows that he was just protecting his father. I am certain that the judge will order his release tomorrow."

"Can you take him in the morning then? Directly to the judge?"

"I am truly sorry, there is no way I can do that."

"But he is just a boy; he has never spent a night away from his family."

The young gendarme was heartbroken for Aziz and, for the first time, he was not happy to be a man of the law. He became quiet for a while, searching for the words to comfort his distraught aunt.

"The station is safe, and my shift has me there all night. I promise to watch over him," he said and quickly turned to Ahrash. "Put your shoes on young man and get your jacket. It is nasty out there."

Ahrash did what he was asked to do; no thought or emotion, not even fear, ran through his mind.

CHAPTER 22

The cemetery stood at the far side of the village, near a thick, wooded area that stretched for miles.

A soft, mourning music filled the graveyard's air.

Sakineh and Sharif were crouching down by a freshly dug grave, both dressed in black. A thin, dark scarf was over Sakineh's hair and a wide black band across Sharif's forehead. From a distance the two mourners resembled a pair of crows, protesting bitterly.

Hajji joined the woeful parents, thumbing a rosary. He sat down and instantly started a quiet prayer. When the last bead of the string slid through his fingers, he leaned toward Sharif and whispered, "May God keep the rest of your family unharmed."

The pain of a grieving father was not unknown to Hajji. He had experienced firsthand the unbearable sorrow of a man outliving his child. During the country's war with Iraq, Hajji had lost two sons in the span of one year. His youngest boy had been blown apart so badly, that they were unable to fully gather his remains.

An energetic clergyman, wearing a green turban and a long black robe, broke through the crowd and entered the scene. Hajji unfolded a chair and placed it at the head of the grave. The man sat down and meticulously straightened his robe over his trousered legs. He directed his gaze rather arrogantly onto the villagers and, without warning, began incanting verses from the *Koran*. His voice was loud and his words were pronounced clearly and with an edge over the now faintly playing music.

Plates of halvah were passed around wordlessly amongst the crowds.

Neloo felt a nudge on her side. An old village matron then handed her a glass jar with a spigot. Neloo knew exactly what she was being asked to do and had been dreading it all morning. She took the jar and reluctantly snaked through the mourners, trickling a few drops of rosewater into each palm. When she returned to her spot, she noticed Hajji was hastily limping away from the throng. She narrowed her eyes and followed his path toward a man and a woman who were approaching the gravesite.

As they neared, Neloo recognized Ahrash's parents. Aziz was carrying a large metal tray and Khalil, his head bandaged with a white cloth, was walking with his hands clasped behind him.

Hajji reached husband and wife. He and Khalil embraced warmly but parted ways after a brief exchange: Hajj returning to the grave site, Khalil and Aziz heading back toward the village.

It was clear that Hajji had advised the couple not to join the mourners.

———————— آرش ————————

From the east side of the cemetery, Ali, alongside three young men appeared, marching toward the dug grave. They were carrying Mahmood's shrouded body atop a large, flat board.

Seeing the procession, the clergyman started chanting, "*La elehe ellallah. Allah Akbar, Allah Akbar.**" The crowd repeated the verses after him. "*La elehe ellallah. Allah Akbar, Allah Akbar.*"

To avoid the sight of the pallbearers, Neloo stared straight ahead at the edge of the woods. There stood a deer and her fawn, perfectly still, as though they were listening attendees. She wondered if the twins saw the deer

The chanting rose to a crescendo as the men put the board down by the grave.

---

* *"There is no God but Allah. Allah is great. Allah is great."*

Ali and Nader removed Mahmood's shrouded body from the board and lowered it into the hole. Shovels started moving in a synchronized motion, throwing dirt onto the body.
Beating her chest, Sakineh wailed and groaned nonstop. She ripped at the ground with her fingernails and threw fistfuls of earth at Ali and the other men, demanding that they stop burying Mahmood.
The theatrical aspect of her grieving made the twins giggle.

As the dirt continued to land on her son's body, Sakineh rose to a stand. She rushed toward Ali and reached for his shovel. Before she could grab it, however, she passed out and collapsed into a heap.

———— آرش ————

The ceremony came to a halt as they moved Sakineh to the shade of a nearby tree. Sharif untied his wife's scarf and splashed water onto her face while two sniffling women fanned her with empty halvah plates.
The clergyman joined them and recited a short prayer. Hajji paid him his wages and he quickly disappeared.

The crowd started to disperse. Some wandered among the graves, visiting their deceased; a much bigger number headed toward the road.
Neloo watched Jafar help three elders, as well as the twins, into his jeep. She was relieved that the boys were finally taken away from the baleful place.
Now that the boys were not present, she could attend to her own disheveled emotions.

Growing up, Neloo had always enjoyed being around Mahmood. Her older brother was witty, fun, and invariably kind to her. But everything had changed over the last two years. Mahmood had become increasingly angry with her over Ahrash. He followed her all the time, teasing her with the most hurtful comments. Still, she had loved her brother, never wishing him any harm. What happened in the shower however, severed the kinship bond between them beyond mending.

"How could I forgive him, be the redeemer of his sin? How could I feel sorry for him, a person whose death had secured my safety?" she bemoaned.

Ultimately, Neloo came to terms with her emotional state.

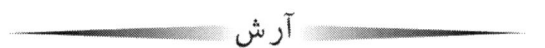

——————— آرش ———————

No one was by the grave site now, except for Ali. He was standing still, leaning his head on the handle of the shovel. Sharif joined him. He stood there for a while, staring down at his son's wrapped body.

Ali put his hand on the grieving man's shoulder but was not able to utter a single word.

Crying soundlessly, Sharif removed his head band and tossed it inside the grave. He then picked up a shovel and motioned for Ali to help him fill the hole.

PART II
Three months later

CHAPTER 23

As soon as Khalil entered the courtroom, he was ushered to his seat by a guard. Sharif and Sakineh were already present, sitting not too far from his assigned spot.

Khalil felt apprehensive – the neighbors had not been in such close proximity since Mahmood's death.

"*Salam-o-alaykum,*[*]" he mumbled faintly, as he passed his old friend.

Not unexpectedly, the greeting was dismissed, left unanswered by the couple.

Judge Kasra, a man in his mid-fifties, strode to the podium. He was short and big at his middle. With a towering forehead, round shape and billowing robe, he would have fit in well with comically drawn nursery rhyme characters.

At his dais, he put on a pair of reading glasses and opened the file in front of him. He read for a couple of minutes, constantly tapping his pen against the splintered wood of the podium.

The drumming of the pen in the quiet room was driving Khalil mad. He tried to focus on the flickering of the fluorescent lights above his head, choosing to see it as a positive sign from the supreme power above.

Flanked by a guard and his attorney, Ahrash, in an oversized orange jumpsuit, entered the courtroom. He sat in a designated chair offset from the center of the room, facing the judge.

---

[*] *a greeting - "peace to you"*

With the sight of Ahrash, Khalil's heart started to pound. "My son has grown in jail," he thought, letting out a loud, soul-wrenching groan that traveled in all directions.

Judge Kasra began to question Ahrash in a crisp voice.

"The police report states that on June 5th, 1982, you, Ahrash Bedel, stabbed Mahmood Mansour in the back, causing his death. Is this statement true?"

"Yes, Sir," Ahrash replied timidly.

"At the time of stabbing, was your life in any way in danger?"

"No, Sir."

"Then why did you attack Mr. Mansour?"

"I do not know, Sir."

Khalil rose to a half stand. "Your honor, Mahmood was sitting on my chest, choking me," he said in broken Farsi.

"Mr. Bedel, you are out of order. You must sit down and remain silent," the judge scolded Khalil and continued his line of questioning.

"Do you always carry a knife with you?"

"No, Sir."

"Why did you have a knife with you on that day?"

"I picked it up from home before I left."

"Before you left for where? To meet Mr. Mansour?"

Khalil looked desperately at Ahrash's attorney. Disappointed that the man remained mute, he stood up again, "Sir, my son…"

"Mr. Bedel," the judge stopped Khalil midsentence. "If you interrupt the proceedings one more time, you will be thrown out of court." He gave this firm ultimatum and promptly shifted his attention back to Ahrash.

"You said that you left the house with a knife. Did you take the knife with the intent to inflict bodily harm on Mr. Mansour?" the judge rephrased his previous question. "Did you?"

"I went after my father, who was going to talk to Mahmood."

"Why did you take a deadly weapon with you? Did you plan to use it?"

"I do not know, Sir. I was very angry."

"You sought to attack Mr. Mansour with your weapon and you succeeded in your attempt to hurt him. Is my understanding of the situation correct?"

"I did not know he would die, Sir."

Amid the aggressive interrogation, Khalil suddenly realized that Ahrash had not glanced his way even once. *"Is he embarrassed about what had happened? Does he feel guilty?"* he wondered, wishing to hold his son in his arms and shield him from the horrors he was experiencing.

The judge's continued questioning became increasingly lost on the shattered father.

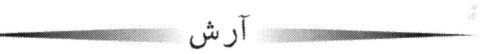

──────── آرش ────────

"Ahrash Bedel," Judge Kasra's stern voice brought everyone in court, including Khalil, to full attention. "You stabbed Mahmood Mansour with the premeditated intent to harm him. His resulting death makes the charge murder. In accordance with the laws of our land, the punishment for murder is the death penalty."

The attorney moved toward the podium and, for the first time, spoke, "Sir, Ahrash was trying to save his father from getting hurt. Mahmood was over 6 feet tall and in top physical shape. Mr. Bedel, as you can see, is a small and fragile man," he said timidly while pointing at Khalil. "The boy had no choice but to interfere."

"Yes, I am aware. However, the law does not permit one to commit murder in order to prevent another's harm. My decision is final."

The judge focused his gaze on Sharif next, "Mr. Mansour, even though the court has decided on death penalty for your son's murderer, you need to know that if the parents of victim elect to change the punishment, their decision will supersede the law. In other words, you have authority to change this court's ruling," Kasra said and paused for a moment, looking at Sharif with even more intensity. "Considering the assailant's young age and immaturity, I earnestly implore you Mr. Mansour to find forgiveness in your heart and lessen the boy's sentence."

Before Sharif could speak, Sakineh rose to her feet and curtly confronted the judge, "I gave birth to Mahmood, I nursed him, I stayed up at night with him – I should be the one to make the decision not his father."

Sharif nodded his head in submissive approval, "Yes, it should be her decision."

"Is it my understanding, Mr. Mansour, that you are transferring your rights in this case to your wife?" the judge asked weightily.

"Yes, Your Honor. Mahmood's mother should have the rights."

Judge Kasra quickly jotted down few lines and sent it to Sharif to sign. He then turned to Sakineh. "Mrs. Mansour, would you consider a reduced penalty for Ahrash?"

Sakineh did not say a word.

"Mrs. Mansour, would you consider a reduced penalty for Ahrash?" The judge repeated his question.

A deadly silence blanketed the room. Everyone was looking at Sakineh, waiting for her response.

Suddenly, Khalil darted toward Sakineh and knelt at her feet. The guards looked at the judge, waiting for his order to stop him. Judge Kasra allowed the desperate father a few minutes, long enough for him to kiss Sakineh's hand and ask for her forgiveness.

"Would you like to have a few minutes alone with your husband to discuss this matter Mrs. Mansour?" the Judge inquired again, hoping that Khalil's pleading had soften the woman's heart.

"I do not need time to think. I want nothing less than the death sentence for my son's murderer."

"Is the death penalty for Ahrash Bedel your final decision Mrs. Mansour?"

"Yes, it is," Sakineh answered with solid decisiveness.

Judge Kasra briefly penned some notes and turned to Khalil. "Mr. Bedel, father of Ahrash Bedel," he recited loud and clear. "At this point, the court sentences your son to death for the murder of Mahmood Mansour on June 5th, 1982. Since the assailant is underage, he will be on death row until six months past his eighteenth birthday. It should be stated that from now until the execution date, Mrs. Mansour has ability to drop the charges against your son or alter the court's decision implicitly."

A violent chill attacked Khalil, deep in his bones. He tried to make eye contact with his son but Ahrash had his head down, avoiding his father.

CHAPTER 24

A burly guard pushed open the solid door and led Ahrash down a long hall dotted with cells. One of these rooms would be the boy's permanent residence for the next five years.

Putting one foot in front of the other, Ahrash tried to stay close to the guard.

The first few cells were empty. In the compartments that followed, most of the prisoners were either asleep or lounging idly.

An elderly man of small stature came into view next. He was standing in the middle of his cell, clapping rapidly. The excited prisoner had his palms near his eyes and was watching them, completely engrossed.

Ahrash inched closer to the guard, believing that the man had gone crazy.

A bald inmate noticed Ahrash. He rushed forward with a large smile, revealing a row of gold teeth. "A boy! Everybody, we have a boy here!" he clamored.

"He is right. A boy is in here!" another prisoner shouted, extending his arm out to touch Ahrash. "Who did you kill, little man? A mosquito?" he cried, laughing hysterically.

The guard pulled Ahrash slightly away from the man's reach. "Just ignore them," he advised.

Sleepy death row was now suddenly awake, fully energized. The inmates stood eagerly by their bars, wide-eyed and excited at the prospect of a child prisoner. They whistled, hollered and gestured lewdly as Ahrash passed by them. And even though they could not see each other, they became engaged in loud conversations about the new addition to the row.

"Quiet everyone!" the guard roared, irritated. "You are scaring the boy."

The boisterous prisoners ignored the order and decided to enjoy the moment to its fullest. Their dull lives on death row had never been so amusing before.

One inmate began banging on his cell wall and others followed suit immediately, hitting their bars and walls with any available object.

The situation turned chaotic in no time.

Frustrated with the riotous gang, the guard yanked at Ahrash's sleeve and stood him in front of a cell. "Stay right here," he commanded. His baton drawn, he started smacking any errant hands escaping the cell bars, while letting out a stream of expletives.

Ahrash's wobbling knees buckled, as he stood alone. He grabbed a hold of the cell bars before him and his eyes met those of the man inside. Amid the commotion, the thickset prisoner sat quietly at the edge of his bed looking at Ahrash. His pacifying gaze sent a calming wave toward the terrified boy.

"Silence! Now! This is an order!" a second guard bellowed into his megaphone. "Another squeak out of anyone and there will be no meals for two days," he said and paused briefly, allowing his threat to sink in. "Is that clear? Everyone will shut up or you will all be hungry for two days."

The prisoners settled down quickly, with the exception of the crazy man, who was now bouncing on his bed as he continued his weird clapping. Upon detecting the silence all around him, the man stopped jumping at once and fell comically from his bed.

The guard, noticing his fall, tried to stifle an inappropriate laugh.

آرش

Ahrash's cell was clean, furnished with a bed and a plastic chair. The bathroom and sink were at the far corner with a four-foot half wall for privacy.

"You get three meals a day: breakfast at six, lunch at noon and dinner at five. Lights are out at 10pm except the hall lights which remain on all the time," the guard explained. "Do you have any questions before I leave?"

"Yes. I had a bag of belongings," Ahrash said in a submissive voice.

"They will bring it to you after inspection."

The guard walked toward the cell door. Before leaving, he turned his head and gave Ahrash a faint smile, "Do not worry about the other prisoners, young man. We have them on a tight leash."

CHAPTER 25

Ahrash sat still at the edge of his bed, gripping his sack of belongings as tightly as he had when he first received it over an hour ago.

In the cell next to him, Babak, a uniquely strange prisoner, threw a shoe at their shared wall. "Hey kiddo, what's your name?" he called out.

Ahrash didn't answer.

He threw the other of the pair and walked to the front of his cell. "I said, what is your name? Did they cut out your tongue, faggot?"

Ahrash remained silent, hunched over the sack in his lap.

"Hey guys," Babak shouted loudly, addressing all the inmates. "I did not get to see the boy. What does he look like? Is he cute?"

"He is cute all right – very puny though," one prisoner responded.

"How old is he?" Does anyone know his name?

"Shut up Babak, you fuckhead. You will get us in trouble again," grumbled another prisoner.

A young, acned man of no more than twenty, rolled a food cart through the door and entered the hall. The loud slam of the door behind him awakened the drowsy prisoners. Picking aggressively at his face, the server moved forward, shoving food trays through slots in the cells. He was fast but careless, not making any effort to minimize the clanging of metal on metal.

Some of the inmates continued to laze on their beds, indifferent to the delivered food; others pounced on their trays right away.

Before long, the food cart arrived at Ahrash's cell. The server picked up a tray, added the slop and turned to make his delivery. Startled by the sight of a boy behind the bars, he suddenly fumbled and dropped the tray with a clatter. "What the heck?" he stammered.

Ahrash kept his head down, feeling his loneliness even more keenly. On the contrary, Babak in the next cell was engrossed by the flying food.

"You ugly, miserable baboon face! Can't you just find a simple hole?" He taunted the worker, gesturing sexual acts.

"Go to hell, motherfucker!" the food man said, while on his knees cleaning the floor.

Babak turned his attention back to Ahrash. "Hey boy," he shouted. "Did I tell you that I love young boys?" he said, cackling with laughter.

On the other side of Ahrash's cell, an inmate named Reza was becoming increasingly infuriated with Babak. He was the same stout prisoner that the boy had had the brief eye contact with earlier. Unbeknown to Ahrash, Reza was once a popular wrestler, well-loved throughout the country.

At his limit with Babak's vulgarity now, Reza rose and walked to the front of his cell. He encircled the bars with his massive hands and roared, "Enough Babak. Shut your dirty mouth right now."

The gravity of Reza's voice stifled Babak at once.

CHAPTER 26

In a vast, harsh land of little vegetation, two men walk on either side of a camel. The majestic animal with its long neck upright and protruding breast looks calm. Nevertheless, the men are firmly grasping ropes attached to its harness.

They move slowly in step, the camel's single hump dips and rises like a mountain in motion. With short shadows trailing them, the travelers appear to be a small caravan from a distance.

A long period of steady strides brings the trio before a well. The men extract fresh water, gulp it down and douse their heads. They attend to the camel next, offering him bucket after bucket of well water. Once the hollow dent under the animal's ribs balloons up, they resume their journey.

A wind picks up and adds miniature cyclones to the landscape. The camel, equipped with mesh eyelids, is not bothered by the whirling winds but the travelers are forced to reduce their eyes to tiny slits. Nevertheless, they keep moving forward.

Nearing the edge of civilization, a figure, tall and lean, comes into view with a long dagger in hand. His feet shoulder width apart and arms at his sides, the man stands still on the road, awaiting the travelers.

No words are exchanged; the nodding of heads suffice as greeting.

The slender man steps forward, lunging his long knife forcefully, deep into the base of the camel's neck. A bloody river gushes from the wound and the men begin to hit the animal on the head with hammer-like objects.

His nostrils flaring, the camel, gradually kneels to the ground without protest. The heavy and swift loss of blood has made him woozy, causing his neck to sway back and forth like a slow-moving pendulum. As life is escaping his body, the motion slows and eventually ceases. The camel's head then lands on Ahrash's bed, its huge, cold eyes aimed at the boy.

آرش

Ahrash awoke with a shriek. Terrorized by the nightmare, he grabbed at his chest to contain his violently beating heart. Fully awake now, he could still see the camel's head next to him and feel the warmth of the animal's last breath on his face. He closed his eyes, seeking refuge in darkness. But the camel's butchery was instantly back in view, crimson blood spurting out of the creature's neck.

 The vivid illusion made the frightened boy lightheaded, as if his own veins were slowly being drained.

Struggling to dismiss his visions, Ahrash reached for the holy book by his pillow. Holding the book tightly against his chest, he curled up into a ball and pulled the covers over his head.

Somewhere on the row, a prisoner let out a sad cry.

CHAPTER 27

Ahrash was awake when breakfast service began. He had survived his first night on death row; nevertheless, the terror of his nightmare remained strong and tormenting.

In his short life, the boy had had many frightening dreams but none had escalated beyond realistic fears of getting caught with Neloo or witnessing Jolfa fighting the wolves. And no matter what images would ambush him, he always woke surrounded by his family, in a place where no horror could lurk.

With no one to shield him now, the nightmare stayed with him, endlessly breeding wild tangents and illusions. The reoccurring scene of the camel's demise gradually began to merge into his own visualized end, his body hanging, lifeless, from a beam.

Ahrash could feel death closely.

— آرش —

A loud conversation erupted in the next cell; Ahrash recognized Babak's voice.

Momentarily, a guard led the crazy inmate out of his cell and down the hall.

Ahrash's tormentor was young, perhaps only a few years older than him. He had a slight frame, piercing eyes, and a wide mouth. His long wild hair, and general visage reminded the boy of a picture he had seen of the notorious Charles Manson.

"So, you are the kid. Not bad! Come closer pretty boy and say hello to your elder," Babak veered toward Ahrash's cell, taunting him with poorly veiled excitement. The guard quickly pulled him away. "Don't scare the kid," he bellowed.

Before disappearing from view, Babak managed to lock eyes with Ahrash, giving the new inmate a boyish smile. His grin was innocently inviting, not unlike a lonely child seeking a friend on the playground. With that brief eye contact, Ahrash was unwittingly offered a window into the man's soul and immediately bore witness to a lifetime of depression and abuse. He pondered the likelihood of Babak even having a family or anyone who cared for him.

The perception brought about a different kind of sadness to the forsaken boy.

───── آرش ─────

The food server was in a good mood today. He was singing and whistling as he collected the trays. He said hello to some prisoners and even tried, a little, to minimize the metal scraping sounds. When he noticed Ahrash was still in bed and that his breakfast had been left untouched, he felt obligated to advise him. "You only have one hour to eat each meal. After that the food will be removed," he said, both hands digging at his pockmarked face. "You need to eat, boy. It is not as if they are going to hang you tomorrow!"

Even though spoken innocently enough, the man's words were harmful, reminding Ahrash of his perishability.

Death is fierce, beyond any child's ability to face bravely. Ahrash had been abruptly introduced to this formidable enemy and could only watch it race toward him. Would he, at only thirteen years old, be strong enough to battle the idea of mortality?

───── آرش ─────

When Babak ceremoniously returned to the hall, Ahrash decided to hide from him. He quickly retreated behind the short bathroom wall and scrunched down there. A pang of loneliness took over him at once. He tried to fight his roaring emotions, but soon, he was sobbing.

CHAPTER 28

Khalil had been to the capital city only once before. For that trip, Hajji had made all the arrangements through a business acquaintance. This time around, unaware of the enormity of the task, the naïve man had decided to travel without asking for any help.

─────── آرش ───────

The Bedel family exited the train station and walked into a busy city street in awe. The multi-lane street was filled with a shocking number of speedy cars, buses, double-deckers and motorcycles, all passing within inches of each other. The sidewalk was also hectic, almost as bad as the street. It was packed with crowds of fast walkers, bicyclists, food vendors, and tenacious beggars.

Khalil who had had every intention of leading the way for his family, felt paralyzed. He was the man in charge but had no idea where to start.

After the initial shock had subsided, Khalil secured his wife and son on the curb and stepped onto the street again. He watched the coming traffic attentively, raising his hand in an attempt to hail a passing taxi. For a time, no car stopped for him. Watching the other passengers, he soon learned that he had to chase after the taxis and scream out the name of the destination. Still, each cab that did pull over was swarmed from all directions by impatient travelers who would nimbly beat the inexperienced man to the vehicle.

He spotted an available taxi and rushed toward it. In his haste, he failed to see an oncoming motorcycle and stepped directly into its path. The cyclist quickly veered, barely missing him. "Watch out, you stupid villager!" he shouted.

By the time Khalil regained his composure, the potential car was gone.

Khalil continued his chase and after an hour of hustling, he finally got a hold of a taxi. He settled in next to the driver and motioned for his family to get into the back seat of the car. Relieved, he handed the address written on a piece of paper to the driver.

The scruffy driver glanced at the paper with a frown. "I cannot take you there. No taxi goes that as far as the prison. You will have to take a series of buses."

Khalil got out of the car and tried, in Farsi, asked for directions to the bus stop.

"It's not far. Walk one block north. Turn right at the first light, go under the overpass and it will be on your left," the taxi driver explained expeditiously.

Khalil looked confused.

The driver repeated his instructions impatiently, even faster the second time. He was clearly irritated with the honking of the cars jammed up behind his vehicle.

Ready to take off, he looked over his shoulder where Issa and Aziz were struggling to get out of the car. The man felt pity for the family. "Tell them to get back in, I will take you to the bus stop," he told Khalil, gesturing toward the mother and son.

───── آرش ─────

The family had been in the visiting room for a while. Khalil and Aziz, glued to the glass, were trying hard to get their son to speak.

"Please say something," Khalil begged Ahrash who was sitting behind the glass, crying quietly. "Is someone hurting you, son?" the worried father asked.

Ahrash gently shook his head no.

"He misses us, Khalil. He misses his home," Aziz said with a sigh, looking tenderly at her son, "Are you missing us, *pesaram?*"

His mother's questions amplified the boy's pain. He lowered himself to a slouch and hung his head, now sobbing.

"You have to share your thoughts with us, Ahrash. Tell us what is bothering you so much. Maybe we could help."

"I am lonely and scared, mom. I have nightmares every night," Ahrash whispered and those words were all he spoke the entire visit.

Stifling a growl, Issa paced the length of the visiting room back and forth. He was unsettled, resembling a frustrated bear in a small cage. To him, Ahrash has always been an indestructible ship, sailing toward a utopian island. The vessel was now sinking and he, powerless, could only bear witness to his brother's catastrophic descent.

Khalil walked away from the glass window and joined Issa.

Aziz remained in her seat, looking up at Ahrash resolutely. Fighting her own tears, she had decided to just talk with her boy rather than ask him any questions.

She started by rehashing the recent events that had happened in the village – all the engagements, weddings, and the newly arrived babies before moving on to talking about Neloo, Jolfa, the sheep, and Koor Akbar.

Having conveyed all she could think of, Aziz then became quiet, folding and unfolding a handkerchief on her lap. She had not been successful in getting Ahrash to speak but at least her tales had stopped his crying.

It was surprising to Khalil and Issa how she, in her fragile emotional state, could remain so calm.

———— آرش ————

A guard entered the room and announced that they had reached the end of visitation.

Khalil returned to the glass window to say goodbye, "I will get you out of here son, I promise," he said and stepped back to make room for

---

my son

Issa.

Issa spoke in a hurry. "Try to be patient, Ahrash. Dad and Hajji are diligently seeking help from lawyers. Until then you have to keep your mind busy by reading and writing. Give us a list of books you would like to have and we will bring them next time," Issa said and paused, brushing aside several strands of hair from his face. Before he was able to speak again, the guard tapped his shoulder and firmly asked him to leave.

CHAPTER 29

Walking back to his cell, Ahrash was in a state of absolute despair. He felt sick and lightheaded. His skin burned so badly it was as if he was wading through murky water and countless creatures were boring into his body.

The guard unlocked the cell and handed him a tissue. "Wipe your eyes and simmer down, son. You will get used to the situation."

Ahrash immediately sought refuge behind the bathroom wall. He sat there, broken. Despite his own despondency during the visit, the sensitive boy could not ignore the wretched condition his family was in. His father looked worn out and older while new streaks of silver painted anguish in his mother's hair. Even Issa, normally a pillar of strength, appeared dispirited.

"I wished I could have at least said how much I love them," he lamented, regretting not having had the composure to speak with his family.

The notion made Ahrash feel like crying all over again, but there were no more tears left for this disheartened child.

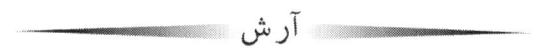

آرش

"Hey boy, where did you go earlier?" Babak asked with a friendly tone. It was clear that he was bored and needed someone to talk to.

Aside from Ahrash, Babak was the youngest person on death row and definitely the loudest. He had no family, no education, and absolutely no social skills. His only possession was a sharp tongue, which often caused him trouble. The arrival of Ahrash on death row, an inmate so close to his age, was a godsend, if only the boy would loosen up a little.

"Are you mute, boy? I asked you where you have been."

Ahrash remained quiet.

Waiting for a response much longer than his patience typically would allow, Babak eventually resumed provoking his quiet neighbor. "What is your name anyway? If you stay silent, I'll call you pretty boy," he said and started to chant. "Pretty boy! Pretty boy! Pretty boy!"

A guard appeared, smacking at Babak's protruding fingers with his baton. "I bet you'd like to sleep hungry tonight," he shouted sourly.

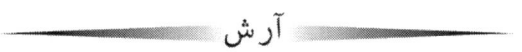

———————— آرش ————————

When the cell lights dimmed for the night, Ahrash crept out from behind the bathroom wall. He rushed to his bed and hid under the blanket, seeking the safety of his other cocoon.

Fatigue fell upon him with a crushing weight but, per usual, the jumble of thoughts kept him awake.

Tonight, the boy's mind bounced around from his family and the news of the village to his feelings of shame and worthlessness – all the while, the ghost of death shadowed over him mercilessly.

CHAPTER 30

Over the next few days, there was an unprecedented amount of activity on death row. More guards were present on the floor at any one time, all well-groomed and attentive. Custodians worked incessantly, emptying trash baskets, wiping the cell bars and scrubbing the hall floors. Tall ladders were brought in as well – men climbing high to wash the windows, remove the cobwebs, and fix the ceiling lights.

Ahrash was relieved when the annoying, flickering light directly outside his cell was replaced.

Early one morning, a doctor entered the cell. He was a stern man, using only a few words during the entire visit. His examination, however, was thorough. He checked Ahrash's eyes for so long that the boy believed something was definitely wrong with his sight.

"You are healthy, but too skinny. You should take more food in," the doctor said at the conclusion of his exam.

A custodian came in next, pushing a cart full of cleaning supplies. He provided Ahrash with a brush and some detergent, instructing him to scrub the sink and the toilet. Adding ammonia to a bucket of water, he then began mopping the floor himself.

The cleaning was almost complete, when a guard entered the cell with a set of bed sheets and a new blanket. He trained Ahrash how to make the bed neatly, military style. "Starting tomorrow, your bed should look tidy before breakfast," he ordered, his voice rough and intimidating.

The guard's face was rather unpleasant. He had small eyes and a big, flat nose. His teeth were crowded together and all significantly embedded in his prominent gums. Two large scars on the left side of his face were indications that he was a survivor of smallpox.

"Pick up the dirty sheets and blanket," he said, opening the cell door and gesturing for Ahrash to follow him.

Leaving death row, they soon entered a small corridor.

"Do you want a haircut?" the stern guard asked and before waiting for an answer, he added, "If you let your hair grow long, you will have to tie it back with a rubber band at all times."

Ahrash decided to get a haircut.

Inside the shop, a barber in a white coat was shaving a prisoner's head. Ahrash sat on a chair and waited. The guard stood above him with his arms folded across his chest.

"A shave or just a trim?" the barber asked Ahrash when it was his turn.

"A haircut," Ahrash answered in a muffled voice.

Using both clippers and scissors, it took the barber only a few minutes to complete the job. He put a mirror in Ahrash's hand and spun him around. "Look, son. I've given you quite a nice haircut."

Ahrash peered into the mirror, looking at his face for the first time in weeks. His image reminded him of a broken porcelain figurine at home which had been haphazardly glued back together.

After his haircut, Ahrash and the guard left the building and entered an annex leading them down a long, dim hallway. The air there was muggy and had a repulsive smell.

Ahrash was thrown into a fright. Not knowing where the man was taking him, he trembled with fear.

They walked in silence. The further they moved, the more the revolting smell intensified.

Halfway down the hall, the guard paused. He casually sized up his young prisoner and continued moving forward.

As they advanced deeper into the hall, Ahrash felt overly sick to his stomach. He thought he might vomit at any moment. He tried to focus on his breathing, but his escalating fear had total control over him.

The guard stopped again, this time in front of a tall cabinet. He removed a set of towels, a jumpsuit, and underpants from the cupboard and shoved them into the boy's hands. He then unlocked a door and sent the miserable child into a shower facility. "Wash well, you have only 10 minutes."

Ahrash stepped inside and closed the door. He was unable to find a lock.

The shower room was long and narrow with numerous shower heads. He used the first head, lathering his hair and body in hurry.

Despite his fear and anxiety, the warm water felt good on his skin.

———————— آرش ————————

Two janitors were mopping the hall floor when Ahrash returned to death row. Inside most cells, the prisoners were in clean jumpers, many with shaved heads. Some inmates were washing their sinks, others making their beds. No one was misbehaving. Death row certainly had a fresh look and feel.

Nearing his cell, Ahrash slowed his pace and peered inside Reza's cell. It was a conscious decision, but he was not sure why he did it. Maybe he needed to see a kind face, an ally. Maybe he wanted to let someone know that he had returned to his cell and that he was safe.

Reza acknowledged him with a smile.

CHAPTER 31

Warden Ramzi awoke at five in the morning. He showered, shaved and dressed himself at a slow pace. As expected, his uniform fit quite loosely, forcing him to slide the buckle of his belt to a never-used notch.

Ready to report for duty soon, Ramzi first joined his wife in the kitchen where she had their breakfast ready on the table.

The couple sat down to their meal.

The kitchen was faintly lit by the rising sun, yet the worry on the pair's faces was clearly visible. Ramzi was anxious to see and inspect the prison after his two-month absence; his wife agonized over his return to work with his health still frail.

"I should have put in an order for a smaller uniform," Ramzi commented, wiggling the loose collar of his shirt.

"It's so nice that you have lost all that weight. You are even more handsome now than when we first met."

Ramzi smiled.

After their short exchange, the husband and wife became quiet – both returning to their individual thoughts.

Warden Ramzi, the son of a shoemaker, was born and raised in a small town. From a young age, it was clear that he was highly intelligent and that he possessed a strong personality. He graduated from high school early and attended a prominent college on a full scholarship. By twenty, he had received his bachelor's degree in psychology. Instead of pursuing a career in this field however, he decided to enroll in military school.

His public service began right after graduating from the academy.

Working hard with absolute dedication and honesty garnered the young Ramzi widespread recognition from the start of his career. He was only twenty-eight years old when he became the mayor of his own town and six years later, he was appointed as the Assistant Warden to one of the capital's largest penitentiaries.

At the time, the prison facility was in a state of sheer chaos. The lack of organization and proper supervision had created a corrupt and unsafe environment equally for the prisoners and the guards. Yet, the sitting warden, already having surpassed retirement age, continued employing his failed method of management year after year.

Aware of the magnitude of the challenge, Ramzi worked with exceptional diligence. He spent long hours at the establishment, constantly searching for solutions to solve the existing problems. He even delayed starting a family until he was able to transform the prison into a manageable, smoothly run operation.

His profound accomplishments awed state officials and when the old warden finally retired, Ramzi was the clear choice as his successor.

Ramzi sat behind the wheel of his car, waiting for his son, Navid, to join him. Navid had made a replica of a crane for his physics class and did not feel comfortable taking his project on the schoolbus.

It was 7am. The sun was already high in the sky, yet the air was still cool and nice. Ramzi rolled down the car window and sat back. A soft breeze wafted in fragrant air from a wall of honeysuckles in the yard. He breathed in deeply and tried to relax. Unfortunately, his effort only renewed the surge of anxiety. The last two months had been the longest he had ever been away from his post. He knew well that many things could have gone wrong during his absence. His assistant, Mr. Davar, was a good man with high moral standards, yet he was too inexperienced to run the organization by himself.

Navid came out of the house with his crane in hand. Ramzi opened the trunk with the click of a button and the boy set his model down carefully.

"Sorry dad, the strings had gotten tangled up. It took a while to separate them," Navid said entering the car.

Ramzi smiled at him and started the car.

He dropped his son off at school and headed toward the prison complex.

CHAPTER 32

His earlier apprehension wholly dissipated the moment Ramzi entered his office. He sat behind his desk and habitually addressed a pile of letters before calling for his assistant Mr. Davar.

Mr. Davar provided his boss an update of the prison's latest ongoings and then suggested they visit the various cell blocks and common areas.

The first inspection was of the prison's kitchen where many of the inmates worked alongside the staff.

The kitchen was immaculately clean and organized. Well-groomed cooks in white aprons, hairnets, and gloves were preparing food in oversized pots while their helpers hustled around them with positive energy.

Ramzi greeted the staff and engaged a few workers in brief conversation, all along assessing the safety and hygiene around them.

He sampled some food next, reviewed the weekly menu, and concluded his visit.

From the smile on his face, it was clear to the staff that their superior was entirely pleased with his checkup.

Passing through a short block, Warden Ramzi and his assistant entered the prison yard next. The weather was exceptionally pleasant for that time of the year. Clearly, the overnight coolness still had the summer heat under control.

They stood in a corner by the edge of a narrow garden and quietly observed the inmates.

Most inmates were gathered in small bunches, playing cards, talking or smoking. A few were exercising, running along the fence, or kicking a soccer ball around.

In one spot, not too far from them, several prisoners were feeding breadcrumbs to a band of noisy pigeons. A guard was among them, participating in their good deed.

As Ramzi looked in the direction of the bird enthusiasts, he noticed an older inmate at the end of the garden. The man was attending to a big azalea bush, removing its dried flowers with care. Ramzi remembered the plant well, it had been a gift from the former warden when Navid was born. It was originally a small plant, head-heavy with a cluster of red blooms. He had had the azalea planted in the prison's yard less than a month later.

A few prisoners noticed the warden and like moths to a flame; they gathered around him instantly. A guard moved to disperse them but stopped when his boss signaled him off. Ramzi listened to the inmates with patience and recorded their concerns in a small notebook. He was earnestly happy to see the men around him healthy and as content as they could be.

آرش

It was during the tour of death row that Ramzi first came across Ahrash, a crumpled, skeletal boy sitting in the corner of his cell.

"He has been here for more than a month, Sir," the assistant quickly explained when he noticed his superior's perplexed look. "He will be here until he turns eighteen."

"There must be a mistake. He is just a kid."

"Unfortunately, Sir, there is no mistake. I saw the Judge's order myself."

Ramzi started to walk away but turned around quickly. He stopped at the boy's cell, staring at him for a while. Ahrash's appearance locked the tenderhearted man into silence.

Mr. Davar was alarmed. It was not too long ago that the news of the murdered inmate ignited his boss's heart attack. He frantically searched for words to reduce the enormity of the situation, but he had no solace to offer. To his relief, however, the inspection of death row came to an abrupt halt. Ramzi concluded his tour and stormed out of the hall.

―― آرش ――

Back in his office, Ramzi asked for the boy's file. He went through the recording lines, many puzzling questions raiding his mind. It was clear that he needed a lawyer's insight.

He faxed the entire file to his cousin, Sepand, who was a criminal attorney.

Shortly after, his cousin called.

"The judge's decision is questionable. The boy was defending his father, not committing a premeditated murder," Sepand stated.

"Can we request that the judge review the case again?" Ramzi inquired.

"Unfortunately, Judge Kasra is not an approachable man. He is headstrong and presumptuous. Any questions about his judgment will upset him and put him on the defensive. Having a high-ranking government official as a brother, this man always parades around, feeling untouchable. All of us in the field try our best to avoid any conflict with him." Sepand went on and on complaining about the arrogant judge Kasra.

The information about the judge was defeating but would not stop Ramzi from trying to course correct. He immediately canceled all his plans for the remainder of the day, instead contacting any agency who could help the young death row boy.

CHAPTER 33

When Ramzi arrived home, the sun had been set for a while. Despite calling earlier and letting his family know he would be late, his wife and son had waited to have dinner with him.

They sat at a neatly set table on the deck where the air was saturated by the fragrant honeysuckles. A steady evening breeze had reduced the day's heat drastically, resulting in pleasant conditions. The capital's famous cool summer nights were, in fact, already in effect.

Ramzi had no appetite. He felt as if barbs were lodged in his throat. "How did the project work out, son?" he asked Navid while rearranging the food on his plate.

Navid spoke proudly of his crane production. He went on in detail, even talking about other students' projects.

"During lunch, we had our models on display in the cafeteria. Nearly all the students and teachers liked mine the best," he explained, unaware that his father could not concentrate on any of his words.

"Why are you not eating much tonight?" Ramsey's wife asked him.

"I do not know. I am just not hungry."

"Did you have a difficult day?"

"Yes, indeed, it was a tough one."

"Maybe it is still too soon for you to go back to work. The surgeon said you need six months to completely heal and regain your strength. Didn't he suggest you start by working part time?"

Ramzi gave her a faint smile. "He sure did, my dear."

"Why are you jeopardizing your health then? You have been gone for more than twelve hours today."

Noticing his mother's frustration, Navid tried to change the subject. "Dad, do you think you could speak at my school's next assembly? In my journalism class today, our teacher asked for parent volunteers with unique jobs who could speak to the students about their experiences. I put your name down before thinking about your busy schedule."

"That is alright son. I will try to make the time for it but it will most likely be Mr. Davar who would attend the assembly," Ramzi said and quickly went back to the earlier discussion with his wife. "I was not planning to stay that long at work, dear. There was a crisis, a serious matter that I could not ignore."

Ramzi's wife did not ask any more questions.

─────── آرش ───────

Later that night, Ramzi felt an urgent need to talk about Ahrash. He gathered his unsuspecting family and told them the boy's sad saga, revealing his own fear of not being able to help him.

The thought of a thirteen-year-old being on death row, awaiting his execution, filled the mother and son with despair. They now understood why the family patriarch never brought home news from the prison.

The family joined hands and Ramzi led them in prayer. They fervently asked God for the boy's safety and his quick release.

CHAPTER 34

Ramzi left no stone unturned in his mission to help Ahrash.

At first, he sought help from local lawyers. Unfortunately, none of them were willing to deal with any cases involving Judge Kasra.

Let down by his community's lawmen, he decided to contact a retired attorney, who was nationally known for several important trials. This time luck was with him. The resourceful lawyer was able to provide him with a long list of distinguished judges across the country. He also gave him the name of a few religious leaders who were experts in Sharia law.

Ramzi entered into correspondence with every single person on the list, pleading with them to examine Ahrash's case.

A week later, Judge Kasra sent word out that he would review the case.

Hopeful and eager now, Warden Ramzi decided to meet with Ahrash.

A guard brought the boy to his office. Ramzi offered him a chair and introduced himself, explaining his position and responsibilities at the compound. He spoke with a calm voice, trying not to intimidate the child who was sitting, with absolute stillness, before him.

"It was a complete shock, son, to find you on death row. We have never had an inmate so young before," Ramzi said, while trying to make eye contact with the boy.

The young prisoner did not allow their eyes to meet.

Ramzi plucked a tissue from its box, moped the sweat off his forehead and spoke again. "I read your file and felt obliged to send your records out to a few respectable judges for review. As I expected, none of them agreed with your sentencing and requested that Judge Kasra revisit the case. And I am delighted to let you know that he has agreed."

Ahrash remained quiet, not exhibiting even the slightest joy at his potential freedom.

Disillusioned by the boy's lack of reaction, Ramzi made an effort to remain positive. He slid a small bowl of candy across the desk. "Have some sweets, son."

Ahrash thoughtfully selected a butterscotch from the bowl and held it in his palm.

"The description of the incident in your file was very brief. I would like to know more by hearing directly from you. You might want to tell me a little about Mahmood's personality and your father's relationship with him prior to the altercation. That will give me a better understanding of why you felt you had to interfere."

Ahrash stated what had happened clearly, but very tersely. Ramzi eyed him for a moment but did not pressure him for additional details.

Something about the boy's extremely reticent manner was alarming. It was clear that he was an intelligent child. He spoke rationally and with an extensive vocabulary, answering every question coherently.

Why is he this withdrawn? Has depression taken hold? The thought was disturbing.

Over the years, Ramzi had witnessed countless prisoners who had become depressed in jail and, unfortunately, many had suffered catastrophic endings.

Ahrash's frail mental and physical state brought about a strong parental sense within the kind warden. He wanted to draw the child into a long hug but instead, he took a big breath, and only offered the boy another piece of candy.

"Listen, Ahrash. Many good people are trying to get you out of here. I do not know how long it may take, but I promise it will happen soon. Meanwhile, you should try to stay strong. I have been told that you have lost a lot of weight. You need to consume more food and remain healthy in order to cope with this temporary adverse situation. Consider your loved ones. Don't you think your parents would want to see you faring well?" Ramzi paused, swallowed hard, and continued. "I will put in an order for you to have a daily outdoor break. Go outside, son, breathe in the air; look at the sky, the sun, and the clouds. These days, however difficult they may be, are still a part of your life. You should not let them go to waste."

Like the slow leak of a cracked jar, Ramzi was gradually losing the boy's scant attention. Still, he could not stop counseling.

"I will tell the guards that you can use our library. You seem to be a good reader. Isn't that right?"

"Yes, sir, I used to read all the time," Ahrash replied.

Just then, the telephone on the desk rang with a rather high volume. Ramzi picked up the phone and immediately sat upright.

Ahrash sensed it was an important call, but he could not know that it was Judge Kasra on the other line.

"I have reviewed the Bedel case as you have insisted. Based on the atrocity Ahrash Bedel has brought upon Mr. Mansour's family, my assessment of the situation remains unchanged," Judge Kasra declared his verdict in a harsh and hostile voice.

Ramzi sank in his chair, so low, it was as if his spine had melted.

"Who do you think you are, Warden Ramzi, questioning my judgment? Are you attempting to ruin my reputation? You had better be careful, if you continue digging into this case, I will take you to court for slander."

Pressing the receiver firmly against his ear, Ramzi shifted his chair away from his desk, trying to protect the young prisoner from hearing Kasra.

"Do not forget that the same way my brother appointed you, he could remove you. It would only take one call from me!" Kasra gave Ramzi his final warning and hung up.

آرش

Over the next few days, no book was checked out by Ahrash, nor did any fresh air reach his lungs. His sleeping remained minimal and fitful, his nights plagued by horrifying nightmares.

The depression was building, creeping deeper and deeper inside the boy's mind and soul.

CHAPTER 35

Back from the fields, Khalil and Issa rounded the last turn for home. Someone was pacing in front of their house. Khalil recognized the man by his limp. "We better move faster, son. Hajji is waiting for us."

There was a panic in Khalil's voice, knowing Hajji was far too busy for a random visit.

"He has news from Ahrash," he muttered under his breath.

At the gate, Khalil greeted his guest. The men hugged briefly and kissed each other on the cheeks.

"How are you, young man?" Hajji patted Issa on the back.

"I am alright," Issa answered plainly.

The trio entered the yard and walked toward the house in silence. Khalil was uneasy; the worry that had started at the sight of Hajji was now growing with each step. He took bigger strides. Nevertheless, the path to the house appeared longer, stretched beneath their feet.

Sensing his father's anguish, Issa asked Hajji, "Are you here with news about Ahrash?"

"No, son. I have just come to visit the family."

آرش

Aziz brought out a tray of small cups filled with steaming tea. She stationed the platter on the rug in front of their guests, secured her scarf tightly over her head, and sat by the men.

"I heard you were at the capital recently to see Ahrash. How did the visit go?" Hajji asked the couple as he picked up his tea.

"We saw Ahrash last week. He was not well at all," Aziz answered with a sigh, tears forming in her eyes.

"God-have-mercy, at least we found an attorney who can get him out of the prison soon," Khalil tried to counsel his wife.

"That is so wonderful Khalil! What is the attorney's name?" Hajji asked.

"Mr. Hekmat."

Khalil reached for a card on the windowsill and handed it to Hajji. "Here is his information. I met him outside of the courthouse on the day the judge sentenced Ahrash."

"Has the attorney been able to take any action?"

"No, not yet," Khalil dropped his eyes, embarrassed. "I cannot afford his fee. Some relatives have promised to lend me money soon."

Hajji studied the card for a while.

"You have to be very careful, Khalil. There are many imposters that will take advantage of people in desperate situations. I recommend that you do not pay him any money until you know more about him. If you want, I can check his background."

The warning about Mr. Hekmat landed harshly on Khalil. He had never suspected the man might be a fraud.

Lighting a cigarette, Hajji took a few short drags and continued talking to the fragile couple. "I have been contemplating your situation for days. In my humble opinion, the first action should be to approach Sharif – battling with the courts is expensive and often fruitless."

Aziz interrupted Hajji, "Sharif put Sakineh in charge. Shouldn't we ask her for mercy, not her husband's?"

"Even so, we should only talk to Sharif," the village elder firmly insisted. He knew Sakineh well. She was his cousin's daughter.

Growing up, Sakineh had always been a defiant and contentious child, one constantly seeking to cause trouble with her siblings, the neighbors' kids and even Hajji's own children. She continued her aggressive behavior at school, disrupting classes and picking fights with students. As a result, she was in detention most days, missing lessons and falling behind in all subjects. She even had to repeat a grade in spite of her high intelligence.

In her early teens, after attacking a teacher with a knife, Sakineh was permanently expelled from school. This rejection, unfortunately, served as a new source of anger, brewing a fresh hatred within the uncontrolled girl. She would wander the village all day, harassing anyone she could, causing trouble. At one point, she had become so violent, even her own parents were afraid of her.

Even though Sakineh appeared calmer and more mature now, Hajji still had his reservations about her. He strongly believed that nothing, not even living with Sharif for all these years, could diminish the woman's innate meanness.

"I think the key to Ahrash's freedom lies with Sharif. He is a good and logical man," Hajji said after inhaling the last of his cigarette. "If you want, I will try to make arrangements to meet with him – of course, without his wife's knowledge."

The thought of approaching Sharif terrified Khalil. How could he face the man after causing his son's death?

"I talked to the clergies in the mosque," Hajji said, bringing up another point. "They think you should offer some blood money to the family."

"I will give away everything I own to have my son back," Khalil voiced right away.

"Do not commit yourself to any amount so hastily, my friend. Remember, you are still responsible for Issa and Aziz."

Khalil nodded in agreement even though he knew without Ahrash, the family would cease to exist.

The discussion continued a while longer. In the end, Khalil and Hajji decided to pay Sharif a visit.

Dinner time was fast approaching. Issa left for the baker's shop. Aziz spread out the sofreh on the rug and invited their guest to share in their meal.

Hajji gladly accepted.

CHAPTER 36

"Where are you going, Neloo?" the twins asked in unison.

"I am going to see Issa. Do you want to come?"

Both boys shook their heads no, yet sneakily tailed her, taking quiet steps. Aware of their game, Neloo decided to play along. She sped up for a while and then unexpectedly stopped. The twins, unable to stop on time, crashed right into their clever sister. They dashed off screaming but returned right away in anticipation of another trick.

Neloo continued toying with them all the way to their neighbor's house.

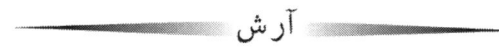

─────── آرش ───────

Issa was milking the sheep when the siblings entered the barn.

"Is that you, Neloo?" Issa's masculine voice filled the air.

Neloo put the box she had brought with her on a low stool and crouched down beside Issa. "Can I milk for a minute?" she whispered.

"What are you planning to do, Neloo?" Issa asked in a quiet voice as he shifted his body over. He knew Neloo was not his only visitor and the twins were probably with them in the barn.

"I am teasing my brothers. Just wait."

The twins, who were stowed out of view, gradually, inched closer – their little hearts pumping rapidly with fear and excitement.

They were in the middle of the barn now, only a couple of feet shy of their sister and their blind neighbor. Too scared to take another step forward, they stood there still, undecided about what to do next.

Finding the moment right, Neloo quickly angled the sheep udder up and aimed. "I got you!" she said, squirting the twins liberally.

The startled boys ran away with a shriek, their sister's laughter following them out of the barn.

"I love those crazy kids," Neloo said, still chuckling. "Without them I would have lost my sanity by now!"

"Children are the true essence of innocence and joy," Issa said as he went back to his milking.

"By the way Neloo, I have been meaning to ask you how the twins are handling their brother's loss. I heard they were very fond of him."

Staring blankly at the rhythmic jets of milk, Neloo gave a low moan. "Hell, is how I can describe what the twins have been through. For weeks, they would scream in their sleep and cry when awake. They had no appetite for food and refused to go out to play. All they wanted was their older brother."

"I am so sorry. Poor children," Issa empathized.

"Well, early on, I was worried the boys would never go back to being happy and carefree again. But a miracle happened. One morning, they woke up, ate breakfast without any fuss and went to the yard to play. Since that day, they have not mentioned Mahmood's name even once – as if their big brother had never existed."

"That is indeed a blessing, Neloo. Not all children are able to block out their sad memories."

"I still cannot believe how they managed to help themselves," Neloo responded.

The discussion on the twins ended abruptly and the two friends gave way to silence. Neloo stood up and took a survey of the barn. She walked among the sheep, patted a few, and fed them alfalfa. She thought of Ahrash and how quickly their lives had been forever altered: Mahmood ending up dead and Ahrash landing in jail for his murder.

She let out a long sigh of despair and reached for her package on the stool. "I have a letter and some sweets for Ahrash," she said, nudging the parcel against Issa's hand.

"Great. Leave them with me and I'll ask my father to take them to him."

"Aren't you going too?"

"No, my father will go alone this time. The trip is too expensive for the entire family to go."

Neloo took a deep breath and with no segue asked, "Do you think Ahrash is mad at me? I have been sending him many letters but have never received one in return."

"Oh dear Neloo, I know the heart can be an organ of pain but remember Ahrash is going through an exceptionally difficult time now. He is like a lone tree in a harsh land, suffering the most violent storm of his life. We all need to be patient with him; he is just trying to survive," Issa said, his voice heavy with sadness and regret.

———————— آرش ————————

When the milking was done, Issa covered the bucket and took it out of the barn. "I am taking the milk to cousin Soraya, she promised to make us cheese and yogurt."

"Why isn't Aziz making them?" Neloo asked trailing her blind friend.

"My mother is too dispirited these days to do much of anything."

Neloo recognized that she had asked the wrong question, given Aziz's trauma. Embarrassed by her own ignorance, she continued walking the length of the yard without saying another word. At the gate, however, not ready to part ways, she tacitly invited herself to accompany Issa.

———————— آرش ————————

Soraya's house was not too far; it was at the base of the meadow.

Waiting for Issa to deliver the milk, Neloo sat outside on a big rock.

The vast, green meadow before her brought back memories of all the times she had walked through that pasture to see her soulmate. She closed her eyes for a moment and imagined Ahrash's bony figure standing atop the hill.

"I miss him so much," she bemoaned.

A door scraping noise, from not too far off, ended Neloo's daydreams. She looked up and saw Koor Akbar, standing in the doorway of his shack with a watering can in hand. The blind man lingered there for a few seconds and then disappeared behind his hut.

"Ahrash really cared for the man," Neloo thought and wondered if anyone in the village ever visited Koor Akbar and if he had heard that Ahrash was in jail. *"Maybe I should approach him?"* She contemplated the thought for a while not being sure what would be more painful for the blind man: feeling that he had been abandoned by Ahrash or the truth.

Exiting his cousin's house, Issa walked to Neloo. She invited him to sit next to her, but he declined. He said that he would like to go for a walk by the stream.

"May I come along with you?" Neloo asked.

"I do not think that is a good idea, Neloo. I wish we could freely meet and talk, but you will certainly be subjected to your mother's rage should she find out," Issa said, awaiting Neloo's response.

Neloo did not say a word. She knew that her friend was right.

"I understand how difficult it is to cope with the situation. You certainly need a confidant, a trustworthy person to share your mind with. Aren't you and Ali's sister close?"

"Shereen is a good friend but unfortunately, she has plenty of her own misfortune. Her mother is seriously ill and the family is deeply in debt. It is not fair to further burden her with my grief."

"Still, you should try to visit her more often. You two can be each other's support systems," Issa said and departed.

CHAPTER 37

The room was surprisingly chilly for a summer morning. The open window must have allowed in the cold mountain air throughout the night.

Ali could hear his mother moaning and wondered if it was her crying that had woken him so early. He stayed in bed for a short time, tossing and turning on the hard floor. Unable to fall back to sleep, eventually he rose to his feet and put on his clothes.

He walked to the other side of the room where his sisters, undisturbed by their mother's groans, were both sound asleep. He closed the window and gently pulled the covers over his younger sister's bare shoulders.

A strange feeling came over him at once, an acute sense of confinement. Not only were the walls of the room closing in on him, his skin felt stretched and taut, not fitting his body right.

Feeling increasingly hemmed in, Ali decided to leave the house.

Outside, he sat on the doorstep and watched the still rising sun. A few feet away, Mahmood's bike leaned against the house. It has been there untouched for over two months. He remembered the day Sharif had brought the bike over; it was exactly one week after his son's funeral.

"I want you to have his bike. It can take you into town," the grieving father said, heartbroken and contrite. He then removed Mahmood's slingshot from his pocket and hung it on the bike's handlebar. "You better have this too. His mother should not see it around the house."

As the sky brightened, a menacing hunger started gnawing at Ali's stomach. He considered going back inside to retrieve the leftover bread from last night's dinner. A peek through the window however, changed his mind; the family was fast asleep, even his mother.

Ignoring his hunger, he then decided to leave the yard. He took a few steps in the direction of the gate only to quickly spin around: *I had better take the bike.*

———— آرش ————

By the time he had reached the village road, the bike's cold handlebars were warm in Ali's fists. He peddled aimlessly, not thinking of Sharif or Mahmood, but of his mother and his two sisters, the three innocent beings who would soon wake to another day of struggle and boredom.

"What does my family have to look forward to in life?" A question formulated in Ali's head and played over and over in a loop.

While it was true that he had never been a stellar provider, Ali had never been so utterly useless either. He worked in town periodically and his wrestling matches often rewarded well. Over the last two summers, he had actually made a decent amount of money working for his uncle in Nonassa.

"I wish I had taken Uncle up on his offer this summer again," Ali chided himself, knowing that he had the ability to improve his family's lives with a bit of effort.

———— آرش ————

Unaware of how he had gotten there, Ali soon found himself before the shack from which he and Mahmood used to steal chickens. He climbed the fence and sat on the top of the gate. Motionless.

After a while, he removed the slingshot from his pocket and aimed for a chicken. He missed with his first shot, sending the chickens darting and clucking.

In the time it took him to prepare another shot, a teenage boy and a woman appeared, wielding large sticks.

"Get the thief!" the woman shouted, running behind the boy toward their thief.

Ali jumped down quickly to the other side of the fence where he faced two angry men, standing before him, arms crossed.

Minutes later, bloodied and bruised, Ali was back pedaling his bike on the road. He had been beaten badly by the men, the woman, and the teenage boy without defending himself or even trying to escape.

آرش

The seemingly endless village road abruptly came to an end, swallowed up by an open and unadulterated terrain. Nestled between the wild path and the far-off wooded forest, was the cemetery.

Arriving there, Ali let the bike fall and hastily walked among the tombstones to his father's burial ground. He had visited his grave many times before, often when he needed an outlet for life's disappointments. Today, crushed beneath a load of shame, the shattered young man needed to be there more than ever.

Ali was fourteen when he had lost his father, old enough to keep many of his memories in his heart.

His father was a selfless man, absolutely dedicated to his wife and children. The farm that he owned, unfortunately, was a bad parcel with poor soil and water problems. To provide well for his family, he had to work harder and much longer hours than other farmers in the village. Yet, in spite of all difficulties, he never expected his kids to help him in the field. He only wanted them to focus on their education.

His children made him proud, especially Ali who did remarkably well at school.

"You are like a powerful river, son; you should never stop until you reach the sea," he would say every time his boy brought a report card

home.

Ali let out a loud cry, knowing the strong stream was now only a stagnant swamp.

From a far distance, a group of mourners made their way toward the cemetery. They were all wearing black and without exception, each one was carrying a child. Their approach angered Ali. He had not been ready to leave his father so soon and had planned to visit Mahmood's grave as well. Since Mahmood's death, it was the very first time he had set foot in the cemetery and it would be a shame if he did not visit his friend's tombstone.

He rose to his feet. Mahmood's grave was clearly visible from where he was standing. He could even see a bunch of flowers resting on the stone, fresh enough to prove a recent visit.

The mourners were moving with a steady stride – uninterrupted. They were now close enough for Ali to recognize them.

"I better leave. I can hide in the woods until they are gone," Ali decided, knowing that he could not indulge in talking to anyone in his condition.

He said a short prayer for his father and rushed to the bike. Pedaling quickly a half circle around the large cemetery, he managed to reach the edge of the forest right before the group entered the yard.

Breathless, he settled on a tree stump. Underneath his feet, piles of broken trees were lying in a graveyard of their own.

While twiddling with Mahmood's sling shot, Ali strolled down memory lane remembering all the times the two friends had spent together. He began from as far back as when they had ditched school to roam freely in town, stealing cigarettes from vendors, pickpocketing unsuspecting folks, and constant brawling with other teens. He further reflected on the recent years – a period filled with wild adventures, climbing mountains, swimming in the river, gambling, and wrestling matches.

Rolling with Mahmood had always carried with it an element of danger too. Ali now made a deliberate effort to push those types of memories out of his mind. Yet one incident in particular glowed brightly in his memories, resurfacing stubbornly.

There was a construction project commencing to expand the town's old hospital. Ali and Mahmood had been hired to work there for one full month. The job was not easy, but paid well.

To save money, they decided to sleep under an overpass close to the worksite and to use the river to wash up in the morning.

At the end of the first week, the young men decided to treat themselves to a meal of lamb kabobs and saffron rice at a local kabob house.

On that particular Friday evening, the restaurant was very busy. It took a long time for them to even be seated and longer still before they could order.

Ravenous, they waited for quite some time but no food appeared. Mahmood called the waiter over a couple of times, asking about their orders to no avail. It was frustrating, especially since they had noticed that some patrons arriving after them had already received their meals.

One young waiter exited the kitchen with two steaming plates of food, heading toward a table just past them. Mahmood stopped him, demanding that he set the food on their table. The waiter somewhat fearfully stated that the food was for his boss's friends.

Mahmood stood up. Hovering over the waiter, he started to shout, using a string of swear words.

From the back of the kabob house, the owner appeared. He was a tall and hefty man in his mid-forties. With a large butcher knife in hand and full of confidence, he approached his riotous customers.

"We do not need trouble here! Get out, you dirty –"

The owner did not have a chance to finish his words before Mahmood threw the plate of hot food balanced in the waiter's hand into the owner's face. He then quickly grabbed the hand holding the knife, slamming it on the back of a chair. The knife dropped to the floor. Mahmood charged and threw the man to the ground, kicking him for good measure.

In a flurry, the two friends exited the restaurant, an angry Mahmood pushing plates of food off the tables along the way. They got on the bike and left quickly before the police could be called or worse, the workers could come after them.

Having traveled several blocks to relative safety, the young men finally stopped at a corner and bought liver kabobs from a street vendor. They ate standing up and then pedaled back to the bridge.

Tired from the day's work and unsettled by what had happened in the restaurant, Mahmood and Ali both opted to remain silent the rest of the night.

They arrived at their place and chained up the bike. Giving each other wide berth, they spread out their sacks and waited for darkness to fall.

Looking at the few early stars and listening to the water running over the boulders was so relaxing that Ali almost forgot about the calamities of the evening. He started calculating how much money he had made thus far and how much he had spent. His plan was to buy gifts for his sisters and mother, or at the very least just for Hannah.

From deep within his reveries, he suddenly heard some rustling noises amongst the bushes. Frightened that it might be a snake, he attempted to get up when suddenly two men wrestled him back to the ground.

About twenty feet away, more men were attacking Mahmood.

Mahmood did not give up easily, but in the end, he was held down firmly by the assailants.

The restaurant owner appeared with his butcher knife in hand. He stood in front of detained Mahmood and without uttering a word, cut open his abdomen.

The avengers disappeared as quickly as they had arrived.

Mahmood's midsection had been split wide open and his intestines were spilling out.

Ali rushed to get the bike.

"Forget the bike!" Mahmood yelled, pushing his intestine back inside their cavity. "We cannot ride in the dark. We must walk to the hospital."

Bleeding profusely, Mahmood held his wound closed with his balled-up jacket and walked more than a mile alongside a panicked Ali. They reached the hospital and with the fervent effort of the doctors, he narrowly escaped death.

We could have both been easily killed that night. Ali shivered at the thought.

The floodgates had been flung wide open now. A series of similarly terrifying episodes attacked Ali's mind, including the many times that an irritated Mahmood, himself, might have killed or injured him.

My mother would never have survived my death. I was a fool letting Mahmood fill my world with peril.

His fury building, Ali reared up and began to walk into the woods. The sun had completely risen by then, yet he felt chilly under the canopy of trees.

Before long, the cold forced him to return to the edge of the forest. He sat down on the same stump, still feeling icy. A pair of squirrels appeared and disappeared among the tree branches. He thought that he saw a deer in the distance, but he couldn't have been sure.

The mourners had made themselves totally comfortable at the

cemetery. They had gathered near a tombstone with tea and snacks, picnicking.

Cold and aggravated, Ali waited for them to leave. Even with all the contradictory thoughts churning in his mind, he still wanted to visit his old pal.

CHAPTER 38

To avoid being noticed, Khalil kept his gaze down as he strode through the bazaar's narrow alley. There were only a few shoppers milling around, yet still he had to pass by an array of vendors before reaching Hajji's store.

From the moment he had entered the marketplace, a young boy with a tray of cigarettes and gum packets, trailed him, begging for a purchase. Khalil finally dropped a few coins onto the tray and sped up. Luckily, no one else stopped him before he reached his destination.

Adjacent to Hajji's store, the village barber was shaving a man's head on the street. A young boy with chubby, tear-streaked cheeks was sitting on the customer's lap, protesting loudly. Khalil knew the barber well and had no choice but to stop and say hello. Fortunately, the distressed child did not allow them to engage in a long conversation.

آرش

Khalil stood at one end of the shop next to a tall stack of rice bags.

Hajji was in the process of signing some papers with two farmers. It took a couple of minutes before Khalil recognized the clients. They were brothers from the Naansa village.

For years, Hajji had bought rice and legumes from farmers and distributed them to the stores in the surrounding cities. The farmers were often in competition to sell him their harvests, finding it a privilege to do business with such an honest and fair man.

Soon, the brothers' deal was complete. Hajji greeted Khalil warmly and, together, they exited the shop.

With their first step out of the store, the same young boy reappeared with his meager tray of wares. Hajji bought two packs of cigarettes and some chewing gum, while inquiring about the welfare of the boy's family.

Passing through the bazaar was not without interruptions either. The shopowners, one after another, stopped Hajji to say hello and to pay him their respects. Hajji tried his best to shorten each visit without being rude.

About half an hour later, the men finally reached the village road and started walking at a brisk pace.

At the last bend in the road, Ali and a young man could be seen. They were smoking by the boulder. Hajji, walked up to them. He asked Ali of his mother's health without mentioning his black eye and ripped lips.

"She is still sick. Next Tuesday, Uncle Jamal will take her to see another doctor in town," Ali explained.

"It is such a shame that she is not getting better. Tell your uncle to contact me if he can. I know several good doctors that might be able to help your mother," Hajji said and quickly limped away. He took big strides to catch up with Khalil, simultaneously making a mental note to send some sweets to Ali's house.

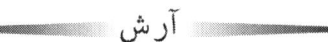

———————— آرش ————————

The twins were playing tag with another boy by their gate. As soon as they saw Khalil, they abandoned their game and hid behind a tree trunk. The third boy stood alone, confused.

The men entered the yard.

Hajji approached the front door – Khalil hung back a few yards.

Sharif, himself, opened the door. He greeted the village elder and invited him to come in.

At the far end of the room, Neloo was sitting on a rug with books and paper all around her. She stood up and said hello to their guest.

"Hello Neloo Jaan," Hajji responded. "Are you ready to go back to school?"

Neloo smiled and nodded politely.

"My daughter is an incredible girl, a precious gift from God," Sharif, out of nowhere, started to praise Neloo. "She is intelligent, responsible, and absolutely kindhearted. I am truly proud of her."

Blushing from the complements, Neloo quickly excused herself to the kitchen.

She had an uneasy feeling; something was amiss about Hajji's sudden visit. She eavesdropped a bit while waiting for the tea to brew but the men were only exchanging pleasantries.

When the tea was ready, Neloo poured it into two cups and placed them on a tray next to two small dishes of sugar cubes and dates. As she turned, she suddenly saw Khalil. He was standing in the yard, not too far from the kitchen window.

Their eyes met briefly. Neloo put down the tray and waved.

———————— آرش ————————

After receiving his tea, Hajji asked Neloo about Sakineh's whereabouts.

"She is at my aunt's house, picking cherries. It usually takes them all day," Neloo responded, rushing back to the kitchen to see if Khalil was still in the yard.

"It is perfect that we are alone, Sharif," Hajji began. "I needed to talk to you privately about an important matter," he said and paused before formulating his next sentences. "Please forgive me for interfering with your personal affairs. I have come here today to ask for peace between you and Khalil."

Khalil's name struck Sharif like a spear in the heart.

"You and Khalil grew up together. Your parents, God rest their souls, were neighbors and friends their entire lives," Hajji went on, twisting his rosary beads rapidly. "I only wish you could see it in your heart to forgive Khalil."

Sharif did not say a word.

"Your old friend is actually standing outside the door at this moment. Be the bigger man Sharif. Open the door and invite him in."

Like a soldier under command, Sharif shot up instantly. He knew if there had been any hesitation, he would likely have changed his mind.

———— آرش ————

Standing by the kitchen window, Neloo witnessed the two shattered friends hug and cry in each other's arms.

The reunion continued inside the house without much conversation at first. The two friends shed more tears; the village elder chain-smoked. When the crying ceased, Hajji took a bundle of papers out of his pocket and placed it in front of Sharif. "This is the deed to Khalil's house. He will put your name on it and leave the village with his family."

Khalil started to cry again.

"Sharif, you have the power to keep Ahrash alive, preventing his family from total devastation. I swear on my children's lives, if you let Ahrash live, God will have mercy on Mahmood's soul," Hajji beseeched.

Khalil sobbed unabatedly, tears finding channels in the wrinkles of his face down to his neck.

"Look at this broken man. If a stone had a heart, it would be melting from the inside."

———— آرش ————

More tea arrived; more cigarettes were smoked. Hajji continued to persuade Sharif to accept the offer and to forgive Khalil and his son.

As the men were discussing Ahrash's fate, a question rang in Neloo's mind: *Would my father be strong enough to act against Sakineh's will?*

CHAPTER 39

Sakineh's sister, Malehe, had several cherry trees in her large yard. Once a year, when the cherries were fully ripened and before they were devoured by the birds, Sakineh spent a long day at her house. She and Malehe picked all the cherries, working for long stretches with minimal breaks.

Both sisters made terrific cherry preserves, sometimes even selling them at the local markets.

———— آرش ————

The sun was beating down directly on her; she was dressed in black with a dark scarf tied under her chin.

She had been walking home a couple of miles in that dreadful heat, carrying two heavy baskets of cherries. The stiff handles of the baskets were digging into her palms, burrowing deeper and deeper with every step.

Despite being hot and tired, the headstrong woman refused to rest the entire way. Now, with less than a mile of her journey left, she was forced to cave to her fatigue.

A small, shade tree was ready to serve her. She rested her load on the dirt and sat down by her possessions. Glad that no one was around, she removed her scarf, unbuttoned her blouse and pulled her skirt up above her knees. Right away, she felt cooler.

A few blisters on her right hand needed attention. They were throbbing painfully. She decided to wrap the sore hand with her handkerchief, hoping the blisters would not burst before she got home.

———— آرش ————

Having gone up and down a ladder all day and carrying heavy cargo for so long, Sakineh was tired to the bone. Yet, in spite of her condition, the ownership of the ripe and succulent cherries was a delight, stretching her mouth into a smile.

"We will have enough jam for the entire winter," she said out loud, excited by the prospect of the stacks of preserves in her pantry.

Still musing about her future stockpile, Sakineh decided to end her rest. She put her scarf back over her head, took in a long breath, and continued her walk home.

The little break had energized her well – she was now able to take longer strides.

"If I'm diligent, the jam will be ready in two days. I just need to get up at dawn," she began planning, unaware of the impending disaster.

Almost home now, Sakineh suddenly saw Khalil and Hajji leaving through the gate. She froze in place. Her hands loosen their grip and the baskets hit the ground.

———————— آرش ————————

Like a raging storm, the angry Sakineh flurried through the door. She shot Neloo a disgusted look and quickly charged at Sharif – roaring, clawing, and biting him with intent. "What the hell was Khalil doing in my house?" she shrilled.

"Calm down, Sakineh. Let me explain," Sharif said, holding his arms up against the barrage.

Sakineh continued her attack, wailing on Sharif and screaming, "You son of a bitch! You traitor! The blood has not yet dried in our son's veins and you are having tea with his murderer's father?"

"Stop shouting! People will hear you," Sharif held his wife's wrists. "Please give me a chance to explain, Sakineh. Hajji brought him over and I could not deny them entry into my house."

Biting Sharif's arm, Sakineh quickly freed her wrist. Her anger now at its peak, she screamed from top of her lungs, attacking again, more viciously.

Neloo shut the window with trepidation.

Wearied by her speedy attack, Sakineh finally stopped beating her husband. She turned her back on him and took a few aimless steps, stumbling. When she was about to collapse, Sharif cautiously helped her sit down. The despaired woman stayed in place for a long time, staring at her husband, reeling at the pain he had caused her.

Neloo was astounded by her own sudden swell of sympathy for Sakineh. For the first time, her mother looked more like injured prey than a savage predator.

Sakineh was breathing with difficulty as if the air around her was too thick, oxygen-less. She struggled for a while but eventually rose to her feet and disappeared into the kitchen.

The father and daughter exchanged a worried look. They had expected the storm, which had arrived so violently, but could not comprehend its quick taming.

Looking desperate and anguished, Sharif sat in a corner. He was torn inside, leading a battle between morality and kinship.

If Neloo felt a wave of pity for Sakineh, her sorrow for her father was like a tsunami, overflowing her world.

آرش

Alas as quickly as it had subsided, the storm returned, wilder than ever. Sakineh, walked out of the kitchen and was hovering over her husband in the blink of an eye. She whipped out a knife and held it to Sharif's neck. "Let Khalil in again and I will kill you in sleep. You know that I will," she said, madness creeping into her eyes. And before Sharif could wrangle the knife from her, she forced the tip in, drawing blood.

Sharif withdrew from his crazy wife. A hand on his neck, he rushed to the kitchen, past a wide-eyed and terrified Neloo.

CHAPTER 40

From the day Sharif brought the small soccer ball home, the twins had been playing with it nonstop. And it wasn't long before several neighborhood boys joined them, establishing the youngest soccer team in the village.

Initially the children held games close by the twins' house. But with all the trees to run into and big, pointy rocks to trip over, the youngsters gradually moved further away until they had almost reached the village road. A wide, flat section adjacent to Ahrash's house was ultimately agreed upon by all the players.

It was rare for any car to travel on the village road, yet Neloo strongly disapproved of the twins' new playground. She forbade them to play there, reasoning that even a run in with a mule could be fatal. "If I lose you, I will have no more brothers left in this world," she said to them time after time, hoping shame or guilt might serve as a deterrent.

Every day, the boys promised to play right by the house, but the minute they stepped outside, they were lured by the coveted field again.

Neloo ultimately brought her worries to Sakineh and Sharif, who chastised her young brothers. Nevertheless, the twins remained incorrigible.

──────── آرش ────────

Late afternoon proved to be the most unsettling time for Issa. During the day, he managed to keep busy in the field. Once he returned home, Ahrash's absence became pronounced and brutally painful. He would sit on the porch bench and think of his brother – often likening him to a baby bird that had fallen too soon from its nest. A nameless, grey void would grow within him and, little by little, become the entirety of his world. Despondent, he would seek refuge in his *ney*, allowing his anguish to seep out through the wooden flute.

The soccer ball rolled into the yard and came to rest at Issa's feet. He picked it up in a noncommittal manner and placed it next to him on the bench.

The twins squeezed their bodies through the gate and with some trepidation, entered the neighbor's forbidden yard. They walked quietly toward the bench and stood a couple of yards shy of their favorite asset, looking at it ardently.

Jolfa, raised her head and let out a short, friendly bark.

A plan had been hatched in the boys' minds and telepathically communicated: steal the ball in one brave move and run away with it as fast as possible.

They inched forward, lockstep, their little hearts pounding faster as they neared the blind man. Gathering his courage, one of the boys finally reached out. Right before he could make a daring grab, Issa picked the ball up, dribbled it a few times and placed it tightly between his feet.

"We need some sticks," one boy suggested.

They searched the yard and found several big and small pieces of wood. Using their new implements, the boys attempted a few more times to break the ball free. Issa, playfully, stopped the brothers each time they were close to achieving their goal.

Their determination blunted, the frustrated youngsters finally ran back, leaving their precious possession in the custody of their blind neighbor.

———————— آرش ————————

Neloo's daily chores had been completed. The house was tidy, the dishes were washed, and the evening's stew was simmering over a low heat. She picked up the letter she had written to Ahrash and left the house.

Just barely stepping outside the gate, she saw the twins, anxiously running out of Ahrash's yard. Pondering the situation, she stood there still, waiting for the boys to reach her and explain.

A hand touched her shoulder next. She turned around to find Shereen and Hannah behind her. "Is everything alright?" she asked, worry flashing across her face.

"Yes, everything is just fine. Sorry that we startled you," Shereen responded quickly. "Mother is with Uncle Jamal. They went to town for some testing. We thought it might be a good time to come and visit you."

Hannah volunteered more information, "Afterward, Uncle is taking Mom to his village, keeping her for the whole week!" she said, excited and animated.

Before Neloo could fully comprehend all the information coming her way, the twins appeared, yanking on her hand. "Come fast. *Koor* Issa has our soccer ball. Come and get it from him," they said breathlessly.

That was the first time Neloo had ever heard anyone refer to Issa as Blind Issa.

"It is not nice to call a person '*koor*.' Either say 'Mr. Issa' or just 'Issa,'" she scolded the twins. "The ball has to wait anyway. We have company right now."

Shereen interjected, "It is alright, Neloo. We can stay here until you come back." She then pointed at the envelope in Neloo's hand. "Is that letter for Ahrash?"

"Yes. I was just taking it to Issa, but it can wait. There is no rush."

In the end, they decided to all walk toward Issa's house. The girls led the way, while the twins kicked up dust behind them.

———— آرش ————

As soon as Neloo saw the soccer ball on the bench, she called out to her brothers, "Boys, it is right there by Issa."

Instead of handing it over, Issa picked the ball up and secured it in the crook of one elbow.

"The twins were looking for it, Issa."

"I know that. Tell them to come and ask me for it. Politely."

"Did you hear what Issa said, my dear brothers? You need to ask him nicely."

The twins caught up to Neloo, each holding onto her skirt. Their sister nudged them forward. "Go ahead, don't be shy."

"Mister, can we have the ball back?" one twin said timidly.

Neloo and Issa both stifled a laugh at the boys' unnecessary bashfulness. Shereen, standing a couple of yards away, smiled.

Once the twins had their soccer ball back, they left the yard with Hannah.

"Are we alone, Neloo?" Issa asked.

"No. My friend, Shereen, is here with me."

Issa stood up and said hello to Shereen. Shereen moved closer. Minutes later, the trio sat on the bench and started talking.

The sun was descending from its highest point in the sky but still was beating down strongly on the village. Noisy birds, not considering settling down any time soon, were still flying in search of food. Some finches were even daringly pecking at the dirt around Jolfa's head.

The setting reminded Neloo of all the times she had shared with Ahrash and Issa on that very same bench. She wished she could travel back in time and stay there forever.

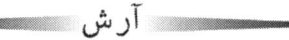

———— آرش ————

It was surprising how quickly Issa and Shereen felt comfortable with each other. Neloo could not remember the last time Issa had been so eager to converse nor Shereen being so talkative and excited. It was clear that they both were really enjoying each other's company.

"Issa, can you play your *ney* for us?" Neloo asked. "I told Shereen how beautifully you play."

"It is getting close to dinnertime and I should go give a hand to mother. Maybe I can play another time," Issa deftly refused.

آرش

Walking with Shereen back to her house, Neloo thought about inviting the girls over for dinner. She knew Sakineh would never approve, yet she still had some hope. Her father often returned home from the field before Sakineh arrived from her outing. "If I ask Dad, he will certainly say yes," Neloo mused.

CHAPTER 41

The village was under a demon's spell; women were all cursed, giving birth to babies without heads. Everywhere, working in the fields, roaming the markets, or walking down the dusty roads, melancholy mothers were either pregnant or carrying headless babies in their arms.

——————— آرش ———————

A warm loaf of bread in hand, Ahrash left the baker's shop and sat on a rock close by. Several noisy black crows started flying low overhead, perhaps hatching a plan to steal his food. Not minding the birds, Ahrash was only focused on the road. He seemed to be waiting for someone, as he would occasionally crane his neck toward the road above the hill.

Two obscure figures appeared in the distance. Ahrash jumped to his feet; he knew it must be them.
Neloo and Aziz descended the little hill. They looked sad and in a haze; their bellies grossly inflated. When they reached him, Aziz pulled her son forward, holding him snug against her swollen stomach.
Ahrash instantly felt on edge as his mother's arms did not hold him right. Her hands felt stony on his back, clutching him tighter and tighter every second. He tried to wriggle free but he was held by an unyielding grip.
Blood started oozing from his ears; his now broken ribs stabbing at his lungs and heart.
Taking his last breaths, Ahrash raised his head to beg for mercy. He saw that his mother had been changed into a spine-chilling creature with hollow eyes and long, razor sharp teeth.

آرش

Sweat-soaked, Ahrash woke amid an unfinished scream. His heart was beating so hard it could have burst through his rib cage at any moment. He sat up on his bed and tried desperately to clear his head from the terror. But in no time, he was back to the doleful village – headless babies floating about, his deformed mother greeting him with open arms.

It was clear that yet another nightmare had leaped over into Ahrash's conscious world – a phenomenon that his fatigued brain could not comprehend.

Sadly, no one was aware that this miserable child had been suffering from a depression whose onset had begun with Mahmood's death. Now, after months of sleepless nights and minimal nutrition, his mind had become so spent that he had started jumbling his lucid moments with those of his nightmares.

This night, Ahrash had been stuck in his dream for so long that if it was not for the regular, midnight bawling of a prisoner, he would not have been able to ground himself in reality.

آرش

In the corner of the cell, right by his bed, a stack of Neloo's letters laid unopened. To distance himself from the dream, Ahrash picked up one envelope from the top of the pile and walked to the cell bars where there was more light from the hall. He wiped his tears away, sat down and read the letter.

My Dear Ahrash,
I am puzzled that you are not answering any of my letters; yet, I know there must be a logical explanation for your decision.

Here, everyone is getting ready for school, except Shereen, who has to take care of her ailing mother.

Approaching the start of school makes me extra sad. It is such a shame that we cannot begin the first year of high school together.

I think about you all the time, wondering how you are passing your days in isolation. Are you allowed to listen to the radio? Do you have access to any paper? What about getting fresh air – do they let you step outside the building?

Neloo continued her inquiries about Ahrash's conditions for some time, longing to understand his circumstances. The letter went on to say:

Wonderful news! Your father was at our house yesterday, having tea with my dad. They made peace, crying in each other's arms for a long time. I cried too.

Ahrash stopped reading. He pictured Neloo sitting with her back against a wall; her skirt pulled over her lap, writing.

Reminiscing about Neloo, miraculously, brought calm to the distraught boy. He closed his eyes and continued musing.

In no time, however, his dreams invaded again: Neloo finished writing and stood up. Her belly was huge, grotesquely oversized.

Ahrash quickly opened his eyes.

Neloo was still there, her eyes fixed on his, begging for help.

A soundless scream escaped Ahrash's throat. He was terrified and shivering, realizing now that he would never be able to sever the umbilical cord of his nightmares.

A voice in his head, maybe even the demon himself, instructed him to fight back and once and for all free himself from all his hallucinations.

The boy obeyed.

Fearful and desperate, Ahrash grabbed his pillow, rushed to the bathroom, and hid himself behind the half wall. Removing a jagged, headless metal spoon from inside the pillowcase he then began to cut his wrists through the skin and veins.

CHAPTER 42

Warden Ramzi received the call about Ahrash before dawn. The news came down on him like an anvil. He hurriedly threw on his clothes and left the house.

―― آرش ――

The military hospital was exceptionally quiet that early morning and Ramzi was able to talk with a nurse right away. Unfortunately, the nurse did not give him much information.

"As soon as I hear from the doctor, I will let you know," she said matter-of-factly, not recognizing the warden out of his official clothing.

Disappointed, Ramzi paced back and forth in front of the receptionist's desk, negative thoughts racing through his head nonstop. There was no doubt in his mind that the boy was in bad condition since he had been brought here instead of the prison's clinic.

"How could he have hurt himself without being seen?" Ramzi was baffled. *I must talk to the guard who was on watch last night.*

The guard arrived shortly after and reported the incident in detail. With his appearance, the hospital staff finally clued in on who had been incessantly asking after Ahrash.

An hour passed. Ramzi stepped outside.

The sun was rising from behind the building with a rushed energy, yet a pale moon still stood its ground, high up in the sky. Birds, plenty in number, were everywhere, darting between rooftops and tree branches. They winged freely and sang excitedly, blissfully unaware of the world's cruelties.

Spotting a bench close by, Warden Ramzi walked toward it. He sat there, glum.

The air around him was filled with a strong smell of the wisteria flowers hanging from the gazebo above his head. The aroma was so intense that even his sad mood could not dampen it.

A few friendly pigeons joined him. Their feathers glinted in the sunlight as they strutted by his feet. A large fowl, perhaps a hawk came into view and started circling high above the pigeons.

Watching the predator hovering over the small birds, Ramzi drew a depressing parallel to the fragility of Ahrash's life: *What if the boy does not make it?* He shivered at the thought.

It was past 8am when the doctor appeared at last. "Your young prisoner is in stable condition and there is no damage to any of his organs," he announced.

"How long will he be in recovery?" the warden inquired.

"A couple of days, but I would like to keep him longer for a complete psychological evaluation. It is very much of concern that this child nearly succeeded in taking his own life."

آرش

Khalil stood over Ahrash, gently stroking his hair. His son's skeletal face was white, bloodless. His neck was too slender and his collarbones were so prominent, as if a beast had scraped them clean of any flesh.

A middle-aged, bubbly nurse walked in and checked the IV. Khalil collected his nerves and, in broken Farsi, asked if his son would be ok.

"Yes, of course, he will be fine. Your son is young and will recover quickly. He just needs a lot of fluids and rest."

Khalil hardly understood the nurse's rapid words but her positive attitude and smile gave him some hope.

The hospital room was relatively dark except for a single blade of sunlight piercing through the curtains. Khalil walked to the window and pulled the drapes back. An enormous cypress tree appeared, standing just beyond the window. He stood there for a while, staring intensely at the majestic tree.

Two young crows flew down in tandem and landed, side by side on a single branch, loudly sharing some tale. Khalil turned to see if their loud chatter woke Ahrash.

His son, resembling a mummified saint, was lying still in bed.

Something suddenly snapped in the sad man. A rush of anger started running through him, an anger toward his creator, the God he had worshiped so obediently all his life.

"Haven't I proved my loyalty to you even after you gave me a blind son and took away my baby girl? Didn't I endure Aziz's depression and years of poverty with an unwavering faith? Didn't I praise you every day for giving Ahrash to us? So why, why is my son here now, far away from home, fighting for his life?"

Khalil's ire soared. His voice was now louder, his face red with rushing blood. He turned his head and faced the mighty tree as if he needed a witness for his grievances and continued.

"How could you not see the hope Ahrash had brought to his deprived brother and fragile mother? How could you not see how hard this child tried to improve his family's dire lives? Tell me – what unforgivable sin could he have committed to deserve such abandonment?"

Harboring this deep indignation, Khalil paced the small path between his son's bed and the window. He was uncharacteristically enraged, muttering further complaints to his maker, waving his fists in the air.

———— آرش ————

Ahrash opened his eyes, his mind muffled and clouded. He was totally confused by his surroundings – the room, the bed, and the machines he was hooked up to. Rubbing his heavy lids, he tried to sustain a rational thought, but he was quickly back to sleep.

When he awakened the second time, he collected his energy to survey the room. He saw his father, asleep on a chair by his bed.

"Dad?" he called out, with a voice scarcely above a whisper.

Khalil stood up immediately and composed himself. "I am here, Ahrash. I am here, son."

Ahrash gave him a faint smile and closed his eyes only to briefly flit them open again. "I am thirsty, Dad."

As if on cue, the nurse brought in a cup of water and two small pills. She helped Ahrash sit up and waited for him to take his medicine

For the rest of the evening, Ahrash would wake momentarily and exchange a few words with his father before slipping back into sleep.

His son being alive and talking, filled Khalil with remorse. He deeply regretted his earlier sin, protesting against God: *Will I be subject to his wrath? Would he now desert Ahrash completely, leaving him to rot in jail?*

A cold sweat ran down the man's back.

At 9pm, the nurse told Khalil that visiting time was over and that his ride was waiting for him outside the hospital.

Khalil stood by his slumbering son and recited a prayer under his breath. He then planted a brisk kiss on his forehead and left the room.

———————— آرش ————————

Earlier that day, Ramzi had made arrangements for Khalil to fly to the capital. The two men had a brief discussion before Khalil could see his son in the hospital.

The warden, speaking in fluent Turkish, greeted the nervous father and cautiously explained how the terrible incident had unfolded.

"I knew Ahrash had been in despair but did not recognize that his sadness had already turned into a deep depression. I should have known better. Being in isolation is a harsh punishment, even for adults," Ramzi ruefully admitted.

Khalil was quiet, intensely absorbing the information with all of his senses.

"I am truly outraged by the judge's decision to keep your son on death row. Unfortunately, I have learned that it is not easy to go against a well-known judge," Ramzi said and paused to contain the lump in his throat. "After what happened this morning, however, I have made a pledge to fight this injustice no matter what it takes. Meanwhile, we all need to be watchful of the precarious situation this child has been placed in – we must all help him survive."

"I will do anything for my son. I'm willing to give my life for him," Khalil interrupted the warden.

"I believe that. I, too, have a son about the same age as Ahrash."

Big drops of tears rolled down Khalil's face.

Ramzi offered him a tissue.

"We should give Ahrash hope, a purpose for living. I know he loves his family greatly. Maybe visiting him more and on a regular basis, will give him something to look forward to.

Heeding the warden's words, Khalil started thinking, trying to eliminate all the obstacles in the way of regular family trips to the capital.

"You should not be worried about the expenses Mr. Bedel. I am sure that we can provide discounted tickets for your transportation or even free passes. As far as accommodation during your visit, I am offering you and your family a safe and comfortable place to stay too."

Ramzi had already given an offer of accommodations some thought. He had decided he would propose his former gardener's headquarters to Ahrash's family. The place was tucked away in the corner of the yard, a room with a bathroom and a small kitchen. Nobody had lived there since his old gardener had passed away last year.

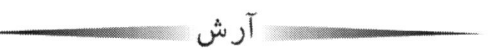

——— آرش ———

A young man in military clothes, picked Khalil up outside the hospital. They rode through the busy streets of the capital for a long while. Khalil watched the traffic in awe. The bright lights of the stores' neon signs strained his eyes, but he could not stop staring at them or the hundreds of people still entering or leaving shops at this time of night.

After more than half an hour of driving, the car finally entered a nice, quiet suburban area. A few turns later it stopped in front of a house with a wide iron gate.

Khalil got out of the vehicle and was greeted by Ramzi.

CHAPTER 43

He climbed the stairs and walked down a long corridor toward Ahrash's room. The door was ajar and he could see him sitting upright in a chair. His son's delicate profile warmed his heart. He stood there and watched him soundlessly until Ahrash turned his head and saw him.

Today was the fourth and the last day Khalil could be with his boy.

The father and son embraced tightly, neither wanting to let go. The smell of the field carried on Khalil's clothes took Ahrash back to the village, to his mother, to Issa. He let out a short sigh, longing for the past, for his simple, yet promising life.

"Have you had lunch yet?" Khalil asked as he put a bag on the serving table.

"No, dad. Lunch is at noon."

Khalil looked at the wall clock, whose hands were both almost on the twelve. "I just barely made it then, I better hurry," he humored.

There were two Styrofoam containers in the bag. In the larger box, two pieces of lamb kabobs laid on a bed of rice, alongside two grilled tomatoes. The other box contained flat bread, feta cheese and a mound of fresh herbs.

"Ready for lunch son?"

"I am not hungry. But it smells so delicious that I can't resist."

Wondering if Ahrash could use his hands, Khalil cut the kabob and tore apart the flat bread.

"You can put my portion in the smaller box, Dad."

"The food is just for you. I had a late breakfast," Khalil explained.

Even so, he brought his chair closer to the table. "It sure smells good. Maybe I will have some."

Much to Khalil's relief, Ahrash was able to use his hands without any problems. He, in fact, appeared to be recuperating very fast. His face was not as pale as the previous days, his eyes less sunken, somewhat glowing. And even though the depression was still with him, his son certainly had his intellectual mind back, capable of carrying on rational conversations.

The father and son dined together peacefully. Ahrash asked many questions about his mother, Issa, Neloo, and Jolfa. Khalil answered them all truthfully.

After having had only a small amount of food, Ahrash stopped eating and leaned back in his chair.

Khalil tried to mask his disappointment at his son's meager appetite.

"How did you find out about me, Dad?"

"Jafar came to the field with the news. We got into his Jeep. After dropping Issa off at home, he drove me to a military airport and helped me with boarding the plane. It could have been very scary, flying in that metal contraption, if I had not been thinking of you the entire time."

Somber, Ahrash looked down. He did not even hear his father's last sentiment as he had abruptly and completely spaced out. It was as though a hand had suddenly spread a dusting of sadness all over him.

Khalil gently touched his son's shoulder and asked him if he was ok. When there was no answer, he cleared the table and sat down quietly.

A silence lingered about them for a while and ended with Ahrash murmuring, "So Issa knows what I have done."

"Yes son, Issa knows. He was with me when Jafar came to the field. Luckily, your mother was not in the village that day and Issa and I have pledged to keep it a secret from her."

The silence returned to the room.

Khalil walked to the window and pulled back the drapes. The old cypress tree appeared, standing even more solidly than before. Searching for the young crows, Khalil's eyes traveled up and down the tree, but the birds were nowhere to be seen. He left the window mildly disappointed and walked back to Ahrash, only to find that he had fallen asleep.

———————— آرش ————————

When Ahrash woke up after his long nap, he did not look depressed anymore. His father, thankful, rushed to the cafeteria and returned with tea and biscuits.

"Dad, do you know how Koor Akbar is doing?" Ahrash asked while drinking his tea.

"Honestly son, I have not seen or heard much about him. I only know that your mother has decided to send him food now. On Fridays, Issa takes a warm dish to him. You should take over that duty once you are back in the village."

Ahrash smiled.

It was past 2pm when Khalil cautiously mentioned that he had to return to the village later that day. "I wish I could stay longer, but after today, the train station will be closed for a week. They are repairing the rails along the route."

Ahrash looked disappointed. "What time does the train leave?"

"At 7pm."

"How far is the station from here?"

"I have no idea. The warden said he will send a driver at 5pm to take me to the station."

Khalil sat in repose for a moment with his hand on his mustache, stroking its bristles repeatedly. He then began to praise Warden Ramzi.

"God bless this man and his family; he owns the kindest heart. Did I tell you that he gave me the key to the cottage in his yard?"

"No, you did not. Why did he do that?"

"Well, he offered for our family to stay there any time we are visiting you. He also promised to provide free bus and train tickets for our transportation to the capital."

"That is so generous of him. I was in the warden's office once but do not remember him well."

A tall doctor entered the room and introduced himself to Khalil as Ahrash's psychiatrist. "I have been visiting Ahrash daily since he arrived here. Your son is an incredibly bright young man; you must be very proud of him."

Aware of his father's limited knowledge of Farsi, Ahrash quickly repeated the doctor's words in Turkish.

The psychiatrist asked a few questions of Khalil, mainly about their village, family life and Ahrash's upbringing. He then requested for him to wait outside until the end of his visit.

آرش

In the waiting room, a young soldier was pacing restlessly while holding a sleeping baby on his shoulder. After a brief exchange, Khalil discovered that the man was originally from his own province and strangely, they both shared the same last name.

The soldier's wife had been hit by a speeding car earlier that day. She had been taken to the operating room where a group of surgeons were trying to save her life.

Khalil extracted his rosary beads from his pocket and suggested to the young man that they pray together.

He was reaching the last beads on the string when a nurse came upon them. "The doctor wants to see you, Mr. Bedel," she said to the soldier with the widest smile.

Khalil knew the man's wife had been saved.

It was almost 4pm by the time Khalil was allowed to return to the room. He was painfully aware that he had only one more hour left with his son.

At the sight of him, Ahrash stood up and threw himself into his arms, crying. "I am so sorry, Dad. Please forgive me."

"You do not need to apologize for anything son," Khalil said and paused, reflecting on another dark season of his life.

"Let me share something with you, Ahrash. You probably heard that before you were born, the family lost a baby girl. That tragedy affected your mother gravely. She mourned her baby for a long time and eventually became consumed by a serious hopelessness. Her condition at the time caused me enormous pain, but I never thought she needed to say sorry. I totally understood what she was going through and that she never meant to hurt or trouble me," Khalil said and reached for Ahrash. He held his thin body tightly in his arms and planted a big kiss on his forehead. "Let us talk about something positive now. Did I tell you that I visited Sharif and that we have made peace? He promised to persuade Sakineh to do the right thing."

Ahrash smiled, not revealing that he had already received the news from Neloo's letter.

A nurse walked in and handed Khalil a big box of candy with a card. The candy was from Warden Ramzi for the Bedel family. Khalil insisted on leaving the box behind, but Ahrash would not accept.

As the parting time was getting closer, the father and son chose to stay quiet. They were both worried, wondering how either one would handle the separation.

آرش

The clock on the wall showed five minutes to five. Khalil reached for Ahrash's hand and held it in his own hand. "You know that I think the world of you son. I trust you to take care of your mother and Issa when I am gone," he said, looking at his son with immense love and admiration. "With all the support we have from the lawyers, Hajji, and the warden, there is no doubt that your freedom will arrive soon. Until then, I expect you to keep your thoughts positive and never attempt to harm yourself again. You have to promise me."

Khalil's voice was gentle, but it had a power and edge behind it.

Ahrash felt a strength in his father he had never known was there.

CHAPTER 44

The tiny kabob house was filled with smoke. The cook, and proud owner of the diner, was vigorously fanning kabobs atop a blackened charcoal grill.

He removed three skewers from the flame and placed them on a platter over a large piece of flatbread. His helper, a thin teenage boy, took the lined-up livers along with more bread and fresh herbs to a man who was sitting at a table with his sons.

"Do you need anything else?" he asked.

"No, thank you."

As soon as they received their food, the man and his children put the livers and fistfuls of herbs on top of their bread and rolled them up, eating their meals with ravenous appetites.

Even though the diner was small, a half wall in one corner had cleverly created a more secluded section for just one table.

Two young men, Abbos and Rajab, were seated at that sheltered table waiting to be served. They were cousins, of about the same age, who worked together on their fathers' shared farm. The men had been regulars since the kabob house had opened, dining there nearly every night.

The helper boy, carrying a bottle in a small paper bag, approached the cousins and asked if they needed more drinks.

"One more to go with the kabobs," Abbos said, pushing their glasses to the edge of the table.

As they were getting their drinks, Rajab suddenly pointed at the entrance of the diner. "Is that Khalil and his son?" he asked and stumbled toward the door to greet them.

"What a pleasant surprise! Khalil and Issa at the diner!" he exclaimed, his hand on Khalil's shoulder to help keep his drunken self upright. "You must come and sit with us."

"Thank you, Rajab, but it is late. We were just going to take some food home," Khalil responded.

"I insist. It is our treat. I have not seen you since Ahrash," Rajab paused midsentence, not sure how to finish what he had blurted out. He looked down, slightly embarrassed. A second later, however, having completely forgotten his blunder, he locked his reddened eyes with Khalil's and managed a somewhat coherent sentence. "Please come and eat with us tonight."

Abbos stood up and kissed the father and son on both sides of their cheeks. "Get glasses for our guests," he ordered the boy who had returned with more drinks.

"Thank you, Abbos, but we do not drink."

"We insist. Just one shot," both cousins begged.

"Sorry. We can't."

"Get everybody kabobs then! Hurry up! And get one extra to go too," Rajab shouted, looking at Khalil, wiggling his eyebrows gleefully. "That is for your wife!"

"No extra kabob, son," Khalil said to the boy and then turned to Rajab. "My wife is in town, staying at her cousin's for a while."

"Why? Is she ill?"

"She is very melancholy. Ahrash's absence is truly hard on her. I thought staying away from home might ease her pain."

Rajab raised his glass and cheered, "To Khalil! Our good man! He then leaned toward Issa to ask something but was distracted by his long hair. "You should cut your hair, man," he said, grabbing the ends of Issa's hair.

Issa, whipped his head back, swift and strong – a crocodilian reaction at being prodded.

Aware of the tense situation, Khalil quickly explained, "Issa has vowed to let his hair grow until his brother's return."

---------- آرش ----------

It was a relatively slow evening at the diner. A few more customers would straggle in now and again to pick up to go orders, but no one else stayed to eat since the father and his sons had left.

At about 8pm the cook abandoned the grill and began to help the boy wipe down tables and put up the chairs. The boy then swept the floor and turned off most of the lights.

The men continued talking in the dim light at the hidden table. The cousins jumped from one subject to another, compensating for their company's quiet presence. At one point, Rajab nudged Issa's arm. "When is your brother coming home?"

"I wish I knew, Rajab, but I do not."

"What do you mean you don't know?" Rajab asked again. This time he spoke slowly, as if he was trying to explain a complex idea to a mentally retarded man:

"I…asked…you…how…come…you…do…not…know…when… Ahrash…is…coming…home?"

Khalil jumped into the conversation and replied for his son, "I offered Sharif my house for Ahrash's release but have not heard from him yet."

"You did what? You are offering your house to Sharif? You must be kidding me, man! Didn't his monster of a son almost kill you?"

Rajab was clearly angry now. "If I were you, I would have given Sharif a good beating for raising that son of the bitch, Mahmood."

"Hold on. Stop right there!" Abbos harshly interrupted his cousin. "It is morbid to speak ill of the dead."

Rajab rose to his feet and gulped the rest of his drink. "Morbid, my ass. I would have killed that bastard myself if the boy hadn't finished the job."

Having difficulty standing level, Rajab shifted his weight from leg to leg, all the while searching his pockets with the concentrated determination of a drunk man. He finally produced a knife. "Do you see this blade?" he asked, dangling the shiny four-inch weapon in front of his cousin's face. "I swear I would have cut Mahmood open if I knew he had been after my sister. Stupid *Baji** kept it from me until the bastard was dead," Rajab continued, the knife unsteady in his hand as he teetered.

Abbos slid his chair back away from the table and got up. A few inches taller than his cousin, he stood in front of him, irritated and angry.

"Shut up, Rajab! I told you not to curse the dead."

"If Mahmood had groped your sister, you would be damning him even more."

"I am warning you cousin, shut up, or I will make you."

The yelling and arguing escalated. Rajab kept brandishing his knife and Abbos, relying on his size, bravely ignoring the threats.

Khalil tried to interfere but any words he used resulted in more fuel for their fire. He planted himself between Issa and the drunken cousins and looked desperately in the direction of the diner's owner for help.

Accustomed to this kind of quarreling, the owner remained in the cooking area, tidying his grill. Once a glass was thrown across the diner though, he removed his apron and marched toward the intoxicated men.

Khalil and Issa slowly inched away from squabble and quietly left the café. They felt awfully bad that the situation did not afford them the opportunity to say goodbye to the generous cousins.

---

* *sister*

CHAPTER 45

Abbos and Rajab sat slumped on a bale of hay, utterly exhausted. Since dawn, the two cousins had been rolling hay amidst a blustering wind. It was certainly the wrong day for the job, but they had had no choice. The grass had been cut earlier that week; another day of waiting and they would have lost it all to the wind.

Abbos looked at his wristwatch and quickly jumped off the stack. "We cannot rest any longer. It is almost time to go."

Rajab, in a childlike excitement, slid down the hay bale. "I am ready. Let's go."

"Not so fast cousin. We need to tie this bundle first; the wind will tear it apart if we leave it unsecured."

آرش

After the evening with the Bedel family at the diner, the two kindhearted cousins spoke constantly about Khalil and the horrible situation his family was in. They genuinely felt sorry for the man who was burdened with a blind son at home and a young boy in prison.

Searching for a way to help, the cousins sought their fathers' advice. Their approach only resulted in harsh paternal scolding.

"When will you two act like grown men and stay out of people's business?" One of the fathers admonished, while his brother continually shook his head in disappointment. "What is happening between Khalil and Sharif is their own affair, not yours; you get drawn in, you invite trouble."

The young men brought the matter to their mothers next, encouraging them to talk to Sakineh. Their mothers, Zeeba and Sadaf, visited Sakineh the very same day, taking with them some sweets and a nice, embroidered scarf.

The women were received warmly at first, but got in trouble once they asked mercy for Ahrash. Sakineh called them dumb and ignorant and wished upon them the same horror of losing their sons. Bombarding them with profanities, she then shoved their gifts into their chests and pushed them out of the house.

Undeterred by their mothers' failure, the tenacious cousins remained hopeful, anxious to find a way to help Khalil.

Rajab soon came up with the idea of kidnapping the twins and thereby forcing Sharif and Sakineh to release Ahrash. Abbos was hesitant at first, but eventually agreed. They decided to take the twins and hide them in their stable. For days they worked out the details of their plan but right before acting on it, Abbos got cold feet. "The police would get involved and we will end up in jail," he reasoned.

A few days later, the cousins finally conjured up the perfect and logical plan, one in which no one would get hurt or be sent to prison.

────── آرش ──────

Long chains thrown around their necks, and thick metal bars in hand, Abbos and Rajab resembled two seasoned gang members, well-prepared to face their rivals. They walked fast, almost sprinting, not minding the stubborn wind riddling their faces with dirt and debris.

After exiting their own land, the cousins strode over a small bridge and reached the bottom of a knoll. Three sharp whistles pierced the air and five more young farmers emerged from different directions, each carrying some sort of weapon.

Every year, after the wheat harvest, the farmers pick a windy day to separate the grains from the stalks. They go to a designated open parcel of land and station their harvests in large, fat rings, giving each other wide berth.

A bull, fixed to a simple machine of rotating blades, loops around each bounty; the contraption behind him, cuts the stalks as he moves. Once the animal goes on to the next section, and before he returns, the farmer uses a pitchfork to lift the broken stalks in the air, letting the wind blow away the unwanted pieces.

Sharif had hired Ali for the entire week to thresh and winnow his harvest as well as to prepare the land for next year's crops. Ali was strong and, when he was in an agreeable mood, an excellent worker. Today, he was very productive. By only midmorning, he and Sharif had already separated half of the grains.

———— آرش ————

The seven young farmers reached the big parcel where, at that point, had had a cloud of dust rising from its entirety. Confident that they would find Sharif, the men marched toward the bullrun.

Sharif noticed the approaching group when they were almost in his section. He glanced at Ali, who was only a few feet from him, sending the stalks high into the air. Ali was totally unaware of what was about to transpire.

In a flash, Sharif was encircled and Ali, caught off guard, was blocked by two of the larger farmers.

Rajab walked closer to Sharif and spoke to him, incensed, "Hey Sharif, did you talk to your wife about Khalil's offer?"

"Yes Rajab, I did. Unfortunately, I could not convince her to accept the offer," Sharif answered, calm and collected.

"You should have forced her then," Rajab shouted, pulling his chain down off of his neck. "Men do not keep children in jail."

Abbos joined his cousin, "We are taking you to town today. You will go to court and get that boy released right away."

The wind suddenly intensified to a gale, sending dust clouds into the air with tornado strength. The floating chaffs, straw, and stalks started dancing in all directions, hitting faces and piercing skin. Along with the violent winds, a thunderous shouting broke out. The circle slowly grew tighter around Sharif. The cousins seized his arms.

"A taxi is waiting for us by the boulder," Abbos said as they moved Sharif forward.

Ali's stomach churned as he watched Sharif leave without any resistance. He turned his head and spit on the ground.

Just then three shadowy figures appeared through the dust, making their way to the agitated men. Once they reached them, Rostam,* the tallest of the three, walked directly up to the cousins and roared, "Let go of Sharif! Now!"

Intimidated by the gravity of Rostam's voice, the cousins reluctantly released Sharif's arms.

Rostam was, by far, the strongest man in the village. Everyone in the community knew about his power, but what gave him the nickname Rostam was his famed battle with a cougar.

Rostam was having lunch inside his house when he heard his dog barking excessively one minute and whimpering the next. He raced outside to find a young mountain lion sinking his teeth into the seemingly lifeless body of his dog.

To scare off the cat, he threw stones, stomped his feet, and yelled as loud as he could. Undeterred, the cougar only raised his head momentarily, his maw dripping with the dog's blood.

In his life, Rostam had had to test his strength against many wild animals, fighting a mountain lion, however, he knew was a different deal. His dog was already dead, but he could not watch him be devoured. So, he pulled his knife from his pocket and jumped onto the beast.

His wife who had run to the neighbors for help, returned with several men. Once they reached the yard, they all froze in place: Rostam, blood-soaked, was sitting on the pinned cougar, his hands in the animal's

---

* *the name of a legendary hero in Persian folklore known for his strength*

mouth, trying to rip it apart.

Rostam spoke sharply, "Have some respect for the man. Sharif is still mourning his son's death."

He looked at the irate young farmers, methodically, making eye contact with one after the other. "Have any one of you ever lost a son?"

"What about Khalil's son who is rotting in jail?" a voice came from the throng.

"No one denies the boy's sad situation but for God's sake, you must give Sharif some time."

The commotion that had ensued eventually attracted the rest of the farmers. One by one, they left their stations and walked toward the pack.

The angry group, now outnumbered, unwillingly retreated – all expect Rajab who was seething with rage, refusing to give up. He swung his chain and slammed it onto the ground by Sharif's feet.

"Listen, Sharif. The boy should be set free soon. If not, as Allah is my witness, there will be more bloodshed. Mahmood deserved what he got. He…"

Abbos stopped his cousin midsentence. He quickly grabbed his shoulders and moved him onward, "We better go now," he whispered.

CHAPTER 46

A white *sofreh* set with colorful bowls of herbs, strawberries, and yogurt was spread atop the rug, looking inviting.

The twins plopped down in their usual spots. "What is for dinner, Neloo?" they asked at the same time.

"Rice and zucchini chicken. We will have to wait though. Dad is not home yet."

The boys were about to complain, when their father entered the house, accompanied by Ali. The children ran to them excitedly and right away were picked up by the tired men.

"Neloo *Jaan*, put out another place setting for Ali," Sharif asked.

─────── آرش ───────

Mealtime went quickly; Sakineh was very verbose, asking Ali too many questions, while constantly encouraging him to eat more food.

Neloo glanced at their guest several times, but he did not look in her direction even once.

The twins finished their food in a hurry and shimmied up next to Ali. They yammered on about completely different topics, restlessly waiting for him to be done eating. The instant the man finished his dinner, they jumped on him wanting to wrestle. Ali tried to entertain them, but his mind was in such a tangled mess that even the endearing twins were unable to help him unwind.

The presence of Ali was certainly a distraction, yet it did not prevent Neloo from noticing her father's anxiety. The man was quiet and withdrawn, barely interested in the twins. He ate very little and, in an uncustomary manner, lit a cigarette before their guest had completed his meal. Neloo was convinced that something serious was burdening him. Her fear grew even more when she considered the recent gossip around the village. It had been rumored that some angry men were planning to beat up her father and burn his harvest.

"Was dad subjected to violence today?"

After drinking his tea, Ali thanked the family for the meal and announced that he must be heading out.

The twins did not want him to leave. They grabbed his legs in disappointed protest. "You cannot go. You have to stay longer!" they cried out.

Sharif had to interfere. "We have had a long day, boys. Uncle Ali must be very tired. Maybe he will join us for dinner again tomorrow night."

"Please, Uncle Ali. Please promise to come again tomorrow!" the twins pleaded over and over.

Ali agreed.

Content at last, the boys released their captive and followed him to the door – happily flopping their too-long sleeves in the air.

For the rest of the night, Sharif remained quiet, chain-smoking. In contrast, Sakineh was in a great mood. She leaned on a big pillow, chirping out a tune while mending the twins' socks. She was even nice to Neloo, asking if the singing was disturbing her studying.

"Is Sakineh reminiscing about the past when Mahmood would have Ali over for dinner?" Neloo pondered the idea, thinking how awful it must be to live only with the memories of your child.

────── آرش ──────

The twins fell asleep as soon as they crawled into their beds. Neloo sat atop her blanket next to her brothers, studying in the dim light. She had a hard time concentrating, reading the same line over and over without complete comprehension.

Sharif took off his shirt and got in bed next to Sakineh. He lied flat on his back with his hands clasped behind his head. Looking straight up at a small crack on the ceiling, he began to speak to his wife.

"Today, at the bull run, some villagers came to me, upset. They wanted us to have Ahrash released."

"Yeah? Did Ahrash kill any of their sons?" Sakineh retorted quickly. "Who were they, anyway?"

"It doesn't matter who was protesting. Everyone in the village knows that Mahmood's aggression caused his death and that now an innocent child is paying the price," Sharif raised his voice.

"Bullshit. My son was never aggressive. He was pure and harmless and he did not deserve to be murdered so savagely."

The word pure describing Mahmood, felt like a knife, further carving into Neloo's deep wound. She shivered in place, remembering the agony of standing nude in the shower stall, her body being devoured by her brother's sinful eyes. She wanted to scream and tell Sakineh that her son was far from pure – that he was evil, a monster.

Sharif was also taken aback by the way Sakineh portrayed their late son. "Have you already forgotten all the complaints from the villagers or the many times you yourself had wished him dead? Now suddenly, in death, Mahmood has become sinless, not to be at all blamed for what happened to him?" Sharif spoke angrily, now looking directly into Sakineh's face.

"Shut up Sharif. You do not know what you are talking about."

"No, I will not stop talking and, this time, you will hear me well. Mahmood caused his own death and no one else should be punished for that."

Sakineh rose to her feet and kicked her husband, hard, in the ribs. "You bastard. You never liked your son."

Ignoring the pain and the unfair accusation, Sharif continued speaking.

"Let the boy free, Sakineh. Forgiveness will lighten your heart.

Think about Aziz, the woman who raised your daughter. How can you allow her boy to waste away in jail?"

There were no words from Sakineh. She just stood above her husband, staring angrily at him for an unsettling amount of time.

"Can't you see that people are angry with us? Nobody buys from me here. I have to rent a truck and lose work time in the field to haul the harvest to other villages. This unnecessary vengeance of yours will eventually destroy us all."

"Dad is right," a quivering voice suddenly escaped Neloo's throat. "There are rumors that—"

Sakineh did not allow her daughter to complete her sentence. "Shut up, you whore," she said, leaping forward to strike her.

Sharif shielded Neloo. "Leave her alone. I am warning you."

"You two traitors are the family's disgrace. If it was not for the twins, I would have slashed both of your throats in your sleep and have been done with the shame. Push me harder and I swear to God, I will do it."

"You want to cut my throat? Do it then!" Sharif removed a knife from under his pillow. "Here!" he said, forcing Sakineh to take the blade. "Go ahead and cut me! I dare you! You maniac!"

Sakineh took the knife and threw it across the room. Her moment of embarrassment somehow triggered her hatred of Neloo. She jumped on her daughter, punching her wildly. Sharif yanked her away and threw her across the room. She landed by Mahmood's bed, the knife within her reach.

A wholly frustrated Sharif slid down into a slump by the kitchen entrance.

He lit a cigarette. The worried Neloo found him quite vulnerable sitting with his back to them: one forceful stab by Sakineh and her father's destiny would mirror that of his son's.

A long and fraught silence permeated the air. Neloo could only hear her rapid heartbeat.

Sharif took his final drag, smothered the cigarette in the ashtray and unexpectedly rushed toward Sakineh.

Neloo was terrified, never having seen her father violent before.

Sakineh grabbed the knife and sat up in a defensive stance. Her husband's leap however was not intended to strike her but to collect Mahmood's bedding spread out beside her.

"Crazy woman! Still setting up your dead son's bed!" he shouted as he opened the door and quickly tossed it out.

A loud wind whistled.

Sharif shut the door and stood there motionless – a statue with its hands squeezing its head at the temples.

Neloo's fear subsided but was replaced by the sadness she felt at what her father has had to bear. He was like a strong stallion half sunken in muck, unable to pull himself out.

How much must a man give in order to keep his wife content?

──────── آرش ────────

Sakineh had settled into bed some time before Sharif could finally bring himself to join her. He glanced at Neloo and gave her a faint smile. His face then hardened as he turned to his wife.

"Listen to me, Sakineh. I have never done anything against your wishes before. But this time is different. I am ransacked by guilt and my conscious will not allow me to keep this child in jail. Today, when they were taking me to sign Ahrash's release, I felt relieved. I wanted to go with them and was disappointed when Rostam interfered. Now is the time for you to accept reality."

CHAPTER 47

Unbearable at first, Ahrash gradually took a liking to his hospital's stay. His room was twice the size of his cell and had a nice washroom with a shower. The large window across from his bed afforded him a view of a majestic cypress, almost from every corner of the room. When he stood by the window, he could see the hospital yard with its beautiful landscape of flowering bushes and well-kept green grass. People would walk past on the brick sidewalks, often holding bouquets of flowers. Watching those moving souls, made the boy feel alive and hopeful.

In addition to having a nice space of his own, Ahrash had numerous opportunities to interact with people. His psychiatrist saw him frequently, helping his mind grow more limpid with each visit. The nurses were in and out of his room throughout the day, showing so much care, as if he was one of their own children.

The lady from food services spoiled him the most. She provided almost any food he liked or craved and when he did not eat much, she would reheat the meal and bring it back to him.

If the cafeteria lady was in charge of Ahrash's nutrition, Eunice, the old janitor, was certainly his main source of entertainment.

Every morning, before breakfast, Eunice would bring in the daily newspaper and place it on the serving table. "Professor, let me know if something important is happening in the world!" he would say with a concerned voice. He then meticulously cleaned the room while telling one story after another.

The old janitor had numerous narratives from his large family, his childhood polio battle, his neighbors' dilemmas, and even the people he had just met on the bus on his way in. A master at creating interesting tales out of ordinary events, Eunice's stories were so engaging that Ahrash preferred to listen to him rather than read the paper.

Every time Eunice was in his room, Ahrash would think: *If this man had had any education, he could have written beautiful stories.*

The friendly atmosphere, proper nutrition, and a steady course of antidepressants improved Ahrash's health quickly. In less than two weeks, he presented so normal and healthy that he could have been easily released. The warden, however, insisted on increasing his recuperation time.

Eventually, the end of his hospitalization arrived and Ahrash's limited freedom had come to a close. He was back in his prison suit, leaving behind his newly found friends, his bright room, the old cypress tree, and all the passersby.

There was no need for him to pack. The boy had nothing in his possession; it was only him and his lucid mind, wondering how the future would unfold.

———— آرش ————

As Ahrash entered the hall, he tried to hide behind the guard, yet he was immediately recognized by the prisoners.

"Hey everyone! The boy is alive! He is back!" the man in the first cell shouted, his forehead pressed up against the bars.

His claim shocked all the prisoners.

When Ahrash was found in a pool of blood on the night of his suicide attempt, the hysterical guard started yelling for help with unbridled emotion. Soon a group of paramedics and doctors stormed into the hall. They were in such a panicked rush that they did not even attempt to keep it quiet.

The noise and commotion of that early morning was so raucous that it forced most of the prisoners out of their beds. The sleepy men stood by their cell doors confused, asking each other about the uproar. Their bewilderment, however, was brief and before long, they all saw Ahrash's lifeless body being carried out on a gurney.

In the days that followed, the prisoners were anxious to find out what had happened to the boy, but none of the guards was willing to discuss the matter. The staff's silence and the absence of the boy convinced everyone that Ahrash had actually died that night.

The first announcement of the boy's return drove most of the inmates to the front of their cells. Everyone wanted to get a glimpse of the resurrected child to have proof themselves that Ahrash indeed was alive.

Death row was now back to life, mimicking the first day Ahrash had entered the hall. The prisoners were happy, clapping and whistling. Some called the boy by his name, welcoming his return, while others extended their arms out for a handshake or simply a touch.

Ahrash was surprised by the way the inmates were greeting him. It had never occurred to him that anyone on the row could possibly care for him. The display of such genuine affection quickly simmered his initial fears. He began to make eye contact as he passed by each cell, smiling faintly.

———————— آرش ————————

With renewed physical and mental strength, Ahrash was determined to remain hopeful as he returned to death row. Nevertheless, once he reentered the pit of isolation, he could not ignore the frightening cloud of sadness that quickly descended upon him.

He sat on his bed.

The crazy Babak could be heard from the next cell, "Welcome back, pretty Ahrash. Glad that you are not dead!"

CHAPTER 48

The first night back on death row was long and grueling. As the lights dimmed, Ahrash went to his bed and curled up under the covers. He was in a downcast mood, unable to concentrate on his earlier positive thoughts.

The maddening nightly ritual in the next cell was now in full effect. The noises were familiar; Ahrash had heard them many nights before. What Babak could possibly be doing in that cell was an enigma that the boy had never understood before and didn't even now with a clear mind.

Ahrash tried to distract himself from the noise. He focused on his father, musing on the time they had spent together during his hospital visit – the time that had given him a chance to discover this great man anew.

His father had always been so gentle and mild-mannered that many, including his young son perceived him weak and submissive. No one was ever aware of his enormous mental strength, perseverance, and unwavering devotion.

Discovering all the good traits in his father, Ahrash now believed in him. He knew that underneath the man's soft exterior, existed a wise and intelligent being who was determined to get his son's freedom back.

The thought of being free was heartwarming. Ahrash shut his eyes and indulged in some reminiscing. Soon he was in Kultappa in a cold winter day. The family was warm under the *korsi*,* eating nuts and dates. He was reciting from *Shahnameh* and everyone was fully engrossed in

---

* a type of low table with a heat source underneath it and a blanket thrown over it

the verses.

Their unity was almost tangible. Even from his lonely, remote cell, the boy could feel its power.

His beautiful thoughts, however, did not last long. They fizzled quickly and were replaced with memories of the past months' events. Ahrash relived the moments, step by step, reflecting on the calamity of his life for the first time with a clear mind.

He could not remember when and how the stabbing had occurred. The scene with the villagers circled around a dying Mahmood, however, was boldly engraved in the deepest folds of his brain.

He recalled Issa standing by him the entire time, his face pale and crumpled. Not too far from them, his father was sitting on the ground, wiping blood from a crack in his head.

Jafar arrived and helped Ali and Sharif put the bleeding Mahmood into the jeep. The shriek that Sakineh let out at that moment was still with him, knifing through his heart.

A cut in the sequence of events, a black void, followed filled only with blips of a hazy image of himself wandering around in Neloo's yard.

Then with startling precision, he recalled the rain and the wind, slapping against his entire body with a colossal force. He was walking with Jafar toward the running Jeep, watching the raindrops and dust dancing in its illuminated headlights. He had a strong urge to turn his head and look at his family who was standing in the downpour, watching him leave. Yet, unable to bear their pain, he just continued walking, toward the jeep.

At the police station, he had felt a crippling coldness in his bones. He shivered violently. Jafar had suggested that he lie down under a blanket, but he had remained seated, trembling in place. He had stayed awake all night.

His trip to the capital, which often manifested in his nightmares, was still frightening. He remembered entering a bus which fully occupied by scary looking men – all in shackles. It was not clear if the men were crazy or criminal or both. He had moved to the back of the bus and a soldier followed him while shoving the end of his rifle into the chest of those he passed. The strained men swore at him in return, throwing out the worst profanities. Finally, at the designated spot, he was ordered to sit between two stern looking soldiers, both sufficiently equipped to go to war.

آرش

It was rather a calm night on the row; all the prisoners were asleep, including Babak. The situation there very much resembled the scene prior to his hospitalization: the dim lights, the quiet whispering of the guards, and his own restlessness. Yet, among all the similarities, there was a missing component that the boy simply could not pinpoint.

Neloo's letters were piled up in one corner of his cell. Ahrash had promised himself that he would read them all, but he felt too wound up to even try one. "I will start reading them tomorrow," he decided. "I have had a tough and emotional day."

Back in bed, Ahrash tossed and turned for a long while. Eventually, he relented and asked for his sleeping pill, which was in the custody of the guards.

The pill sent him into slumbers rather quickly.

He was in the last moments of his wakefulness when the missing element suddenly popped into his head. It was the lone prisoner's midnight wailing…

CHAPTER 49

He opened his eyes. The sunrays, filtering through the small skylight in his cell, were revitalizing. He knew he had made it through the night.

"You have a note from your neighbor," a guard tapped at the bars.

Ahrash sat up in his bed, looking frightened.

"Do not worry, son. It is not from Babak; it is from your other neighbor. You can trust him. He is a good man."

The message was only one line, penned elegantly. "If you ever need to talk to someone, consider talking to me. –Reza"

Ahrash did not answer his neighbor right away. A few days later however, he wrote to him, revealing his constant fear of Babak: *He makes strange noises at night, claiming that he is cutting through our shared wall.*

Reza's response was quick and succinct: *I will ask the guards to check his cell.*

The next day a man entered Ahrash's cell. He was an older officer and his uniform was embellished with military insignia. He sat on the bed and motioned for the boy to sit down next to him. Ahrash lowered his body to the edge of the bed and with much trepidation asked, "Is something wrong with my family?"

"Your family is fine son," the man said and immediately dropped his voice to a whisper. "I understand that you have some concerns about Babak, the prisoner next door."

"Yes sir, I am afraid that he is cutting through the wall."

"The reason for my visit today is to put your mind at ease," the officer said, looking at Ahrash in a fatherly manner. "Earlier today, we searched your neighbor's cell thoroughly. Everything was as normal as could be – no sign of cuts or holes in any walls. There were only some scuffmarks near his stall, likely from him punching or kicking the walls. The inmate has no tools in his possession either, except for a few broken spoons. He probably used those to gouge and scratch his bathroom sink."

The kind man paused briefly and shifted his body into a more comfortable position. He placed his hand on Ahrash's slumped shoulder and made his last attempt to dispel the boy's fears. "Babak is certainly a disturbed individual. But I assure you he has zero chance of getting to your cell. Trust me son, you are safe in here."

The information Ahrash received on that day was absolutely comforting. It also made him wonder what power Reza held in this place to make that inspection happen so quickly.

Over the next couple of days, there were more exchanges between the two cells, mainly concerning Babak. Then, rather abruptly, the correspondence changed topics to Ahrash's constant struggle with depression. The new acquaintances also segued into speaking through the bars instead of sending notes via the guards.

Reza was an educated man, capable of viewing the world from a wide-angle lens, even from behind his cell bars. He was a smooth talker, an excellent listener and a master advisor. The words he used in each interaction were always well-thought-out, crafted to give the child prisoner strength and confidence.

From the start, he insisted that Ahrash follow his therapist's recommendations of writing daily to reflect his emotions. He also persuaded the boy to record positive memories from the past, no matter how minute they might be. His finest advice, however, was about passing time in isolation.

"Reading is the best weapon against boredom. You should request books from the warden or your family. I can also ask my wife to bring you magazines each week when she visits."

آرش

In no time, a bond of friendship formed between the two prisoners which grew stronger with each passing day. Reza, aware of the boy's high level of maturity, spoke to him straightforwardly, never fooling him or giving him false hope. Ahrash, as a result, quickly developed a deep trust in his row mate, sharing with him his innermost thoughts and feelings.

Getting to know the boy even faster than the therapist, Reza soon became a beacon of hope, a lighthouse in the storm. Any time that Ahrash felt sad or lonely, he was able to derail his thoughts and protect him from certain downfall.

The staff on death row was amazed at how a quiet and reserved man like Reza had become such an involved adviser to a thirteen-year-old village boy. What they didn't know was that helping Ahrash survive had become Reza's last mission in life.

CHAPTER 50

Where Ahrash was imprisoned, the residents on death row were not allowed to have any outdoor breaks. The officials there assumed that the small skylight in each cell would supply sufficient sun exposure for the criminals who would soon be executed.

Warden Ramzi, bent the rules for Ahrash, allocating him a daily break. The boy, however, had refused to step outside even after he had returned from the hospital.

His unwise decision disappointed Reza.

"Take advantage of the warden's offer, Ahrash. You have a unique situation. Unlike all the prisoners here, your freedom might arrive at any time. You must stay healthy until then to be able to enjoy the rest of your life," Reza argued over and over until he convinced his young row mate.

آرش

A strange sensation came over Ahrash the moment he stepped outside. Like a newborn baby, just out of the womb, his senses were quickly under siege – eardrums vibrating violently with foreign sounds, eyes struggling with the brightness of the outside world. And as he gulped at the crisp air, his young heart started pumping hard, sending blood to his face, flushing his cheeks.

The air had the slight chilly bite of an autumn morning; the blue sky harbored countless dense clouds. Ahrash stared at the beauty above his head, mesmerized by the clouds huddled in the shapes of mountains, snowy castles, and various animals. It was an amazing feeling to trade his concrete ceiling for the captivating sky.

Only a portion of a much larger field, the assigned yard was small and separated by a razor-wire fence. Both areas were surrounded by acres of lands which were stripped of all vegetation.

What was barely passable as lawn covered Ahrash's entire space with the exception of a narrow concrete walkway between the grass and the back of a building.

Ahrash stood at the edge of the yard, not sure what to do next. After a while, he started ambling across the lawn where weeds conveniently popped up anywhere they could. He moved from one intruder to the next, squatting down to touch and smell their flowers.

A pair of dragonflies appeared and fluttered among the dandelions in the lawn. He watched them with delight, fully regarding their freedom.

Eventually he settled himself on the sidewalk, choosing a position that afforded him a better view of the distance. The massive Alborz mountain range and its striking, snow-covered Peak Damavand attracted him instantly. The faraway mountain reminded him of The Hill in his village, the knoll his family used to climb and picnic at in the summer. He knew very soon The Hill would be blanketed white and wondered when the snow would fall in the capital city.

A cat leapt from the awning and landed on the sidewalk with a thump. The beautiful calico was either pregnant or burdened by a tumor, for she had a big, dropped belly.

The feline looked at Ahrash and decided it was safe to approach him. Ahrash stroked her back. Soon, the cat was curled up next to the boy calmly purring.

The presence of the friendly animal flooded in the warm memories of Jolfa. Ahrash let his mind drift and quickly found himself in the meadow sitting under the willow tree with Jolfa by his side. In the distance, the flock was grazing on the grassy hillside, their coats tight and sleek.

Suddenly, the smell of grass intensified in the yard.

---- آرش ----

Ahrash remained seated in the same spot until he heard the guard's blaring call, "It is time to get back inside."

He patted the cat one more time and walked toward the guard. Just then a group of prisoners, loud and vulgar, rushed into the adjacent yard. The strident men were so busy taunting and pushing each other that none of them noticed a child in a similar jumpsuit on the other side of the fence.

Eager to write about his revitalizing outdoor break, Ahrash passed through the hall speedily. A few prisoners acknowledged him along his way and he timidly responded.

Inside the cell, a rather large box was sitting on his bed without any label. Ahrash was puzzled: *It cannot be from my family, they had visited me just two days ago.*

Another guard let himself into the cell. He was a young man named Dawood, one of Ahrash's favorite guards. He was by far the happiest staff member in the place; his unique, loud laugh was discernible from anywhere on the row.

"This box is from Warden Ramzi. Let's open it," he said, seemingly more anxious than Arash to find out what was inside.

Ahrash carefully peeled back the packing tape and opened the flaps. The box was full of essential school supplies.

"Take them out so we can see what is underneath," Dawood said, his head hovering over the box.

"Hey, look. These are photos of famous soccer players!" he shouted, pulling out pictures from a small, card-sized box. "Look, this is Pele."

Ahrash did not recognize that player nor the next few that Dawood enthusiastically showed him.

"How come you do not know them? Don't you love soccer?"

"I never played or developed any love for soccer. My brother is blind and growing up, I only played the games he could play."

Dawood picked up another small box. "What about wrestling?" he asked.

"I am more familiar with that sport. I often watched the competitions among our villagers."

"These are the wrestlers with multiple Olympic gold medals, let's see if you can recognize any."

Searching among the pictures with devotion, Dawood quickly found a card and handed it to Ahrash. "You should know this one for sure."

The athlete in the card looked very familiar. It was as if Ahrash had seen the man recently. Yet still, he could not place him. "I thought I knew him, but I do not," he muttered, slightly embarrassed.

"Look again. I'm sure you know him."

Ahrash stared at the picture again but still could not recognize the man.

"He is your next door neighbor, Ahrash. He is Reza Gheydari, a four time Olympic gold medal winner."

The boy had seen Reza a few times since coming to death row, but the man in the picture had a different vibe. He had longer hair and appeared taller. Posing in wrestling gear with all the gold medals around his neck, Reza certainly looked powerful and fierce.

"You were probably a toddler when he was the world champion. I was about your age then."

"Why is he here?" Ahrash asked with curiosity.

"Sorry friend, I am not allowed to talk about other prisoners," Dawood appeared to resent the question.

After removing the smaller objects, including sports magazines, crossword puzzles, and brain teasers, three thick textbooks appeared, resting at the bottom of the box. Right then, Dawood realized that he had forgotten to give Ahrash the message he was meant to deliver.

"These textbooks belong to the warden's son. He used them last year when he was in ninth grade. Warden Ramzi wants you to study them. When you are ready, he will make arrangements for you to take the required tests."

CHAPTER 51

Ahrash woke with a jolt, his entire body covered in an icy sweat. Still in a trance, he sat up and put his hands on his fast-beating heart. *The same dream again!* He heaved a deep sigh.

While the antidepressants greatly tempered his wild and spooky dreams, one particular nightmare continued to visit Ahrash on a regular basis. In those night terrors, he often saw himself and Issa undergoing surgeries so that Issa could receive an eye from him. Sadly, the operations would leave both brothers blind each time.

"These dreams are a reflection of your deep love for your brother. You must not dwell on them as much as possible." His therapist's words circled in the boy's mind. He consciously tried to follow the advice but the residue of the nightmare had already thickly settled in his mind.

How is Issa pulling through in my absence? Who is he spending his free time with? Who is reading him poetry? Thinking of his brother, Ahrash was suddenly struck by a terrifying notion, "If I were to be executed, who would be with Issa when our parents are gone? Will his future be like Koor Akbar's, somewhere alone in a shed?"

The sad thoughts continued wheeling in Ahrash's head like a wicked spell, preventing him from falling back to sleep. He tossed and turned, periodically looking up at the skylight, beseeching morning to arrive.

آرش

"Why are you up so early, young man?" Reza called out to Ahrash as soon as the boy abandoned his bed.

"I had a horrible nightmare and could not fall back to sleep."

"I heard you crying. What caused you to feel so bad?"

"Thinking of my brother and the promises I had made to him."

"Did you try to divert your thoughts to something else?"

"I could not," Ahrash sighed. "I messed up badly, Reza. All my life, I wanted to be a savior for my family. One moment of insanity and I managed to tear down the bridge that could have taken them to a brighter future."

"You still have a chance to reach your goals. Your freedom might be right around the corner."

"I cannot not fool myself. I know I will die here. The shadow of death is getting closer every day and rightly so. I failed my family and deserve this fate."

Ahrash started crying again.

Reza allowed the sad child to sob a while before speaking up. "You saved your father's life and should be proud of that. You are an honorable man, forced into the body of a boy. Honorable men always protect their family."

———————— آرش ————————

The sudden staccato of steady footsteps in the hall interrupted the conversation of the two friends. Then in a flash, two burly and unfamiliar guards passed them and stopped at the next cell. Ahrash could hear them talking to Babak in quiet, hushed voices. Before long, however, all hell broke loose. There were thumps and bumps against the walls. Babak shouting and cursing.

Eventually, the guards yanked Babak out of his cell, feet in shackles and hands cuffed behind his back. They succeeded in making him take a few steps forward before he began to resist again. He sat in an awkward position on the floor and held firm against the guards' pull. His face was ashen, his hair even wilder than usual.

Like a trapped beast, Babak moved his head in all directions, snarling and snapping at any arms or legs within reach.

Another guard joined the first two, twirling his weapon in his hand. Every attempt to bite or spit, earned Babak a visit from the baton.

The situation reminded Ahrash of a dog he saw once encircled by several village boys, beaten with rocks and sticks. He was sure that just like the dog, Babak would eventually surrender to his destiny.

Somewhat tamped down now, Babak was lifted to his feet by the trio and forced to move forward.

Many prisoners woke up to the noise in the hall. They rushed to their cell bars, eager to find out what all the commotion was about.

The rows of spectators gave Babak a new audience for his anger. "What the fuck are you looking at, you bastards?" he swore and growled as he passed each cell. And then, with a deafening slam of the metal door, he was out of death row.

"Are they going to execute him?" Ahrash asked Reza.
"I believe so."
"Do you know what he was guilty of?"
"No, Ahrash, I don't know what his crime was. But I heard that his punishment was just right."

Reza knew well of Babak's monstrous acts, but didn't see a reason to poison the boy's mind. Babak had tortured, raped, and killed several young boys over a four-year period. He claimed that he had killed his first victim when he was only fourteen.

"He was unusually quiet last night. I wonder if he was scared," Ahrash said, suddenly feeling hollow inside.

"Death is a powerful phenomenon, my friend. It is certainly capable of terrifying us all with its finality."

CHAPTER 52

The first snow arrived early and with power. It came down uninterrupted for two days, meticulously blanketing the entire village. On the third day, a strong and unexpected wind found its way down from the mountain, making the situation even more worrisome.

As the chaotic weather continued, the residents became alarmed at the prediction of an imminent and dreadful snowstorm.

The year prior, at about the same time, a similar snowfall had turned into a blizzard without any warning. The blusterous storm uprooted trees and tossed them into the air, shattering windows and collapsing roofs.

It was a frightening time in the village. The shopkeepers closed their stores and the clergymen locked down the mosque. Everyone rushed home and stayed with their families, all except for the children who had gone to school earlier that day.

Returning students back to the village, the bus driver was faced with a colossal challenge. He was an experienced driver and had traveled the same road hundreds of times over years. Yet, maneuvering the large vehicle in such conditions was a seemingly impossible task, dangerous and risky.

Two thirds of the trip had been successfully completed when the blizzard suddenly hit. The blast was wild. It shook the bus violently, bombarding it with flying snow, broken branches, and stones. With virtually zero visibility, the driver was now forced to navigate essentially from memory.

The inevitable eventually happened. The bus slipped off the road and nosedived into a ditch. Twenty-two students, of all ages, including

Ahrash, Neloo, Hanna, and Shereen, were catapulted from their seats, landing on top of each other in the front section of the bus.

Miraculously, no one was seriously hurt. There were only a few minor cuts and bruises on some of the kids.

Night soon arrived with its bitter cold. The students huddled together to stay warm. A large box of animal crackers that had been saved for an emergency, was opened and divided amongst the children. Even so, everyone remained cold and hungry throughout the night.

It wasn't until noon the next day that the students were finally rescued.

Today's wind was not strong enough to induce a blizzard, yet school officials decided to send the students home ahead of the advancing storm. With the memory of last year's disaster still fresh in their minds, they simply could not risk the children's safety.

Neloo was delighted by the early dismissal; she had important news to deliver to Shereen. If the bus had kept its regular schedule, it would have been dark by the time she arrived home and unsafe to go out.

Shereen could have graduated from high school this year but had decided to stay home to care for her ill mother. Her resolution, burdened Neloo heavily, setting her on a quest to find a workaround.

At the onset of the school year, the loyal girl launched a vigilant campaign, approaching administrators and counselors, as well as Shereen's former teachers. She even sent letters to the district superintendent, seeking guidance and help.

Neloo's effort paid off well. Today, Mrs. Zaker, the literature teacher, handed her a packet. "This is for Shereen. The district has approved independent study for her," she announced, giving Neloo a wide smile. "Shereen is lucky to have such a tireless advocate as a friend."

آرش

Neloo stepped off the bus, lopsided from the weight of her heavy bag slung on one shoulder. She was eager to visit Shereen; the last time she had seen her was more than a month ago, the day that school had been closed for a national holiday.

First, however, she needed to stop at Ahrash's house.

Bolting from her doghouse, Jolfa dashed toward her before Neloo had even entered the yard. She sprung about in a circle around her old pal, wagging her tail with excitement. Neloo lowered her body, and cradled Jolfa's wet head in her arms.

The front door opened. Aziz stood in its frame with Issa standing behind her. "Do not stay out there in the snow, come in and warm up Neloo *Jaan*," she called out with her usual kind voice.

"Thank you, Auntie, but I am on my way to visit Shereen. I just wanted to find out about your visit yesterday with Ahrash."

Aziz and Issa, both stepped outside and stood with Neloo under the awning. The door remained slightly ajar. Neloo could see Khalil was sleeping under the cover of the *korsi*. "Is Ammo Khalil ill?" she asked Aziz.

"He is resting. The trip to the capital always makes him tired."

Neloo took another peek through the door's crack and then returned her focus back to her original thought. "So, how was Ahrash?"

"*Shohkran-lel-Allah,* Ahrash looked good. He has put on some weight and the color has returned to his face. No crying – none at all – even when we were saying goodbye!" Aziz happily detailed. She then raised her hands toward the sky in a prayer pose, "*Shohkran-lel-Allah*, Neloo *Jaan*, God has given Ahrash back to us."

As Aziz was praising the Lord for his kindness, Issa disappeared through the door. He returned quickly and handed an envelope to Neloo. "You have a letter from him."

Neloo tucked the letter in her bag and insisted that the family go back inside. She then walked toward her house with a joy she hadn't known in some time. Her excitement, however, fizzled, when she reached the house, recognizing at once that she could not read the letter in Sakineh's presence. She stopped right at the door and looked at Jolfa who had followed her all the way there. The canine had the same apprehension, not wanting her to enter the house.

"Maybe I should go directly to Shereen's," Neloo thought, but right away rejected her own idea – carrying her heavy school bag in the snow was not feasible.

"Goodbye, Jolfa," she heaved a resigned sigh and slipped inside.

The twins right away rushed to her from under the korsi cover, bringing with them warmth and identical smiles.

Sakineh was nowhere to be seen.

"Where is your mother, boys?"

"At the neighbor's house. She left a long time ago and we are hungry and bored," one twin grumbled.

"Mother said the wolf will eat us if we go out," the brothers said in unison.

How could Sakineh leave these kids alone with charcoal burning under the korsi? Anger washed over Neloo. Yet, despite her exasperation, she decided to focus on how to deliver her package.

Leaving the twins behind, unsupervised, was obviously not a possible option. But if she lost today's opportunity to visit Shereen, it might be a while before she could hand her the form. *"What if Shereen misses the application's deadline?"* Neloo pondered her dilemma for a while and eventually concluded that her best choice was to take the twins with her.

"I will fix your lunch now my dear brothers. If you eat and put on your snow gear quickly, we can all go visit Shereen and Hanna," she suggested.

The twins gladly agreed.

It took Neloo only a few minutes to prepare lunch. She put the plates of food in front of the hungry boys and sat down, slipping under the korsi's cover. It was now time for her to read Ahrash's letter.

Ahrash began by writing about his studying, explaining the type of textbooks he had been using and how far he had advanced in each subject.

"I did not expect the ninth grade to be so easy. The textbooks I have are almost repeating everything we have already learned in previous years. Hopefully, it is not the same with your books. If yours are also too easy, you should request to move to higher level classes. It is a shame to be held back like this."

Reza, the champ in the next cell, was mentioned many times in the letter. Ahrash portrayed him as the epitome of mental strength and wisdom.

"Even when I am at my absolute lowest, he can magically lift my spirits."

There was also talk about a cat.

"I have a pet now, a calico cat. She comes to me every day. I thought at first that she was pregnant, but she is not. She has a big growth below her abdomen which I believe is harmless; she looks too happy and healthy to have a malignant tumor. I did not name my cat and am open to suggestions."

After being cold all day, Neloo felt the warm blood finally circulating in her body again. It was heartening to know that Ahrash had the support of a good man, that he was studying, and that he now has a pet. She wished to read the letter one more time but knew they had to rush out.

Hiding the letter in her backpack, Neloo hastily wrote a message to Sakineh. She put on her coat, and walked to the door to fetch her boots. She found her little brothers both standing by the door, completely ready to go.

───────── آرش ─────────

Taking a single step out of the door, the twins stood still, looking timidly at the endless snow-covered land. They had seen snow last year, yet they dreaded moving forward, clasping each other's hands tightly for support.

"Come on boys, it is fun to walk in snow. Even if you fall, your gear will keep you dry," Neloo tried to motivate her brothers.

"What if the wolves come to eat us?"

"Do not worry. No wolf would dare hurt you with your big sister around."

With full trust in Neloo, the twins eventually started to walk. They took small steps at first but in no time, they were kicking the snow, sending powder in the air.

They scooped up snow but did not know what to do with it. Neloo patiently demonstrated how to make a ball by pressing and circling the white stuff in the palm of their hands.

Mastering the skill quickly, they used the snow to make other things, including a couple of figurines. They gave names to their creations and started to play with them.

Once, when one twin dropped his figurine, both brothers scooped up the broken pieces and put them on top of a boulder. They performed a brief burial ceremony, crying and praying while covering their deceased with more snow.

Watching the boys reenact the exact ritual of Mahmood's burial made it evident to Neloo that she had only been deluding herself – the boys had not forgotten their big brother and what had happened to him.

It was early in the day, not even noon yet, but Neloo was getting more and more anxious about the short window of light available at this time of the year. With the playful mood of the twins, it took more than twenty minutes for them just to reach the boulder. They had at least a mile left to go and the snowfall hadn't yet ceased.

"Look Neloo! I caught a snowflake! I am tasting it!" one twin said, his tongue protruding.

"Stop eating them! You are finishing them all!" The other twin pushed his brother to the ground and sat on top of him, trying to wipe the snow from his tongue. The snow eating twin fought back and soon both brothers were rolling around, their faces the color of beetroots.

Neloo was amused but had to interfere. "There are plenty of flakes for everyone. Let us all eat them!" she declared. So, for a while, all three siblings kept their mouths open as they moved forward.

آرش

Wonderful news awaited Neloo at her friend's house. Once she entered, she saw Shereen's mother out of bed, sitting on the floor with a tray of food on her lap. She looked well, with brighter eyes and a fuller face. Her turnaround was truly remarkable. Over the last six months, Neloo had only seen her in bed, moaning in pain.

"I am so glad that you are feeling better," Neloo said sincerely.

"Thank you, Neloo *Jaan*. But I would not be alive today, if not for my dedicated daughter."

Shereen's face turned red. "My mom is mistaken. It was her doctor that made her better, not me," she said humbly. "The treatment she received actually made her sicker at first before she started progressively feeling better. We were even taking a short, daily walk in the yard before it started to snow."

Shereen brought out tea and offered some *klucheh* and dried figs to her guests. Hanna took hers and the twins' shares and moved to one corner of the room, entertaining the boys with her extraordinary talents.

"Where is Ali in this crazy weather?" Neloo asked.

"Today, he is working for Hajji at his rice storage facility," Shereen's mother answered.

"That is so marvelous. Maybe Hajji will offer him a permanent job one day."

Shereen shook her head in disappointment, "Hajji has already made that offer, but Ali refused it," she said and quickly changed the subject. "How is everything at school this year?"

"Oh, I almost forgot. I have something for you."

Neloo unzipped her jacket and pulled out the envelope.

———— آرش ————

The moment Shereen and her mother learned about the independent study, they became overly excited and emotional. They screamed, hugged and kissed each other and Neloo over and over.

Shereen was beside herself. She held Neloo's hands and jubilantly, jumped up and down. Hanna and the twins quickly joined them, bouncing and laughing, without knowing what they were so happy about.

After the initial excitement settled, Shereen's mother cried quietly. It seemed as though she was overwhelmed with the enormity of the news.

"I am forever grateful to you, Neloo *Jaan*," she said as tears rain steadily down her face.

CHAPTER 53

Her midnight barking was not of much concern at first; Jolfa would regularly warn of any warm-blooded creature passing by. As her agitation persisted however, Khalil sat up in his bed, alert.

Minutes later, a loud pounding at the front door woke Aziz and Issa as well.

Khalil slipped his dagger out from under his pillow and leaped across the room to the door. Issa joined him right away and shouted, "Who is there? What is your business at this time of the night?"

The beating on the door continued.

Trapped inside the sheep house, Jolfa was becoming frantic. Growling vehemently, she ran back and forth alongside the fence, slamming her body into the heavy wooden slats, determined to break down the barrier. Her loud and incessant barking sent the neighborhood dogs into their own frenzies, pushing back the loitering wolves into the forest.

And then, as abruptly as it started, the pounding at the door stopped at once. The family's fear, however, did not subside. With only a door between them and impending calamity, they were beyond terrified, each breathing heavily.

Another explosive sound broke the short-span silence. Khalil spun toward the shattered window and watched the glass shards flying inward like fragmented icicles.

"Who is out there? What do you want?" he shouted.

"Come outside, Khalil. Come outside, you fucking coward! It is time to get even."

"It is Ali, dad. He is drunk," Issa whispered.

Ali rounded back to the door and resumed his hammering. "Come out, you bastard and face your worst enemy!" he demanded again.

Khalil and Issa stood, scared stiff. Neither man knew what to do nor what might be coming next. Behind them was Aziz, a holy book clamped tightly to her chest, murmuring prayers.

A light appeared in the distance and gradually grew brighter. A villager, with a teenage boy alongside, reached Khalil's house. He raised his lantern high and shined it onto Ali who was now kicking at the door.

Ali paused briefly, only long enough to shoot the man a disgusted look.

"It is one o'clock in the morning, Ali. You are waking everybody up," the villager protested.

Heedlessly, Ali continued his attack, rattling the door with each thwack. "Come outside, Khalil. Be a man!"

The villager took a couple of small steps forward. "Go home and leave this family alone before we call the gendarme," he commanded.

Ali landed another heavy kick at the door and turned around. "You want the gendarme? I'll go get fucking Jafar myself. I have business with him too. If that son of the bitch did not drive like a girl, Mahmood would be alive today," Ali said, frothing at the mouth with rage.

He took a few stumbling paces away from the house but having forgotten what he had intended on doing next, he stopped. Looking confused now, he planted his stick in the snow, clutched it with both hands, and rested his head on top. He stayed in that position for a while, so still it was as if he had turned to stone.

"Are you alright, Ali?" the villager reluctantly called to him while shining the lantern out toward the drunken man.

A new furry was ignited. Ali charged, swinging his stick at both father and son. "Do not you fucking understand? I am not leaving until Khalil comes out!" he bellowed.

The frightened villagers quickly retreated.

Another light approached and shortly after, Sharif reached Ali. Towering over him, he stood solidly, his presence commanding as usual. "Stop making such an uproar, Ali," he said. "You are scaring the twins and all the neighborhood kids."

Ali turned his head toward Sharif. "Tell the boys that I must avenge their brother," he said, acting as if he was sober and in total control.

"You are drunk Ali. Let me walk you home. Your mother is probably worried about you."

"No. I am not leaving until I kill him. Mahmood is gone because of this weasel man!"

Sharif craftily removed the stick from Ali and discarded it behind himself. "Listen, Ali. I am in as much pain as you are. We are two broken men – you have lost a friend and I have lost a son. If Khalil is guilty, we will make him pay, I promise. But not right now and not like this."

Sharif threw his arm around Ali's shoulder and pulled him in close. "Let's go home, son."

Ali whimpered wretchedly, his pain anchoring him in Sharif's arms.

CHAPTER 54

Unannounced, Warden Ramzi entered death row through a private door. He took a few silent steps inside the hall and positioned himself such that he had the broadest view of the cells. For a while, he observed different inmates until his eyes became fixated on his youngest prisoner.

Ahrash was sitting on the floor with books and papers scattered in a wide perimeter around him. He had his knees up, creating an easel with his legs, against which he had placed a pad of paper. From the way he was concentrating, it was clear he was tackling an arduous problem.

"He seems comparatively healthy, but still underweight," Ramzi thought, staring at the boy whose head appeared too big for his narrow neck and thin appendages.

——————— آرش ———————

Being kindhearted and sensitive had always conflicted with Ramzi's practical disposition. When he was young and fresh out of college, he had the greatest difficulty with this personality division. As time went on, however and largely due to his profession, he was gradually able to give more weight to the pragmatic aspects of situations rather than his own emotional considerations. In the case of Ahrash, it was clear that the man's tender side had always cast a large shadow on reality.

Watching the boy sitting alone in a prison cell sent waves of pain over Ramzi. He compared the boy's life with his own son's, barely a year older than Ahrash: *Navid must be back from his music lessons by now. He is probably working at his desk. Maybe he is listening to a favorite song or talking with a friend on the phone. I'll be home soon and the family will all sit down to dinner and talk.*

The chasm between the two young lives was vastly troubling, impossible to ignore.

What has happened to our humanity? Why are we keeping a child behind bars? If this moral slide is called justice, I am ashamed to be a part of it.

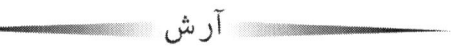

——————— آرش ———————

Ramzi had never disclosed to anyone the amount of effort he had to put in to make life easier for Ahrash; neither had he mentioned the hurdles he had had to overcome requesting the smallest of favors for the child. Every step he took in a positive direction for Ahrash, Judge Kasra made sure to block immediately, exercising a fervent power. It was unclear if the man's intent was to punish him or his prisoner.

One of the toughest challenges with Kasra was over Ahrash's education. Kasra had a motto and was perfectly firm about it: *No money should be wasted on inmates condemned to death.*

It took Ramzi several appearances in court and the support of two philanthropic lawyers to finally make Kasra relent, allowing Ahrash to continue his education while incarcerated.

Still holding his steadfast gaze on the boy, Ramzi walked back to the door and turned the key in the lock, almost soundlessly. Even so, Ahrash raised his head and the two locked eyes briefly. They both smiled.

——————— آرش ———————

In the morning, before breakfast was distributed on the row, a desk, with a matching chair, was delivered to Ahrash's cell. The desk had one small and one larger drawer with a compact hutch attached, perfect for holding several books. A note on top of the desk said: *I hope this set makes it easier to study. Good luck, Warden Ramzi.*

Ahrash had never received a gift so substantial in his entire life.

CHAPTER 55

The first time Ahrash heard about the Mullah Killings, he had been in the hospital.

For months, mullahs had been stabbed to death in the quiet alleyways and streets of the capital. Some were even found dead in their homes, grossly mutilated.

As the count of murders grew, a deep, pervasive terror began to sink in throughout the community. Mullahs, panic-stricken, remained in their homes with extra locks on their doors. If they had to leave the house, they would shed their robes and turbans in an attempt to hide their identities.

The police force worked laboriously, following all leads to find the assassin or assassins. Nevertheless, in spite of all their efforts, without murder weapons, fingerprints, or witnesses coming forward, the crimes remained unsolved – an enigma.

———— آرش ————

"Have you heard the big news?" Dawood, the jolly guard, asked Ahrash. "The Mullah Killer turned himself in, confessing to all the murders."

Ahrash was relieved by the news. Since he had left the hospital, he often thought about the murders, wishing he knew if the violence had been stopped.

"Did he say why he did all those awful killings?" he asked Dawood.

"No. He just walked into the police station and said, '*I killed thirteen of them, one for each year of my son's life on this earth.*'"

Everyone knew of the horrible crimes the Mullah Killer had

committed, but only a few knew why.

After the Iranian revolution in 1979, most generals and high-ranking officers from the previous regime were briefly tried and executed, leaving the army in the hands of novice military men and the country in serious peril. It was then that the shrewd Iraqi Leader, Saddam Hussein, attacked his vulnerable neighbor, starting a war that lasted for almost a decade.

In the early stages of the war, Saddam's forces had captured the port of Khoramshahr, an important city of the Khuzestan province and the country's main source of crude oil. The strike was quick and unexpected, not giving the local army regiment a chance to put up a resistance.

The Iraqi forces did not show any mercy, killing soldiers and civilians alike. They set fire to oil wells, official buildings, as well as residential houses. Men, women, and children who were unable to flee or hide, were killed throughout the city.

In only a few weeks, the metropolitan Khoramshahr had been turned to rubble, almost a ghost town, with only a thousand citizens remaining.

During their occupation, the Iraqis troops planted countless mines all around the city, making it deadly for Iranian soldiers to reach them. Simultaneously, they placed battleships in the Persian Gulf, blocking the navy from accessing the city via the waterways.

Many attempts by the military to regain the control of Khoramshahr failed, one after another, only causing further casualties and more destruction. The absence of solid and seasoned generals and a lack of proper tactics was clearly hampering the Iranian defense.

As the enemy began advancing toward other oil-rich cities, the Islamic Republic Army, under the direction of Iran's leading imam, turned to the public for help. They asked the young Muslims to step forward and fight for the liberty of their land and protection of the revolution.

The imam's message was well received. Immediately, a massive number of young and devout Muslims volunteered to go to the war zone. Without any training, fearless of bullets and mines, these brave men charged toward the Iraqi troops on suicide missions.

After several fierce and bloody battles, the Iranian young army finally freed Khoramshahr from her aggressor.

Victory, however, was not achieved without cost; countless lives were lost on both sides and the city was completely leveled to the ground. The fighting had been so bloody that Khoramshahr, the green city, came to be known as Khoninshahr, the blood-soaked city.

Many sad stories had been reported during Iraq invasion, some so bizarre that they seemed more like rumors than reality.

There were accounts of groups of donkeys being chained together and prodded ahead of the soldiers through the battlefields fraught with danger. When the mines exploded, chaos ensued. Terrified, the surviving animals would run back, becoming entangled and inadvertently trampling the soldiers.

After that failed strategy, a more horrific approach was selected – children from orphanages served as frontrunners, clearing the road for the soldiers.

Families were also asked to let their youngsters participate in the war. When the requests were denied, some children were taken away without their parents' knowledge. Randomly, trucks would stop at schools and pick up a large number of boys. The children were given a necklace with a key on it, the key to the heaven's gate. They were then taken to the minefields, chained together and sent forward.

When his son and a few of his classmates did not return home from school, the Mullah Killer panicked. He looked everywhere for his missing boy, asking the police for help, hiring detectives, even traveling to the war zone himself.

After months of searching in vain, the man was convinced that his son and his friends had been taken by the army.

On the first anniversary of his boy's disappearance, the distraught father suddenly snapped. Bloodthirsty, he was determined to avenge his only child.

———————— آرش ————————

The presence of the Mullah Killer on death row, constantly reminded Ahrash of the grisly images of the crime scenes from the newspaper. He was now even more scared than when Babak was his neighbor. Unable to sleep or study, he became increasingly angry with the man, uncharacteristically wishing for his quick demise.

The Mullah Killer was executed exactly one week after his arrival on death row.

CHAPTER 56

Mornings for Ahrash always began with Reza inviting him to talk. The two prisoners would converse for a while, often describing how they had slept the night before or if they had had any significant dreams. A subsequent, shorter chat often chased the morning meal after which Ahrash would head outside with a book.

Today, Reza did not initiate an exchange and when Ahrash was leaving for the yard, he saw him still lying in his bed, facing the wall.

Ahrash recalled Reza's nasty migraine from two weeks ago: *He probably has another massive headache.*

───────────── آرش ─────────────

Outside was chilly and a bit windy. With only a light jacket over his prison jumpsuit, the cold rushed over Ahrash the moment he stepped out into the yard. He pulled the collar of his jacket up and took long strides over the pale grass. The grasses' icy blades crackled under his feet like dried leaves.

As he neared the elm tree in the middle of the lawn, his cat jumped down from the roof and trotted toward him. Ahrash picked her up and walked to a chair which was a new addition to the yard. He settled into his seat. The cat kneaded his thighs briefly, assessing the best way to curl up on his lap.

The wind picked up. Ahrash raised his head to the sky. The clouds were so saturated with water that they seemed ready to overflow at any time. With the wintery cold and all the moisture in the air, the village boy was certain that the capital would have its first snowfall within a day or two.

Looking back at the heavy snow they had had in the village, Ahrash suddenly found himself inside the school bus, stuck in a ditch.

It was exactly a year ago, when he, Neloo and a bunch of the village kids had to stay in the middle of the road, battling the bone chilling cold.

Unruffled by the scary situation, Neloo moved from one child to the next, carrying the first aid kit. She calmly attended to any cut, no matter how small, while consoling the panicked students.

After taking care of the injured, she encouraged everyone to turn in any food they had in their bags, explaining the importance of rationing in these types of situations. She then equally divided the food and the cookies that the bus driver had kept for emergencies. "Don't finish your food all at once. We do not know when help will arrive," she advised the children.

Neloo remained awake throughout the night, looking after all the children. If anyone needed to go to the bathroom, she would wake both Ahrash and the driver. They would all go out together, surrounding the child, well aware that they were under the surveillance of hungry wolves.

"I do not believe any adult could have handled that calamity better than Neloo," Ahrash thought, keenly missing his girl.

A bird's shriek from somewhere on the roof alerted the cat. The feline stood up quickly with an arched back, her hanging underbelly touching Ahrash's knees. She looked around briefly and decided to cozy up again in the same spot.

Ahrash read his book for a while but only managed a couple of pages. He had been consumed with an uneasy, imprecise feeling the entire morning. He closed his book, and while petting his cat, allowed his mind to drift freely.

Reza took over his thoughts and the one question that had him completely perplexed, surfaced again: *What could this man with such a caring disposition have done to land him on death row?*

━━━━━ آرش ━━━━━

A few inmates appeared in the adjacent yard while Ahrash waited for his usher to show up. He nervously eyed the prisoners on the other side of the fence, wondering why they did not send for him yet.

The number of inmates grew quickly. By the time the guard finally arrived, the main yard was teeming with loud and unruly men.

"I totally forgot that you were here, pal," the merry Dawood said when he showed up. "We better rush back now before I get in trouble."

They moved toward the building.

Still thinking of Reza, Ahrash timidly asked, "Do you know why Reza is here on death row?"

"I am surprised that you do not know, young man. I heard the champ has adopted you," Dawood gave a half-suppressed laugh.

"He does indeed treat me like a son but he never talks about himself."

Dawood's face crumpled with a dejected frown. He brought his head closer to the boy. "You did not hear this from me," he whispered. "The champ is a political prisoner. They found out that he was plotting a protest against the current regime."

━━━━━ آرش ━━━━━

Reza was still in bed and under the covers when Ahrash returned to his cell. The boy desperately wanted to talk to him but decided to wait.

A couple of hours later, when there were still no words from Reza, Ahrash became very anxious: *Maybe he is seriously ill. I better call out and speak with him.*

It took longer than usual for Reza to respond.

"We did not talk today at all. Do you have another migraine?" Ahrash asked when Reza finally came to the front of his cell.

"I am not feeling very well, but it is nothing serious," Reza responded.

"I wanted to tell you something, but I better not bother you now. It can certainly wait."

"That is alright, Ahrash. What is on your mind?"

"Well, today I found out why they put you on death row."

"Glad to hear that. Now, there are no more secrets between us," Reza said and excused himself to go back to bed.

─────── آرش ───────

The light had been dimmed for a while, but Ahrash could not fall asleep. He was thinking about Reza and the fact that this great man was on death row only for opposing the regime. At school, he was taught that the Islamic revolution had brought a true democracy to his land. *If what they claimed was true, why then can't Reza freely express his opinion? Why must he die without having committed an actual crime?*

Outraged and depressed, Ahrash left his bed and started pacing the cell with quiet steps.

Right away, Reza whispered to him, "Are you awake, Ahrash?"

Ahrash darted to the bars. "Yes, I am awake, unable to fall asleep. How about you? Is your headache gone?"

"I feel slightly better," Reza answered. "What were you doing with your sleeplessness my friend?"

"Just pacing and thinking."

"Thinking about what?"

"Many things but mainly of Neloo and Issa," Ahrash intentionally left out Reza's name.

Reza did not ask any more questions and was quiet for a while.

The silence that enfolded around them was heavy and the boy did not know how to break it. He just stood by the bars, idling.

"Listen, Ahrash," Reza eventually spoke. "You should know by now that no one remains on death row for very long. Babaak was here a short time, the Mullah Killer, even shorter," he said and paused to swallow a lump in his throat. "I am sorry that I did not prepare you for this before, but I have to let you know that they will be taking me at dawn."

Ahrash's heart suddenly sank in its cavity. "Taking you? You mean..."

"Yes, my friend. It is my turn now to exit this world."

Ahrash began to shiver, picturing a noose closing around Reza's neck. "You must be terrified."

"Yes, I am. Death is final and I am not ready for it," Reza's voice cracked. He was at the edge of tears, unaware that Ahrash's tears were already running down his face in sheets.

"You had better go and try to get some sleep now. I just couldn't leave without saying goodbye to you."

"Can we talk until they come for you?"

"No, Ahrash, you need to sleep and I need to write a few letters. Please try to stay strong. I promise to watch over you if I can."

آرش

The first snow had indeed arrived in the capital that night, coming down steadily until dawn. It was as though all the angels in the world had shed their white wings to mourn the death of a great man.

PART III
Four years and six months later

CHAPTER 57

"What is with all these books, young man?" the good-humored Dawood asked as he plunked down a heavy box by Ahrash's feet.

"There is nothing else to do in here except read. Besides, books give me knowledge and expand my horizons."

"Ok then, my dear scholar, allow me to open the box for you," Dawood said, attacking the taped-up package with his pocket knife. It took him only a couple of minutes to unwrap the box and remove its contents. To his disappointment, there was nothing else in the box except several college exam practice guides.

Ahrash started to sort through his newly found treasures. It was comforting to him to see Navid Ramzi's name written on front of each book. *He must have been saving them for me from his preparation classes.*

With three years of high school successfully completed, Ahrash, now a senior, was confident that he would easily pass all the required tests to graduate this year. What concerned him the most at this point, was the Concours, the University Entrance Exam.

The Concours is a stringent, nationwide exam that takes place only once a year in Iran. It consists of several comprehensive and rigorous tests, designed to place only the very top students of the country in its seat-limited public universities.

Each year, approximately ten percent of the 1.5 million applicants receive admission, forty percent of which are preselected based on veteran status or a strong Islamic background.

Ahrash's apprehension was not without basis. In Iran, as with many other nations, the privileged students from wealthy families always had a better chance of being accepted by the top universities. They often attended the schools with above average academic standards and could afford to pay for the expensive Concours preparation courses. For a self-taught boy like him, who had never set foot onto a high school campus or received any guidance from instructors, the odds of excelling at the Concours was certainly near nil.

Ahrash knew he must study intensely.

──────── آرش ────────

Thumbing through one study guide, Ahrash noticed that Dawood was still standing next to him.

"Sorry, Dawood. I did not realize you were waiting for me. Do you want the box back?"

"No, you should keep it. Use it as storage, there is no room left on your desk."

"It is alright. I still have some empty spots under the bed." Ahrash said and pointed at the stacks of books visible underneath his bed.

Dawood took the box but instead of leaving, he busied himself folding its edges. He looked atypically tense.

"Hey pal, did I tell you what I am going to do today?" he asked Ahrash without preamble.

"You did not. Are you borrowing one of my books?"

"No. I am going to do something much more daring."

Ahrash was now intrigued. He closed the book in his hand and laid it down on the bed. "Let me guess, you are going to ask a girl to marry you? Right?"

"Yes! How did you know that?"

"Just a wild guess. Who is the lucky girl, Dawood?"

"My cousin, Zari. I have been in love with this girl for as long as I can remember," Dawood said softly, his demeanor, less animated than usual. "After my shift today, I will go to my uncle's house to ask permission to marry her."

"So exciting. I am truly happy for you."

"Well...Zari has a couple of other suitors, ones with more education and better jobs. I am afraid I will not be her first pick."

"You will never find out unless you ask. Besides, you are a good man and I am sure your uncle and his daughter both know and appreciate that. Have faith in yourself."

"I'll only know if I ask. That is a good advice," Dawood said with some confidence, his usual smile fastened back onto his face.

CHAPTER 58

It was Ahrash's fifth fall in the capital city and, one way or the other, his last.

Autumn had long since arrived, yet the elm tree in the yard stubbornly held onto its green leaves. By contrast, far away on a gentle hill, fall colors of gold, red, orange and purple were strikingly on display. And beyond the array of leafy colors, stood the majestic Alborz Mountain, its snow-covered Damavand peak piercing the sky's chest like a giant spear.

Ahrash stared off into the distance for a while, marveling at the beauty of the hillside. He drew in his gaze to the acres of flat land surrounding the compound. The large expanse of evenly trimmed dried weeds instantly took him back to Kultappa, to its golden wheat fields after a harvest.

"If Issa was here, I would describe the surrounding splendor to him. I would tell him about the gilded fields. I would tell him that the Damavand peak is so white that it hurts the eyes to look at it," Ahrash murmured. "And Issa would add to my sentence, '…as though a million gardenias have descended upon it.'"

Feeling more and more nostalgic, Ahrash made a conscious decision to derail his thoughts before sadness completely consumed him. He opened his book and started to read.

The book that he was reading was, unfortunately, beyond sad. It was the complete narrative of Nazi Germany, the darkest chapter in recent history.

An hour later, as the pages of the book had become soaked with the blood of innocent Jewish families, Ahrash found it unbearable to continue reading. The atrocities that had happened during the war left him feeling shameful for ever having complained about his own hardships. There was no comparison between his pain and the suffering of those children who were ripped away from their parents, shot, gassed, or burned, the children who died of hunger or had their heads smashed against the vehicles by German soldiers.

How could humans be so savage to their own kind?

Gloomy, Ahrash, placed his hand on his sleepy cat, and started stroking her fur. The feline stretched her body out to twice its curled-up length and resumed napping – her paws dangling in midair.

A small flock of Tula gray geese appeared in the sky. They landed in the middle of the field, one after another, like a group of paratroopers. Their loud arrival scared the tiny, yellow birds who were feeding, almost invisibly, at that very spot. The small birds took flight and, in the blink of an eye, fanned out high and wide, resembling an exploding firework.

The cat calmly glanced at Ahrash through a narrow opening of one eye, acknowledging the wing fluttering noises.

"Do you know that we have those exact geese in my village?" Ahrash told the cat. "My dog, Jolfa, teased them relentlessly, chasing the poor birds in and out of the stream whenever he saw them."

The cat was back to sleep, yet Ahrash continued talking to her, "When I left home, Jolfa was almost three years old; she must be getting old now. I hope I get to see her again."

Neloo's latest letter, placed inside the book, beckoned Ahrash. He resisted for a while but eventually picked it up, flattened the pages against his chest and started reading it for the third time.

The letter began with news from everyone Ahrash knew and cared for: his parents, Issa, Koor Akbar, Hajji, the twins, Ali, Hakim, Jafar, Shereen, Hannah, and even the village baker. Neloo then wrote about her preparation for the college exams.

"Thank you for sharing your notes. I study them all the time: at school, on the bus, and at home, of course, when the twins are asleep. The little devils are so energetic that I cannot concentrate when they are around.

Some of the math problems in the study guide are difficult to understand; I do not believe they were ever covered in my classes. I have been trying to get help from Mrs. Amini at lunchtime. She is very welcoming and supportive.

How is your progress? Do you ever need help understanding the material? I wish we did not have to study apart."

In the last section of the letter, a new suitor was mentioned, a young man who had totally captivated Sakineh.

"Fareed is a medical student who also teaches science at my school. He is from a prominent family; his grandfather used to own many villages, including ours and Naansa. Sakineh thinks of him as a godsend. My father also agrees that he is a good choice for a husband, especially since Fareed wants his wife to pursue a college education."

Even though Neloo had spoken of many other suitors before, finding out about her new admirer, disheartened Ahrash gravely. This suitor appeared to be a perfect choice, one even approved by Sharif.

Ahrash heaved a big sigh and continued reading.

"Sakineh cannot contain herself. She is so excited that she does not even mind when my dad discusses your freedom with her. Her enthusiasm can be harmful as well. I am afraid that her behavior gives false hope to my suitor, making him believe that one day my heart will unite with his."

آرش

Over the last years, Ahrash had often pondered where the relationship between him and Neloo would stand if he were to be set free. "Would any family allow their daughter to marry her brother's murderer? Should Neloo lose her parents over a boy who had grown up in jail, without any prospects?"

Neloo deserves the best, not me.

The cat rose to his feet after a long nap. She kneaded Ahrash's lap briefly and jumped down with an exaggerated meow. Seeking more attention, she then rolled onto her back at her companion's feet, all four paws in the air. Ahrash leaned over and rubbed her stomach, being gentle around the underbelly growth.

"If I am ever released, you will not be bothered by this tumor anymore," he told the cat. "I will take you to the village and Hakim will remove the nasty growth."

Unaware of Ahrash's elevated emotions, the cat soon got up and walked toward the lawn. She sniffed around briefly and started to nibble on some weeds.

"Do not eat the grass the silly cat! It will make you sick!" Dawood entered the yard, stomping his feet and yelling at the cat.

It was a relief to see Dawood. The young guard had disappeared for a while, right after the day he had disclosed his proposal plan to Ahrash.

"Good to see you, Dawood. Where have you been all this time? I was getting worried about you."

"At home, alone," Dawood answered, his shoulders dropped into a defeating crouch.

Ahrash immediately knew that his friend had experienced a bitter rejection by his uncle and Zari.

"Well, that is life, I guess. What can you do when everything is against you? You love a girl all your life, dreaming of making a family with her. A stranger then comes along and snatches her from you, collapsing your whole world at once," Dawood said flatly.

Not knowing how to counsel him, Ahrash followed Dawood out of the yard without uttering a word. They took several steps together in silence when suddenly Dawood turned around. He grabbed Ahrash tightly and lifted him up off the ground, "I was kidding, Ahrash. I was kidding! My uncle and Zari – they both said yes! I am the happiest man on earth!" he shouted, spinning Ahrash in the air.

"You are a big tease, man! But you better put me down before you drop me on the hard concrete!" Ahrash chuckled.

"You were right all along, pal. My uncle told me he was impressed with the man that I have become. He also said that he had promised my late father he would watch over me and that marrying his daughter helps him fulfill that duty."

"That is so wonderful! But where have you been all this time?"

"Well Zari had to agree too. So my uncle invited me and my mother to go on a trip with them to Mashhad. He let me spend hours alone with Zari to talk. Do you know what the first thing she said to me was?"

"What?"

"She said, 'What took you so long, cousin? I almost had to say yes to another suitor!'" Dawood said, his pride ringing loudly.

CHAPTER 59

Issa was easy to spot anywhere in the village. He had a distinctive physique and always walked with a certain confidence, head high and chest forward. In addition, he was the only man in the village with sleek auburn hair that now fell well past his shoulders.

As the school bus eased onto the village road, Neloo saw Issa walking toward the bakery. She grabbed her bag and headed to the front of the vehicle so she could be the first one to get out.

"Stop, Issa! Stop!" she shouted, scrambling off the bus.

A good distance away, Issa froze in place. He knew something must be seriously wrong. Neloo would never call out to him so boldly right in the heart of the village.

"Is everything alright with the family?" he asked as soon as Neloo reached him.

"Family is fine. But we need to talk about Ahrash."

"I am getting *naan* and will be home soon. Let's meet at my house when I return."

"No. We need to talk now," Neloo pulled on Issa's sleeve, striding toward the boulder.

Issa moved with her with apprehension. He was truly concerned with the rumors that had been circulating in the village about the two of them. Being alone with Neloo in a hidden spot now would certainly brew more malevolent gossip.

"I have a disturbing letter from Ahrash. He seems to be badly dispirited," the words spilled from Neloo's lips hurriedly as she scurried with Issa behind the boulder. "He claims that he is damaged goods, a murderer, and that my parents would never accept him. He even wants me to marry someone else, a suitor that I hardly know."

Neloo paused and removed Ahrash's letter from her pocket. "Listen to what he wrote here. *'Think of me just as a boy you heard about in a story. A boy who loved the blue sky but grew up in darkness, a boy who wanted to soar high but died with broken wings in a cage.'"*

Her grief renewed, Neloo stopped reading. She imagined Ahrash's lifeless body lying alone on the floor of his cell. She took a step closer to Issa and rested her head on his shoulder. "I am horrified, Issa. He might try to harm himself again."

Issa stepped back, gently forcing Neloo to lift her head.

"You are right, Neloo; this letter is alarming. After being strong for so long, Ahrash appears to be teetering on the edge now. He certainly needs help, but we must approach him cleverly and with caution. Actually, this matter is too important to be discussed on the side of the road."

"I can come over to your house this afternoon. We can go over the entire letter with your parents and decide what to do next," Neloo said and turned to leave.

Issa reached for her arm and stopped her.

"I have changed my mind, Neloo; you better not visit my house after all. I am becoming more and more convinced that we must completely cut off all the contact for the remainder of Ahrash's sentence. The next six months are critical. We cannot afford to jeopardize his freedom. Any more gossip about us might upset your parents and have a negative effect on their final decision," Issa explained with a serious tone of voice.

CHAPTER 60

"Ouch, be gentle, it hurts!" Hannah complained as Shereen combed through her long hair.

The two sisters were sitting on the bench in their yard trying to draw some warmth from the anemic sun.

Not far from them, inside an elaborate pen, a young chicken was running around, clucking incessantly. The tiny fowl was out of control, walking from corner to corner, climbing over perched hens, pecking at the trees and running into the fence, all the while protesting loudly.

"Is she going to lay an egg?" Hannah asked her sister.

"Nah, she is too young."

When Neloo entered the yard, the chicken was still clucking. "What is wrong with your bird and why are you sitting outside in the cold?" she questioned the girls.

"It will snow soon and then we will be stuck inside. Besides, it is fun to watch this crazy chicken," Shereen answered, grinning.

Neloo walked toward the loud bird to take a closer look. She noticed a new and elaborate chicken pen in place. The pen's large perimeter was fully fenced with chicken wire tightly secured onto equally spaced vertical strips of wood. The roof was comprised of more chicken wire and was partially covered by a tarp. In one corner of the pen, two small, built-in troughs stood for water and food; in the opposite corner was a two-leveled coop with a wide door.

"When did you get this marvelous hen house?" she asked.

"Ali built it last week. He was tired of us losing chickens to the foxes and coyotes," Shereen explained.

"He did a great job! I am glad he is finally showing some motivation in life."

"I know. I think working for Hajji has made him more responsible."

Shereen gathered Hannah's thick hair into a ponytail at the side of her head. She then divided the hair into sections, braiding each part separately. She was about two thirds done with the braiding when her mother called to her from inside the house.

"Neloo *Jaan*, could you check on my mom? If I let go of Hannah's hair, all the braids will come loose."

Neloo went inside and returned after a few minutes. "Your mom was thirsty," she said and paused, suddenly uncertain about her visit. "Is your mom's sickness coming back? She did not look very well."

"I do not think so. My uncle says she probably has a bad cold and that he should wait a while before taking her to the doctor. He is very busy, you know, preparing to go to Mecca.

"Can you or Ali take her?"

"I guess we could do that. I will watch her closely, but I am sure it is just a cold."

Neloo sat next to the girls, deep in thought. And for a while, everyone was quiet, except the young chicken.

A few minutes later, Shereen glanced at Neloo and right away noticed her red, puffy eyes. "Have you been crying again, Neloo *Jaan*?" she asked.

"Yes, off and on all day."

"Did something bad happen?"

"Sadly, yes. Now that we are nearing the end of our long journey, Ahrash is losing his mind. He wants me to marry someone else!"

"Marry who?" Shereen asked.

Before Neloo could answer Hannah abruptly said, "I know who. He wants you marry Issa, doesn't he?"

"Are you trying to be silly, Hanna?"

"No, not at all. Everyone knows you and Issa are in love. People saw you together holding hands and..."

Neloo stopped her young friend midsentence. "I love Issa like a brother. He is my rock, a strong shoulder to cry on."

"So it is a lie! You never held his hands or kissed him?"

Neloo did not respond.

Wrapping all the braids around the base of the ponytail, Shereen secured them with pins on the side of Hannah's head. She picked up a mirror from the bench and held it in front of her sister, "How do you like it?"

Hannah looked in the mirror from different angles but instead of answering her sister, she reworded her question to Neloo, "So *everything* is a lie and you two are not in love?"

"Maybe you are still too young to understand the meaning of loyalty, Hannah, but I assure you that neither I nor Issa would ever betray Ahrash. We both love him immensely, missing him every day, all the time. And that is all I can tell you," Neloo stated rather roughly.

Shereen entered the conversation. "Sorry Neloo *Jaan*. Hannah is only repeating what people are saying without putting any thought into it," she said and then timidly whispered, "Now, that we are talking about love, can I trust you two girls with a secret?"

"What?" Hannah became excited.

"I think I have a crush on Issa. Every time I see him, my heart sinks in my chest, wishing one day he would fall in love with me."

"I do not blame you. If I was not genuinely in love with Ahrash, Issa would be my first choice to spend the rest of my life with. He is bright, caring, and totally handsome. You two could actually make a perfect couple."

Summoned by her mother again, Shereen left the yard.

Hanna scooted closer to Neloo. "I am sorry for being rude earlier," she apologized, her face exploding with charm and sweetness. Neloo, in response, placed an arm over her shoulder and pulled her in even closer.

The clucking of the young bird reached its peak and then suddenly stopped. A couple of minutes later, she calmly walked out of the coop leaving behind a tiny, bloody egg on a bed of hay.

CHAPTER 61

The first time he laid eyes on Koor Akbar, an instantaneous fear overcame him, a fear so powerful that it gave the boy of almost fifteen recurring nightmares. Even now, after four months of delivering food to him, the youngster shuddered with horror every time he was in the presence of the blind man.

———— آرش ————

The years of isolation, bad hygiene, and insufficient nutrition had turned Koor Akbar into a beastlike creature. He had become very thin and had developed a hunched back. His grey hair and beard had grown long and wild, both dreadfully infested with lice. His milky eyes had sunken deeper into his skull; his eyelids were completely covered by moles of various sizes.

Koor Akbar's previous caregiver had been relatively tolerant of him. He had even developed some affection toward him over time. Every week he cleaned the hut, groomed the man and put him in a set of clean clothes. When the weather was good, he encouraged him to bathe in the river while taking him to the public bath during the cold seasons. His tasks were often frustrating, but under no circumstance would the young man's conscience have allowed him to shirk his duties.

He continued looking after Koor Akbar until he graduated from high school and joined the army. To replace him, Hajji had hired different teenagers but none of them could handle the responsibilities properly.

———— آرش ————

With every step toward the shack, the boy's hatred of Koor Akbar swelled. It was bone-chillingly cold; his gloves were thin and his bundle too heavy to carry in the snow. He walked cautiously yet had difficulty finding solid ground for his feet. Every time he stumbled and ice entered his rubber boots, a current of rage passed through him; making him swear involuntarily.

The snow in his boots was hard pack now, hurting his toes on contact. He decided to speed up and almost immediately landed in a hole between two snow-covered boulders. His bundle crashed a foot from him, its contents flying in the air.

With his sudden fall, his eyeglasses also had come off and disappeared into the whiteness. He started searching. It took him a while, with his poor sight, to finally retrieve his glasses and collect the containers of food.

Cold and miserable, he moved on, yearning for the demise of the blind man before winter's end.

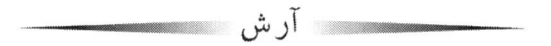

───── آرش ─────

From a distance, the door to the shack appeared to be wide open.

"The idiot doesn't even close the door when he goes out to pee," the boy said aloud and instantly recalled the profound odor always exuding from the hovel.

When he reached the shack, the door was still open. Koor Akbar was nowhere to be found.

"I do not need to wait for him to come back," the boy dropped the bundle inside the door and left the sorry place in a flash.

He took a new path this time, a route closer to his house. Without the burden of his load, he now tucked both hands in his pockets and moved forward steadily; the prospect of thawing out under the *korsi* warming his heart.

Large flakes of snow started falling without any preamble. Every chunk that landed on his hat quickly turned to ice, taking up residence on top of his head. Nevertheless, he was content, the promise of home was just within reach.

After a few minutes of fast walking, when he was distanced enough to feel safe, the boy stopped and took a peek back. The shack's door was still ajar with no sign of Koor Akbar. "Where is the damned blind man? How long does it take for him to go to the bathroom?" he muttered, taking even longer strides forward.

From his new angle high up on the hill, he now was able to see behind the shack. Something colorful there caught his eyes, something familiar. He wiped the snow from his glasses and peered out again. "It looks like Koor Akbar's pajamas. Why is he lying in the snow?" Puzzled, he stopped for a moment and gathered his thoughts: *I have done what I was paid to do.* And with new resolve, he continued home, promising himself he would not look back again.

The snow was more compact now and he could even see the smoke from the chimney of his home. He just needed to speed up.

But he could not speed up. A powerful force was holding him back – a force of good that he never knew he owned.

He turned around.

———— آرش ————

Shaking profusely, he summoned his courage and peered inside the shack. Suddenly, a pair of snowbirds darted out of the hut, passing over his head speedily. Their unexpected appearance startled the boy. He leaned on the jarred door for support, his hand pressed against his volatile, young heart.

"Koor Akbar, come back to your house!" he shouted from the top of his lungs and waited, expecting to hear the man's footsteps. But in that vast, snowy field, the only sound he heard was his own heartbeat.

He called again and started walking away from the perceived safety of the hut.

As he moved toward the back of the shack, crimson stains began to appear in the snow and grew larger with every step forward. The smell of death rose from the shameful ground and the boy saw a horror that will be forever seared into his mind: an island of bloody snow scattered with torn pieces of Koor Akbar's clothing. And, in the very center of the blood bath, sat a skull, mostly stripped of its flesh.

———————— آرش ————————

Koor Akbar's sad death caused a grand stir in the village. Kultappa had always been a land of wolves, but it had been decades since someone had been killed by them.

The overall consensus among the villagers was that the blind man had been ambushed by the wolves while relieving himself at night. Issa, thought differently though. He was certain that man's demise was not an accident, but rather a deliberate attempt by him to end his life: *Koor Akbar was an intelligent man. He had survived many winters in that shack, knowing well to never go out after dark or to wander too far. Besides, if he had planned to return, he would not have left the door open to his hut, inviting the bitter cold in.*

CHAPTER 62

Khalil woke at dawn after a restless night's sleep. He remained in bed for a while and, as with any other morning, he first thought of his far away son. Today's rumination was quite specific – Ahrash would be eighteen in a few months and his future was still unknown.

"What will happen then?" The question circled in the man's head over and over without any resolution.

Years of tenacious effort by him, Hajji, and Warden Ramzi had all failed to free his boy. What else could be done now except to pray – pray for a miracle that would soften Sakineh's stony heart.

———— آرش ————

Ever since Khalil had been reunited with Sharif, the two friends periodically met in their fields. They mainly talked about their harvest and other farm related issues, sometimes commiserating on their sons' catastrophic lives.

In his most recent appearance, Sharif had come across very hopeful, inspiring optimism about Ahrash's future. He had said that Sakineh was so excited by the prospect of Neloo getting married that she hardly mentioned Mahmood's name anymore.

"She is more approachable now, we were even able to discuss Ahrash without her having a tantrum," Sharif reported with confidence.

Khalil, too, felt a similar vibe coming from Sakineh as of late. At the previous *Nowruz*,* Sharif and Sakineh had come to Hajji's house where Khalil's family and two other couples were already visiting. Sakineh could have excused herself and left, but she chose to stay. Her decision

---
* Persian New Year

was surprising as the two families had not been under the same roof since Mahmood's death.

"Could it all mean that Sakineh will set Ahrash free?" Khalil knew he needed to pray more ardently.

———— آرش ————

Still pondering his boy's future, the disheartened father left his bed and walked to the window. He pulled back the drapes, expecting to see darkness. Instead, he found a full moon hanging in the early morning sky. The round face of the moon was so bright that Khalil could see the yard even through the frosted window.

Suddenly, the image of Ahrash appeared, sitting alone, and shivering in the cold.

Khalil took a step backward, distancing himself from the window.

The image gradually morphed into shadowy figures, a family of wolves, prowling in the yard. Khalil followed the animals' movement, until they disappeared behind the snow-covered bushes.

The trespassers' presence shifted Khalil's thoughts to Koor Akbar and his tragic death. He pictured the blind man's last moments: the wolves' warm breath on his neck, their teeth plunging into his throat. *What a horrible ending!*

He put his hand on his chest and somberly said a prayer for Koor Akbar's soul.

Just then, Issa turned in his bed, switching from his back to side, facing his father. Khalil looked at him and could not return his eyes back to the window: *What a noble man my son has grown into. He is strong like a bull and dignified like a lion.*

———— آرش ————

The prayer bundle on the windowsill beckoned the grieving man. He picked it up and spread its rug out on the floor, neatly straightening its four corners. He stood there on the rug, facing in the direction of Mecca.

Suddenly a grim thought popped into his head, mirroring Ahrash's concern: *Would Issa's future parallel Koor Akbar's – alone in a hut, perishing in the worst way?*

Sometime later, when Aziz woke to pray, the broken Khalil was still standing on the prayer rug, unable to surrender his heart to his almighty God.

CHAPTER 63

It was the second time Ahrash had been in Ramzi's office. His first visit had been about four years ago, a month after he had arrived on death row. At the time, he was a despondent and confused boy, completely buried in a delusionary realm.

He remembered walking into the office, trembling. The place had had the aura of a dungeon, its formidable master standing tall and sinister at the door. His memory, however, suffered a sharp decline after that point, leaving everything behind in darkness.

———— آرش ————

Ramzi offered him candy, just as the first time he was there. Ahrash reached into the bowl. His skinny wrist tore at the warden's heart.

"How are your studies coming along young man?" Warden Ramzi started the conversation.

"It is promising, Sir. I am perfectly ready to take the exams for my senior classes. As far as the Concours, I probably will need more rigorous studying."

"The Concours is difficult. I used to tell my son, 'Study hard, as you can never be over prepared for this exam,'" Ramzi said and handed Ahrash a thick folder. "This package contains your college application. It arrived earlier this morning. Read the directions well before filling out the forms. If I remember correctly from my son's application, it requires a signature from one of your parents too," he explained.

"I will start working on it right away, Sir. I have been waiting to participate in the Concours since I was in middle school."

"Your aspirations are commendable son. I am truly proud of you."

Over the last four years, Mr. Namat, a retired educator, had been administering all the high school exams from within Ahrash's cell. He simply brought in the assigned textbooks at the start of each semester and visited later for the midterm and final exams.

Taking the Concours on the other hand was not that easy.

"As you probably know, the Concours is given on the same days and at the same times across the country. To take the exam, each applicant must be present at the designated universities," Ramzi explained.

"I was wondering myself how I was supposed to take it."

"Well, I had a drawn out and frustrating battle with Judge Kasra over your situation. He certainly had the upper hand, but I was not willing to give up. Miraculously, before our final appearance in court, he sent an unexpected letter, authorizing you to take the exams at Tehran University."

"That is wonderful, Sir. I truly appreciate all your help and support."

Ramzi offered more candy to Ahrash and picked one out for himself. He took a few steps around his office, unwrapping his treat. It was clear, that he was not looking forward to discussing the next topic.

"I have to let you know that unfortunately Judge Kasra could not acquiesce without attaching a condition. He wants you to be in your prison jumpsuit and shackles the entire five days of the Concours. I personally believe the order is too harsh and unnecessary. If you would like, I can make further attempts to remove this stipulation."

"It is a privilege to participate in the Concours. I am willing to take it under any circumstances."

Ramzi let out a sigh of relief, "Good thinking son. It is not wise to entice the snake out of its hole. Now, you had better get back and start working on your application."

آرش

Outside the warden's office, Dawood was waiting to take Ahrash back to his cell. The young men met and walked together out of the building.

Curiosity wired into his psyche; it took only a few minutes for Dawood to start his interrogation. He asked about the folder in Ahrash's hand and the reason for the meeting, not being satisfied until he received all the information.

"You must be kidding me!" Dawood stopped, planting his feet firmly on the ground. "You must not accept being in shackles while taking the exams. That man is just a donkey."

"I have no choice, Dawood."

Angrier now, Dawood held up his fists, "If you allow me to, I would love to teach that judge a lesson. Who does he think he is, ordering you and the warden around?"

"I appreciate your concern but there is no reason to make a mountain out of a molehill. Besides, I live at the mercy of this man's whims; agitating him might cost me my life."

———— آرش ————

After Ahrash left his room, Warden Ramzi picked up the phone and dialed the number written on a small post-it note.

A delicate voice came from the other side, "*Jahan*[*] Daily News. How can I help you?

---

[*] *world*

PART IV
Three months later

CHAPTER 64

Ahrash stepped onto the university campus flanked by Dawood and an officer. The three men walked only a few yards before they were stopped by a thick wall of human bodies.

Tens of thousands of young students were standing inside the gates, anxiety etched deeply on their faces. Ahrash had never seen such a big crowd, except in some photos from Hitler's or Ayatollah Khomeini's rallies.

The sheer number of people was, at first, only overwhelming. Once more students arrived behind them, Ahrash began to feel confined and claustrophobic. The noise was even more disturbing; it was as if a swarm of restless bees were continuously buzzing around his head.

At seven o'clock in the morning, the sun was still unfolding its many arms, yet it was powerful enough to make everyone sweat. Being in a prison jumpsuit and shackles, Ahrash felt very hot and somewhat nauseated.

"I wish I had skipped breakfast this morning," he thought, as his sickness started to grow.

A water fountain was spotted close by. Dawood took the shackled Ahrash to it. They both drank a good amount of water and quickly reported back to the officer.

"My card says Sina Exam Hall. Shouldn't I try to find the building, Sir?" Ahrash timidly asked the officer.

"They will soon announce where to line up to get to your assigned hall," the officer explained. "The order of the call is based on the applicants' last names. Your last name starts with the letter B, so you will find out before most of the other students do."

Dawood quickly jumped into the conversation with a sarcastic remark. "It might take a while though. We are two hours early for no good reason."

آرش

The presence of Ahrash, a strange contender, in his prison getup, was seemingly first noticed when he stood in his designated line. Heads began to turn, starting with the students standing in front and behind him, travelling along both sides of the queue in a domino effect.

Avoiding all gazes, Ahrash directed his attention at a crew of photographers who were standing on a higher ground, setting up fancy cameras on tripods. "Maybe I will take some photography classes," he fantasized, forgetting for a moment how slim his chances were to attend university.

A nudge at his side interrupted Ahrash's daydreaming.

"Look at the soldiers up there," Dawood said in a hushed voice, motioning with his head at the rooftop of a nearby building.

Heavily armed soldiers were standing in a line on the roof, looking down intensely at the crowd. There were even more militia on the balconies and behind the windows of the other buildings.

Finding the campus to be like a military zone was a jolting experience for the young Ahrash. He had always envisioned universities as peaceful places, somewhere that young minds could grow and flourish without being watched and beleaguered.

"Hey Ahrash, guess when my son will be born?" Dawood asked excitedly.

"In about three months."

"How did you know?"

"I have been keeping track since you first told me the good news."

Dawood pondered that momentarily. "I'll bring him to you as soon as he is home from the hospital."

"I do not think that is a good idea, Dawood. Shouldn't you take some time off then, to take care of the baby and your wife?"

Dawood pondered again, this time a bit longer. "Well, I guess I should. In that case, you have to promise to visit us if you are released before I am back to work."

Amused by the conversation of the two young men, the officer pinned a tepid smile on his face which did not go unnoticed by Dawood.

"Ahrash's prison term will be over soon, Sir," he addressed the officer with elevated emotion. "I have been taking care of this young man since he was only thirteen. He is like a brother to me."

———————— آرش ————————

Inside the exam hall, every student had an assigned seat. Ahrash was placed in the front row and his custodians stood only a couple of feet away.

Four ceiling fans were hard at work, but they could not keep the large hall cool.

With handcuffs on, Ahrash struggled to wipe the sweat off his face; yet, he remained patient. He knew that the officer had strict orders to keep him in chains until the test had been administered.

Once all the students had taken their places and their IDs had been checked, a delivery man appeared. He rolled in a cart to the front of the room and transferred several boxes to a table. The proctors quickly removed the test packages from the boxes and stacked them in equal heights. They started counting the tests.

The clock on the wall showed ten minutes to nine when the tests were all distributed. Ahrash was, at last, free from his shackles.

Minutes later, a young man entered the room with a video camera perched on his shoulder. He stood by the door, gave a short wave to the testing staff, and started recording.

There was an interesting logo on the cameraman's shirt: a picture of the earth with her ocean's waves turned into individual letters, spelling, "*Jahan* Daily News."

Finding the logo clever, Ahrash watched the man a little longer, not knowing how quickly his recorded images would change the course of his life.

--- آرش ---

By the time Ahrash returned to his cell that day, it was past 7pm. His dinner had been served a while ago and looked cold and unappetizing. He picked up a piece of flatbread and deposited the rest of the food in the return drawer.

Exhausted, he laid down on the bed, nibbling at the bread in his hand. He was content with the day's test and hoped that he would perform at the same level over the next four days.

That night Ahrash slept the longest and soundest he had in almost five years.

CHAPTER 65

On the second day of the Concours, Ahrash awoke early. Unlike the previous day, he felt relaxed and well-rested. His breakfast tasted good, and although he had planned on not eating altogether, he devoured the entire meal with an unfamiliar appetite.

Soon Dawood appeared and ushered him out of the building toward their parked jeep. When the officer arrived sometime later, they all got into the car, Dawood behind the wheel, speeding away.

For a long time, they drove through a rural area with small orchards on both sides. A group of tiny houses appeared next, children of all ages running around in their cluttered, fenceless yards. There were no farm animals in sight, yet Ahrash detected the unmistakable scent of livestock through the cracked window. The smell was strangely intoxicating. He rolled the window down ever so slightly, not sure if his fellow travelers would mind.

The houses gradually became more sparsely spaced and eventually yielded to miles of rolling green fields. Ahrash extended his gaze at the endless grandeur of the hills, wondering how he had missed all this yesterday. He knew he had to fully take in these serene moments before they were lost to the chaos of the capital's rushed traffic.

———— آرش ————

Finding a parking spot turned out to be a disaster this time. They had arrived only a half an hour later than the day before, but there was absolutely no space to be found. Not only was all the metered street parking taken, the university's oversized parking garage and the three private parking lots in the area were all at capacity as well.

Dawood drove wildly, checking all the corners and alleys, while constantly cursing under his breath.

After driving several blocks in all directions, he concluded that the only way out of this mess was to drop Ahrash and the officer off at the university entrance. His idea, however, was dismissed every time he suggested it to his superior.

In one alley, almost four blocks away from the campus' entrance, Dawood finally spotted a tight, but empty space. He cut in front of another car and quickly squeezed the jeep into the slot, not paying any attention to other driver's honking and swearing.

Their troubles, unfortunately, did not end there. As the men were hastily exiting the car, several motorcycles entered the alley and parked right behind their vehicle. A throng of reporters quickly jumped off of the bikes and ambushed Ahrash. They encircled him so tightly that the car's door could not be closed behind him.

Terror struck Ahrash. With his wrists and ankles fastened, he felt completely vulnerable. He craned his neck, his eyes helplessly searching in all directions for Dawood.

Oblivious to his fear, the reporters continued jockeying for position, shoving microphones into his face, and shouting questions.

The officer and Dawood tried to cut through the group and make way for Ahrash to move forward. Dawood was confrontational, constantly yelling at the mob, "He needs to get to campus on time! He will be late for the exam!" Yet, in spite of all the shouting and pleading, the trio could only take a few steps forward before being blocked again.

As the number of reporters multiplied, the fear that Ahrash would miss the exam intensified. The thought of that calamity made Dawood's anger swell, compelling him to use his fists on the reporters. The reporters, in response, returned punches.

A fight amongst the throng started quickly and did not stop until the officer removed his firearm from his belt and shot it in the air. The sound of gunfire sent a few policemen into the alley. They acted quickly,

DEATH ROW BOY

beating the reporters into submissions with their clubs while threatening arrest.

Once the menacing crowd dispersed, the policemen escorted Ahrash and his company all the way to the university. They entered the campus just in the nick of time.

---آرش---

What had transpired in the past twenty-four hours to draw all those reporters toward Ahrash was a well-thought-out plan, one the boy could not have possibly imagined.

Failing time after time to bring the law on his young prisoner's side, Warden Ramzi finally decided on a bold move. Three months prior to the Concours, he had contacted the Editor-in-Chief of the capital's most prominent news agency, the Jahan Daily News. *He shared Ahrash's saga, in detail, with the editor and pleaded for help.*

The editor promised to bring the story out when it would be the most effective.

The two men had met several times. Working with a group of writers, they had crafted an article, explaining Ahrash's agonizing journey.

The newspaper also recorded an interview with the warden in which he spoke of Ahrash with particular regard, admiring his intelligence, moral values, and his immeasurable devotion to his family. Throughout the interview, in addition to praising Ahrash's character, Ramzi strived to deliver two crucial facts to the public: Ahrash had been a child when he had committed his crime and, moreover, he had done it to save his father's life.

When the first day of the Concours was over, the *Jahan* Daily News had run both the article and Ramzi's interview in their paper, sending them out early the next day. A large photo of Ahrash taken during the exam held center stage on the front page, while another smaller photo of him was placed in the left lower corner. In that picture, Ahrash was a boy of thirteen, entering prison in his oversized orange jumpsuit. The caption read: "Death Row Boy – From Prison to The Concours."

Within a few hours, Ahrash's story exploded like a bomb, totally shocking all its readers. It also caused competition among news outlets, sending their reporters into a frenzy.

The media's aggressive behavior continued to escalate, reaching uncontrollable heights for the remaining testing period. Every day, Ahrash had to be ushered in by a bevy of officers in order to make it safely to the exam hall.

CHAPTER 66

After the powerful exposé by the *Jahan* Daily News, Ahrash's story quickly appeared in other prominent national papers. Radio and television started to report as well, using youth crime as the underlying topic of debate and discussion.

The enormity of the news, as it was expected, shook the public at once. Condemning a child to death, locking him up for years, was so bizarre and hideous that it seemed to be more like fiction rather than a real story. Yet the evidence was indisputable – the pictures of the boy in his cell and the interview with the warden were folded in the pages of almost every magazine and newspaper.

The nation was heartbroken. Across the country, complete strangers to the Bedel family lit candles in mosques, praying for Ahrash's freedom. Some brave citizens reached out to the authorities, demanding that Judge Kasra recant his decision; a few even picketed outside the courthouse, carrying mounted pictures of Ahrash.

One particularly courageous editor wrote:

Discussions on Death Row Boy have become impassioned debates among scholars. While many I have interviewed find it to be a decline of morality to sentence a child to death, hardcore lawmen in robes disagree. They argue that Islamic rule, Sharia law, is always just and must be followed without exception.

The support of the Iranian citizens for Ahrash in that chaotic revolutionary era was truly admirable. Everyone championing for the boy's release well knew that they could easily be labeled a defector of the system, landing themselves in jail or worse.

——— آرش ———

It was on a Tabriz radio station that Neloo first heard the discourse on Ahrash. Initially, she thought the panel was having a general exchange of views on juvenile crime and punishment. But soon she was convinced that the focus of the program was Ahrash. Her Ahrash.

No one was home at that particular moment. The twins were playing in the yard and Sakineh was out, probably at her sister's. Nevertheless, Neloo was nervous. Not knowing when Sakineh might return home, she lowered the radio's volume and neared her head to its speaker. She listened raptly, her heart palpating with every mention of Ahrash's name.

Halfway through the program, it suddenly occurred to her that Ahrash's family should hear the broadcast as well. She called the twins in and asked them to rush to the Bedel house. "Tell Aziz to turn on the radio right away. Say it is very important," she told the boys and quickly closed the door to avoid their usual endless stream of questions.

Over the next few days, Neloo was able to collect several magazines that had articles about Ahrash. This victory happened with the help of Jafar, the village gendarme.

In the summer, Jafar periodically gave rides to a few enthusiastic kids who wanted to go to the public library in town. He dropped the children off at the library in the morning and picked them up when he was done with his duties at the station.

Neloo now decided to get a ride to the library alongside those kids. She was well aware that getting permission from Sakineh would not be easy. But she was determined to go even if it required her father's interference.

Her efforts paid off in a big way. At the library, she was able to find a few magazines with articles about Ahrash. She read them, one by one, as time allowed, copying the name and the issue numbers of the remaining unread papers. Later, when Jafar returned to pick up the group, she asked him to stop at a magazine shop before going back to the village.

At home, Neloo lodged the magazines between her book piles in the corner of the room, reaching for them whenever she was home alone. She read the articles, multiple times, cherishing every piece of information. What solaced her the most however, was seeing the photos.

In the past, she had often tried to conjure up an image of Ahrash all grown up, but each time, only his boyish face would flash in her mind. Now she knew how the boy in her heart looked as a young man.

آرش

One morning, the magazines were strewn about, when Neloo suddenly heard Sakineh. She was returning home unexpectedly, humming a tune in the yard. Fearful, Neloo shoved the magazines under her textbooks and ran to the kitchen just before Sakineh entered the house.

"What have you done girl? You look like the cat who just stole our dinner," Sakineh remarked with suspicion. She then hastily dumped a sack of walnuts on the kitchen floor, "I need half of the nuts shelled by tomorrow."

Neloo nodded in acquiescence but, Sakineh had already left the kitchen without looking at her.

After that close call, Neloo was constantly worried: *It would be a disaster if Sakineh discovered the magazines. I must discard them all.* But how could she part with the photos? She had only just found them.

In the end, the logical girl cut out one small picture of Ahrash and saved it in a book. She concealed the rest of her treasures in a bag and asked Shereen to deliver them to Aziz.

CHAPTER 67

For decades, Mohammad Reza Pahlavi, the Shah of Iran, had allocated a large budget for military advancement. He had purchased the most modern defense weaponries from Europe and America and had sent his officers abroad for education and training. By the year 1979, and before the Islamic revolution had begun, Iran was a military powerhouse and a reliable guardian of peace in the region.

Unfortunately, the new leader who replaced the fleeing monarch dissolved the Shah's strong military in no time.

A year later, Saddam Hossein, then the ruler of Iraq, made a sudden decision to attack Iran's southern border. He speculated that the revolutionary chaos and massive purge of generals had rendered his neighbor grossly unprepared for war.

Unforeseen by Saddam, his neighbor put up a great fight against his invasion. With most of the population still fanatically supporting the Islamic governance, Iranian soldiers and volunteer fighters were sent on suicide missions. Using 'human wave' attacks, they defeated their enemy in battle after battle. As a result, within only a few months, the war had shifted decisively in the favor of Iran. The Iraqi military had sustained a series of defeats and had been driven out of the occupied lands.

As Saddam's army was falling apart, Iran seized the upper hand, invading Iraq to depose its government. Emboldened by this move, the West now had an excuse to support Saddam: If Iran's army wasn't stopped, it might slice through Iraq to the oilfields of Kuwait and Saudi Arabia.

Therefore, the bloody war continued, lasting another eight years and costing 1.5 million more lives.

Throughout the long war, the edge constantly oscillated between the two neighbors: Iraq by receiving support from the world's superpowers – Iran by turning its youth into expendables.

After years of fierce battles between the two countries, a new and even uglier phase of the war began. Saddam, a heinous leader, ordered the use of lethal nerve agents against Iranian troops, while both the US and UN turned a blind eye to this atrocity.

With the massacre of Iranian fighters by poison, much younger groups of soldiers were now being called in.

Parents panicked. Many moved to different proveniences to hide their younger boys from the authorities. Numerous families even decided to smuggle their children to other countries via the mountainous Afghani border. Some succeeded, while many more were conned by human traffickers and other criminals.

Every day the news of different sorts of crimes on children were printed in the paper, continuously adding to misery of Iranians. A top government official even went so far as to advise, "Your children are better off dying with honor for their country than being raped or mutilated by a stranger in the mountains."

———— آرش ————

The demise of Iranian troops with deadly chemicals along with the draft of much younger soldiers, quickly dampened Ahrash's well received story.

Undeterred by the situation, Ramzi solemnly tried to bring the boy's name back to the media's forefront. His requests unfortunately were declined by all the agencies.

"As long as families are struggling to save their own children, they cannot cradle someone else's child," the *Jahan* chief editor argued. "We need to wait for another window of opportunity to be effective."

If the media, the last frontier of hope, had deserted Ahrash, who would save him now?

CHAPTER 68

"In this night of awful darkness
Who can say in what state we will be
when dawn breaks?
Will the morning light make
the frightening face of the storm disappear?"*

It was a terrifying time. The court would convene within two months to finalize Ahrash's fate and nothing seemed to be going in his favor.

Neloo was in a desperate state, crying privately. Aziz and Khalil, incapable of going through their daily routines, stayed mainly at the mosque, praying for a miracle. Even the unshakable Issa was crumbling. He spent hours alone in the meadow; his *ney's* sad tunes piercing the souls of humans and animals alike.

Hope had left hearts, sheer terror setting in harder than mortar.

———————— آرش ————————

Then, a miracle occurred.

The results of the Concours came out. Ahrash had earned an almost perfect score ranking twenty-seventh among one and a half million participants.

The news of his achievement exploded with an unbelievable power. Performing at such a high level on the Concours for a self-taught child was an absolute phenomenon. The fact that this village boy had been residing on death row for years made the news even more sensational, capturing the nation's attention to its fullest.

---

from Nima Yooshij's "It is Night"

Ramzi was energized. Knowing how little time they had, he took two weeks off from his official duties to attend numerous television and radio programs. He was hopeful, believing the public outcry would eventually seize the attention of someone in power, a conscious lawman in a black robe or a well-respected clergyman wearing a white turban.

Contrary to what the media outlets had assumed, the mourning parents, even the ones who had lost their sons to the recent battles, became true advocates for Ahrash. They sent letters to the heads of clergies and the Department of Justice, begging for mercy for the young man.

The country's scholars and highly regarded scientists also spoke up, asking for the reversal of Judge Kasra's decision or at least a new trial. They labeled Ahrash a prodigy and his execution a waste of a brilliant mind.

———————— آرش ————————

Ahrash's story was so widely spread this time that it could no longer be hidden from Sakineh. The photo of her son's murderer was now in every paper, his character and intelligence praised by the masses.

Seeing Ahrash's pictures and hearing his name around the village agitated Sakineh heavily, making her more and more irrational. Sadly, and per usual, Neloo stood at the receiving end of her lunacy.

Sakineh extended her brand of crazy to strangers as well. The first and last news crews to visit Ahrash's village for interviews, encountered a mad woman who ran after them, throwing rocks and cursing.

———————— آرش ————————

As judgment day approached, the controversial debates on the radio and television heated up exponentially.

Ramzi was invited on to the nation's most viewed television program to discuss Ahrash's sentencing. He was on a panel alongside a distinguished clergyman and two prominent judges. During the program, the clergyman suggested offering Mahmood's parents substantial blood money. Ramzi commended the idea and mentioned that Hajji, a philanthropic man in the village, had already started a fund for Ahrash and that many village families had participated to the extent possible, and some beyond their financial abilities.

The television program was still on the air when people started calling to donate money.

Within a day, an account had been established with Ramzi and Hajji as its trusted keepers. Donations big and small, arrived from every corner of the country, reaching over 2 million *toman** in less than a week.

Ramzi appeared again on the same program to express his gratitude to the kind donors. He announced that the entirety of the money collected to date would be offered to Mahmood's parents and that any incoming donations would go toward Ahrash's education.

*"Will the morning light make
the frightening face of the storm disappear?"*

Iranian monetary unit

CHAPTER 69

She sat upright in the wooden chair, her intimidating presence unnerving the three men. Fully aware of her supremacy, she looked beyond them as though they were of no significance. It was no secret to her why they had all gathered in her yard that evening. The men had only one mission. They wanted to buy Ahrash's freedom with her son's blood money.

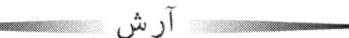

آرش

For days, Sharif had tried desperately to persuade his wife to accept the collected donations. He had even arranged a day trip to Tabriz, her favorite city.

They first visited Sakineh's cousin who had recently given birth to her eighth child. Sakineh was delighted to reminisce and catch up. She had not seen her cousin since she was a mother of only three kids.

They headed to the Bazaar next, the city's biggest shopping center. Sharif had never liked shopping, but this time, he patiently accompanied his wife, trailing behind her like a dutiful child.

Sakineh purchased a complete set of silverware from one vendor and a fancy tablecloth from another. "These are for Neloo's dowry," she said sweetly, winking at her husband. Sharif smiled. He knew Sakineh had been preparing for their daughter's wedding ever since Neloo had turned fifteen.

From the Bazaar they went directly to Shah Goli, a beautiful public garden full of entertainment and activities. The couple had been there only once before. They were newlyweds at that time; Sakineh had been three months pregnant with Mahmood.

They walked leisurely in the garden for a while, allowing its serenity to calm their nerves. As the sun started to set, the husband and wife took a boat ride on a small manmade lake to reach a cozy restaurant tucked away on the other side.

Waiting for their dinner of lamb kabobs and saffron rice to arrive, Sharif repeated his mantra that had been the theme of the day. "Be smart, Sakineh. This money is substantial. It can improve our lives drastically. Think about the twins' education, Neloo's dowry, a bigger house, or maybe even my early retirement." Sharif went on and on, trying to convince Sakineh to set Ahrash free and accept the donated money.

Sakineh was mostly quiet. Perhaps, she did not want to spoil the good time or maybe she was truly mulling over the idea.

Two days after their trip, Sakineh agreed to see Khalil and Hajji.

———————— آرش ————————

Khalil had his head down, trying to conceal his rising distress. He was in his work clothes and had probably come straight from the fields. Next to him, Hajji was sitting with a metal box on his lap. The village elder looked uneasy as well, constantly tapping the box with his fingers.

Sitting opposite her guests with her husband by her side, Sakineh appeared calm and in total control.

The sun was starting to set, but there would be at least another two hours of light. The earlier wind in the afternoon was stronger now, pushing cooler air in from the south. Birds, big in numbers, were still scattered about the yard. Their dramatic singing overpowering the soft melody of rustling leaves.

Sharif had watered the area right before his guests' arrival, bringing about an earthy smell, pure and pleasant.

In another world, another time, it could have been a lovely summer evening at the end of a long, hot day.

Neloo arrived carrying a small tray. She said hello and offered tea and *klucheh* to everyone. She then chose to sit on a flat rock close by. Sakineh flashed her an angry look but, the girl remained rooted in place, defiant.

Unlike her mother, she acknowledged their guests, looking at them with a friendly smile.

The three men around the table, all appeared anguished but, it was Khalil's condition that worried Neloo the most. He had aged beyond recognition. The wrinkles on his face were so deeply etched, it was as if all the liquid had been sucked out of his tissues.

Neloo wished she could embrace and comfort the broken man.

A group of noisy sparrows landed in the cherry tree near the group. As Neloo followed their movement, a single pair of cherries, tucked away on a high limb caught her eye. They were the only fruit on the tree, left there untouched by the birds. "Why isn't any bird going after them?" she thought, remembering a discussion she once had with Issa over destiny and fortuity. She eyed the cherries for a while, wondering if it was fate or will that had granted the pair's survival.

After draining the last of his tea, Hajji transferred the box from his lap to the table. He raised his eyes to the domineering woman next to him and spoke plainly. "We know that no amount of money can ease your pain, cousin Sakineh. Still, I urge you to accept this offer from the humbled Khalil," he said, sliding the box forward. "Two million *toman*, as well as some jewelry."

Sakineh opened the box, reluctantly. She glanced at the money and the jewelry inside and immediately pushed the box back to Hajji. "I cannot accept any of this."

Sharif jumped out of his seat so frantically, as though he had been charged with a thousand volts of electricity, "What the hell are you talking about Sakineh?" he shouted.

There was no response from Sakineh.

Fuming with anger, Sharif turned to his guests, "I do not understand what game my wife is trying to play. As God is my witness, we had come to an agreement!"

Hajji spoke again. "Listen, cousin, I forgot to mention that Khalil is offering his house in addition to the collected money. He will sell his field and once Ahrash is back, his entire family will leave the village for good."

"This is all true. Khalil is just asking for permission to stay here one week longer. He wants to sacrifice a lamb and distribute the meat among the villagers," Sharif added to Hajji's sentences but suddenly stiffened, recognizing he had just revealed his secret contact with Khalil.

Sakineh shot an angry glance toward her husband and firmly reiterated, "Still, I cannot accept."

"What is wrong with you, Sakineh? Didn't you agree to this after we came back from Shah Goli?" Sharif bellowed.

Loosening her scarf a notch, Sakineh rose and faced her husband, "You stupid man. Can't you see how much your daughter is still in love with Ahrash? They have been writing to each other all these years. She even sleeps with his picture under her pillow!" she said and before Sharif had a chance to digest her words, struck him at his chest with both fists. "Weak, pitiful excuse for a man! You would not even care if Mahmood's murderer married our daughter!" she shrieked, attempting to hit her husband again.

This time, Sharif swiftly intercepted the blow by grabbing both of her wrists.

Sakineh, unable to free her hands, started to kick and bite.

Hajji moved in to separate the husband and wife. "You both need to simmer down and say a *salavaat**!" he said. However, the brawl was only escalating and he could not pacify either party.

**a salutation upon Muhammad, the prophet of Islam, sometimes used to calm oneself*

Khalil remained quiet. His face was very pale, almost white. It was as if a vital artery had been slashed internally, depleting his body of blood.

A large raven dove toward the noisy sparrows, sending them away from the cherry tree. He sat on the high branch and started picking at the lone pair of the surviving cherries.

Neloo sighed at the scene, realizing that no will, however strong, would ever overpower destiny.

She rose to her feet and slowly walked toward Sakineh, murmuring to herself to be strong. As she moved, her hair danced with the wind and her loose skirt flew up from the ground. The beautiful Neloo resembled an angel who was on a self-sacrificing mission.

Stopping a few feet short of Sakineh, she drew in a big breath and summoned her courage, "If you let Ahrash live, I will marry any suitor you choose."

"And you expect me to believe you, darling girl? What guarantee do I have that you won't change your mind?" Sakineh spoke without concealing her anger. "Answer me Neloo! What guarantee do I have?"

A shrewd monster was at play and Neloo's nerves were too overwrought to think of a response. She looked at her father and Hajji for help but neither man had an answer.

Everyone became quiet at once, even the chatty birds.

"Think Neloo. Think hard. You must save Ahrash," Neloo commanded herself, her palms over her temples, holding her head like a vice.

Within seconds, she was standing right in front of Sakineh, looking directly into her eyes with a confidence unknown to herself. "I will get engaged now and will get married once Ahrash is released. Hajji, Khalil and my father are all my witnesses," she said, her voice solid and imposing.

Content with the results of her ploy, Sakineh couldn't suppress a triumphant smile.

"Ok then. I will tell Fareed's family that we can hold the engagement celebration this week."

CHAPTER 70

Under the blistering midday sun, Sharif and Sakineh meticulously washed and scrubbed Mahmood's tombstone until it appeared as shiny as its first day. They then sat down by the clean grave, each murmuring a prayer.

"Mahmood would have been 25 years old today, probably married with children," Sakineh sighed woefully.

Sharif scooted closer and tenderly guided her head to his chest, his towering torso shielding her from the sun. Clearly, the gracious man had forgiven his wife's latest outburst, even though this time she had completely humiliated him in front of their guests.

"Mahmood's death is the worst tragedy of our lives. Yet, we must stay strong for the sake of Neloo and the twins. If I could, I would have given my life to change his fate even if..." Sharif could not complete his sentence. Fraught with sadness, he sat there quietly, holding the weeping Sakineh tighter in his arms.

The cemetery was unusually quiet that day. No burial was in progress and no one was visiting. There was not even a single bird in the sky or creatures scurrying about. In the eerie landscape of the vast graveyard, there was only the statuesque entanglement of Sharif and Sakineh.

After a long period of crying, the grieving parents started walking down memory lane, reminiscing about Mahmood – the day he was born, his mischievous childhood, his teenage rebellions and his undeniable charm when the mood was right. Some stories made them cry, others made them laugh. They sought comfort in revisiting the life of their firstborn son. It was a healing moment, one of unity and of acceptance, a time for a connection that had been years overdue.

The door to the morgue on the east side of the cemetery opened. Two men carrying a body on a stretcher marched out. Trailing behind them were a few obscure figures.

Sakineh got up quickly. She tented a hand over her eyes and started looking in the direction of the incoming group. "Is that Ali's family?" she asked, rather bewildered. "Did his mother die?"

"Ali's mom passed away at dawn today. I did not want to share the news with you on Mahmood's birthday," Sharif responded in a downcast voice. "We should go and pay our respects."

Sakineh shook her head, "You go, Sharif. I want to stay with my son a little longer."

آرش

The caravan of Ali's family finally reached the designated site. Ali and the cemetery worker put the body down on the ground next to a dug grave where his sisters and uncle were standing.

Shereen and Hannah were crying quietly.

As Sharif hastily weaved through the graves toward the mourning family, he saw Neloo and the twins approaching them from a different direction. Neloo had a black dress on. The boys were in clean and tidy outfits, their hair neatly combed back from their faces.

The siblings reached the burial site about the same time as their father.

The boys immediately rushed to Sharif, seeking his attention.

Ali and his uncle, a middle-aged, diminutive man, lowered the wrapped body into the hole and started to cover it with dirt. Sharif allowed Ali to toss in only a couple scoops of dirt before edging toward him and reaching for the shovel. Holding Hannah's hand, Ali then stood by his sisters, as their mother's tiny body slowly disappeared in the ground.

CHAPTER 71

For years, Ahrash had endeavored to travel a tough academic terrain. No one was alongside him – no teacher, no guide – it had been only him and a steeply rising road. Yet, despite the difficulties, his studying turned out to be a blessing and, at times, the sole means for his survival. Once the big exam was over however, Ahrash had become numb, hollow inside. He could not sleep at night and his previously meager appetite diminished to a dangerous level. Without another goal to keep him buoyant in life, he just floundered about in his cell, not knowing how to pass his time.

———— آرش ————

"Sakineh has finally accepted the money, son," the electrified Khalil gave the news to Ahrash. "She and Sharif will meet with the judge on September sixth to sign your release. We can pick you up as early as noon on the same day."

Ahrash could not remember seeing his father so happy before. His old man was so excited that he could not remain in his seat during their visit.

Khalil talked excessively, explaining in detail, the pilgrimage trip he and Aziz had planned, the leasing of their field, and the offers they had received for their livestock. He covered every piece of village news, every little change regarding anything and anyone with one exception – he didn't reveal the sacrifice Neloo had had to make.

———— آرش ————

The cat was combatting a large black spider who had taken up residence in a corner created by two walls. Ahrash did not stop her but chose to avoid watching the struggle of the creature to stay alive.

Dawood entered the yard with a fancy pet carrier in hand. He cheerfully walked to Ahrash and placed the crate before him. "What do you think of this, my pal?"

"Wow, I can't believe you have already made it," Ahrash responded, totally amazed with Dawood's commitment.

To travel home together, Ahrash needed a carrier for his cat. Dawood had promised to make it for him if he could be provided with a design.

After receiving the sketch, the day before, Dawood bought the materials on the way home. He ate his dinner in a rush and started working on the project right away. The design was rather involved and with the limited tools that he owned; it took him several hours to finish. It was well past midnight, by the time Dawood was able to join his nine-month pregnant wife in bed.

"It looks great. Let's introduce it to her," Ahrash removed the top of the carrier and put it next to his cat. The cat circled the container a couple of times and nudged its corners with her nose. She then leapt in, cozying herself atop the floppy, soft mat which was tucked inside.

"She has six days to get used to it."

"I think she already loves it. Thank you, Dawood. You are a good friend."

By protocol, Dawood should have been back on the row by now. But he decided to sit next to Ahrash for a while and talk. "The warden told me to get boxes for your books and other belongings. I have them all in my car. Do you want to start on it after lunch? If you finish packing today, the books can be shipped tomorrow."

"Sounds good, Dawood."

"You must be very excited, going home. Aren't you?"

"I do not know. I suppose I should be. It is hard to believe that it is actually happening."

"Nothing is above freedom," Dawood said, stretching his hand toward Ahrash, offering him a piece of paper. "I have written my address and telephone number here. You must come and have dinner at my house whenever you are in town."

Ahrash took the paper. "I will visit, I promise," he said and threaded his hands between his bony knees, giving way to the silence.

A few minutes of quiet appeared too long for Dawood. "What are you thinking about?" he asked.

"About the dream I had last night."

"What was it about?"

"Never mind, it was disturbing."

"I have to know. You must tell me."

"Well, I was dead and wrapped in a shroud. But I kept screaming from inside the ditch asking my brother to put me in a box."

"What do you mean, a box? Like a coffin?"

"Yes. I want to be buried in a coffin."

"Muslim do not do that."

"I know. I had a lengthy discussion about this with my brother when I was thirteen. I made him promise to bury me in a coffin when I die."

"You are a weird guy, man," Dawood patted Ahrash on the back. "We better get going now, you have books to pack."

CHAPTER 72

Once Sakineh agreed to release Ahrash, Khalil set in motion the plans he had been quietly contemplating for years.

The affairs were settled smoothly and in sequence: their field had been leased for five years, their Persian rugs had been sold along with all the animals except Jolfa, and most of the family's belongings had been sent to the city of Tabriz, secure at his sister's house.

With the purchase of a sacrificial ram, the family was now perfectly ready for Ahrash's return.

آرش

Two fabric bags had been sitting by the door since early morning. Aziz in a new outfit and a nice green scarf, had been ready to leave since dawn. She was restless, arranging and rearranging the bags' contents over and over.

Khalil was glued to the window, waiting for the taxi to appear. They were not scheduled to leave for some time, but they could not afford to miss their ride.

The husband and wife were leaving the village five days prior to the court date. They would go on a pilgrimage to the holy city of Qom before claiming their son at the capital.

A series of loud honks announced the taxi's arrival. Khalil picked up the bags. "We will be back next Wednesday around noon," he told Issa as he rushed out of the house. Aziz scurried after him only stopping to give her son a tight hug.

Half an hour later, the taxi dropped the anxious couple off safely at the bus station.

While Khalil stowed their belongings in the belly of the bus, Aziz got on board and selected a seat by the window. She leaned her head against the glass and calmly gazed out.

It was early September, but the aura of spring was all around. The sky was as blue as it could be with clusters of puffy white clouds. The lush green land that stretched from the road for acres, was dotted with sheep grazing calmly on its fat hills.

Aziz looked further on at Aladaglar, Tabriz's famous rainbow mountain. The mountain chain was painted with hues of copper, red, green, blue, and yellow – an amazing display of Mother Nature's artwork. She had been traveling on this very route for five years but, surprisingly, she had never noticed these colorful mountains until today.

"Ahrash should see all this beauty," Aziz made a mental note to remind her son on the way home.

Ever since the family decided to leave for Tabriz, there had been a rumbling in Aziz's heart. Starting anew in a foreign place was certainly challenging, yet she was happy to leave this sorrowful land. The Kultappa village, for her, was only a pit, a keeper of her shattered dreams. It was there that she had lost her baby girl and for a time, her sanity; it was there that they had stolen Ahrash from her.

"Maybe this move will bring happiness back to the family. Khalil is still young. He can easily find a job as a gardener or a fruit packer. We might even be able to buy a small house and send Issa to a school for the blind," Aziz thought and heaved a euphoric sigh. She continued her musings and soon found herself far into the future, surrounded by Khalil, her sons, their wives and many grandchildren. "The family must never be separated again," she resolved.

Khalil didn't quite share his wife's sentiments. His emotions were odd and unfamiliar to him. In spite of everything moving so positively for the family, he constantly felt as if a strong force was propelling him toward a sudden grief. The last time he had seen Ahrash, his son was too thin, resembling a walking skeleton. He appeared saddened, not even excited by the news of his freedom. "Is he embarrassed to be seen in the village," Khalil pondered and then abruptly thought of his boy's impending shock at the news of Neloo's engagement: *Ahrash will be devastated.*

He turned to Aziz to share his thoughts but found her asleep.

Aziz's head was resting on the window, her head scarf, down, bunched up at her neck. She had a faint smile on her face, perhaps the preamble to a joyful dream.

Khalil turned to his wife and gently pulled up her scarf. Suddenly, a warm feeling flooded over him, remembering the day, he had purchased that green scarf.

Before leaving for the fields, Khalil sat down by Aziz who was stretched out on her side with an enormous belly. He took her hand and tenderly placed it in his own.

Aziz opened her eyes and smiled. Her innocence and beauty melted her man's heart.

Khalil's mother joined them after her prayers and started talking in a hushed voice. "Don't go to the field right now. Wait until Issa wakes up," she told Khalil while covering young Issa with a blanket. "You have to keep your boy out of the house today."

A competent midwife, Khalil's mother had assisted in the delivery of dozens of babies in the Nonassa village. Seven years ago, she had delivered Issa in the same room and now she had returned to bring another grandchild into the world.

It was a beautiful day in late March, the ideal time to work in the field. Khalil, however, was too excited to be productive.

As noon approached, he decided to quit for the day and take Issa to a kabob house for lunch. The anticipation of having another child was so joyful that Khalil had completely forgotten his inherent shyness. He greeted total strangers at the diner, even having conversations with people he hardly knew.

After lunch, the father and son spent the afternoon at the market. Khalil bought a pair of warm socks for his mother and a new, nicer ney for Issa.

In one store, a delicate georgette scarf caught his eyes. It was a beautiful piece, a vivid green, Aziz's favorite color. The scarf was too expensive for their budget but, Khalil decided to purchase it anyway. He knew it would make his wife happy.

When Khalil and Issa arrived home, Aziz was sitting on the rug, leaning on a large pillow against the wall. In her arms, a beautiful baby was nursing.

"God has given you a healthy boy, son," Khalil's mother gave him the happy news.

———————— آرش ————————

Khalil was pleasantly lost in his memories when the bus arrived at their stop. He reluctantly put his thoughts on hold, woke Aziz up, and started gathering their belongings.

Hopeful and excited, the couple left the bus, and continued on to the next leg of their journey.

CHAPTER 73

The sun had been up for hours, beating at the room's single window with its long, scorching arms.

Awake for a while, Issa had chosen to remain in bed. He could hear the neighborhood kids playing soccer outside and knew it had to be past eight. The boys never started their games any earlier.

At midmorning, the heat finally forced Issa to get out of bed. He turned on a fan at the corner of the room and sat in front of the blades, contemplating how to start his day. Perhaps he could eat breakfast or play his *ney*, but he had no appetite for either. Without any duties to fulfill or someone to talk to, Issa was totally adrift, an aimless blind man – another version of Koor Akbar.

A sudden uproar rose outside among the soccer players. The boys were apparently having a row about a goal. Sparked by the noise, a few dogs in the area started to bark. Their protests reminded Issa that he needed to let Jolfa out of the sheep house. He hastily put on his shoes and left the house, wearing only his pajama bottoms.

As soon as he set foot outside, a strong metallic smell struck his nose. The ram!" he cried and immediately reached for the rope that had secured the animal to the house. He jerked the line and felt full resistance. Tracing the rope, he moved forward; the smell of blood intensified until his foot butted up against a stationary, solid mass.

"The ram is dead," Issa murmured.

He leaned over the animal and ran his hand around its neck. There was no wound or laceration at the throat and the body was warm to the touch. Checking the underbelly, he found it intact as well. The situation was puzzling.

Hair bouncing around his shoulders, chest smeared with blood, Issa took off. Moments later, he appeared before the soccer team, resembling an injured caveman.

The panicked boys scrambled to safety; the twins called out for their sister.

Neloo intercepted Issa at the halfway point between their houses and briskly walked back with him to the trouble zone.

———— آرش ————

"He has lost a lot of blood, but he is still alive," Neloo told Issa after a quick inspection of the sheep. She then turned to the twins who had been shadowing them the entire time. "Go get Hakim, boys. Go quickly!" she instructed.

The ram had a big gouge at the side of his head near his left eye. The cut was deep and still bleeding.

Neloo wrapped the wound with a clean towel that Issa had fetched from inside the house. "Keep pressure on it until Hakim arrives," she told Issa, guiding his hand to the source. "I will look around, maybe figure out what happened."

Her initial search did not reveal any signs of foul play. No footprints of any kind, human or animal, were in sight except for that of the ram itself. The dirt in the area was also undisturbed, indicating that there had not been a struggle with a wild assailant.

She followed the bloody trail from the injured animal back to the porch, carefully looking for clues. Once she got close to the house, she believed that she had found the answer. A wide section of metal siding on one wall was separated at the joint, curving upward, its sharp edge covered with dried blood.

Ali arrived, breathless, carrying a small medical bag. "Hakim is behind me. He will be here soon," he said, while checking on the sheep.

Over the last two years, Ali had been receiving training from Hakim. Even though he was still employed by Hajji, he had permission to go along with his mentor to visit sick villagers or their sick animals. Hakim had found the young man exceptionally talented in the field and started lending him his medical books to study. Soon, Ali became a reliable assistant to Hakim, working diligently towards a paramedic license.

By the time Hakim arrived, Ali already had a serum running through the animal's veins and had begun sewing the laceration. The master watched his young apprentice at work with keen eyes, constantly nodding his head in approval.

Neloo started washing the blood from the ram's face. As she and Ali both tended to their patient, their eyes locked. The moment was short and not repeated but was long enough to show how much love and admiration still existed in Ali's heart for her.

"Congratulations on your engagement," Ali said and quickly steered his eyes away.

"Thank you, Ali."

Neloo's face felt so hot, as if her cheeks were on fire.

The three men moved the ram cautiously into the shade of the bench. Ali asked for a shovel and started covering the blood on the ground with dirt.

When Neloo told Hakim about the bloody metal siding, the experienced man agreed with her theory. He had seen many adolescent rams injure themselves, sometimes in an attempt to fight their own reflection in glass or other shiny surfaces.

Their job completed, the medics started to pack their bags. Hakim handed another serum bag to Neloo. "Use it after the first one is empty. We will check on him again this afternoon. By then, he should be up and walking."

"You need to clean the blood off of yourself," Neloo advised Issa after Ali and Hakim had left.

"I can wash up in the creek, I suppose, but it might take a while."

"It is alright. I'll stay here until you return. I have nothing to do except to watch over the twins," Neloo stood up, looking in the direction of the soccer players. "And I can see them perfectly from here."

———————— آرش ————————

Issa's absence was indeed long, but Neloo did not mind. First, she let Jolfa out of the barn. She felt badly that the poor dog had been trapped inside the sheep pen and likely fretting about all the commotion around the main house.

After giving Jolfa plenty of attention, she then decided to check the house to make sure traces of blood hadn't made their way in with Issa.

The moment Neloo entered the house, she was bombarded with childhood memories. They were all from the happy times, yet they made her sad and emotional. "I should hurry up. I can't stay in here too long," she murmured, noticing her growing sadness. "I'll just follow the path Issa would have taken to get the towel."

The house was, as always, tidy and clean. Nowhere and nothing was soiled with blood either.

Relieved, Neloo was ready to leave when her eyes landed on stacks of books belonging to Ahrash. The books had been undisturbed in his study corner for all those years.

The scene ripped at her heart. She stood there for a while, sobbing quietly.

When Neloo returned to the yard, the ram was shivering. She rushed back inside and fetched a blanket to cover the convalescent animal.

Sometime later, Issa returned from the creek. He looked clean and tidy with his hair gathered at the nape of his neck by a rubber band.

"You have the longest hair of any man I have ever seen. Are you going to keep it that way?" Neloo asked.

"Of course not. I am waiting for Ahrash to cut it himself," Issa smiled and quickly changed the conversation. "How is our ram doing? Any improvement in his condition?"

"Well, he opened his eyes a couple of times and then started shaking. I covered him with a blanket and he seems to be ok now."

No other words were exchanged between Neloo and Issa for a while. The two friends sat next to each other on the bench, giving way to the silence. The ram, not too far from them, was at peace; his breaths rising and falling in steady, rhythmic waves.

"Do you know about what time they will arrive?" Neloo's voice finally filled the air.

"Around noon," Issa answered. "Only two more days left; the lost Joseph will be back to Canaan at last."

CHAPTER 74

Neloo looked stunning that morning. She had on a pale, yellow dress with tiny white flowers. Her hair was gathered loosely to one side, tumbling over her shoulder. A simple row of pearls, a gift from her future husband made her long, delicate neck even more graceful.

She pinned a fresh cut lily above her ear and threw a thin scarf over her hair. The white flower against her glossy brown hair looked exquisite, even though it was partially covered by the scarf.

Blessed with natural beauty, Neloo had never attempted to make herself more attractive. Today, however, she was a different girl, wanting to look feminine – pretty and desirable.

── آرش ──

The neighborhood boys were engaged in their midmorning soccer play. As Neloo approached, the game came to an abrupt halt, each child yielding to her. She was so pleasingly beautiful that even a pack of rowdy young boys could not ignore her presence.

"You look very pretty, Neloo. Where are you going so dressed up?" one of the twins asked.

"I am going to greet an old friend."

"Who? Ahrash? Is he really out of jail?"

"Yes. Ahrash is coming home today."

Issa was sitting under the shade of the boulder, playing his heart out with his wooden *ney*. The anticipation of his brother returning home had brought about the most infinite and deepest love, an overwhelming emotion that he could not fully identify. Maybe, only Rumi could describe his feelings with his line: "There is a void in my soul, ready to be filled."

Neloo crossed the village road and reached her blind friend minutes later. She quietly sat beside him on a small blanket and pulled the flared skirt of her dress over her knees.

Being there, in the heart of the village, without worrying about Sakineh's wrath, she felt wholly liberated for the first time in her life.

"How is the ram doing?" she asked Issa when he finished playing his song.

"He is as good as new. It is hard to believe he was fighting for his life less than forty eight hours ago."

"He is a tough fellow. I hope you have tied his rope somewhere else, away from the house. That sharp siding looked very sinister."

"Actually, there was no need to move him to a new location. When Ali came to check on the ram yesterday, he offered to fix the siding. He even sprayed it with some frosty material to make it less shiny."

"So thoughtful of him. Ali has matured greatly in recent years."

"I agree. This poor man experienced a long, harsh descent after your brother's death. Now it is time for him to rise. As they say, the wound is the place where the light enters you.*"

Issa and Neloo continued their discussion a while longer until Ali's sisters arrived and sat by them. Soraya, Issa's cousin, joined them next with two little boys in her wake. She had brought a plate of *halva* with some thin bread, cut into small squares.

Issa played more songs.

As noon approached, the boulder's shadow rose above itself, diminishing the shade to a sliver. The group decided to move forward, congregating at the head of the village road for more shade and a better view. They were just settling down in their new spot when Hajji arrived with a big entourage.

A hand landed on Issa's shoulder and a forceful kiss on his cheek.

---

a quote from Rumi

"Your brother will be home at last!" Rahim shouted cheerfully, now sober, and as always, with good intention.

Hashem joined his cousin with two other young men, circling Issa under Jolfa's suspicious watch. "We should all celebrate tonight at The Kabob House. You must come and bring Ahrash with you," Rahim suggested.

"I love the idea, but we should probably give Ahrash a couple of days to rest," Issa answered, genuine in his response.

At about 1pm, the baker and his helper arrived, pushing two big carts. He started passing out sweet breads and candies to the crowds that had been lined up on either side of the road. Having always had a great respect for the boy, the baker was beyond happy that Ahrash had survived his terrible ordeal.

A woman started playing a *daff*. Rahim jumped into the middle of the road and began to dance; Hashem and his friends immediately followed suit. The kids were the next to join, even the macho, preteen soccer players.

Neloo could not help noticing several women pointing at her. She did not mind that they were likely talking about her, nor did she resent them. The love story between her and Ahrash was not a secret in the village anymore. Everyone also knew she had recently become engaged to another man. The women's attention, however, brought back the questions she had avoided all morning, "Was her presence here unethical now that she had promised her heart to someone else?"

A car materialized in the distance. The dancers quickly exited the road while the daff player switched to a faster, more rhythmic beat. The pack started cheering. The children were running around, clapping; many of them did not even know why they were so happy.

At the first sighting of the car on the road, Neloo started shaking. Her legs, as if they belonged to a newborn foul, became too weak to hold her weight. She reached for Issa's arm, willing power back into her limbs.

A taxi stopped before the crowd. It had only one passenger.

Sakineh emerged from the vehicle. Her mourning outfit had been replaced with vibrantly colored clothes; her thin scarf barely covering half of her hair. Beaming with pride, she walked forward, head high with a large grin on her face. She appeared taller than usual.

Hajji rushed to her, "Where is Sharif, cousin Sakineh?"

"He preferred to stay with Khalil's family than to accompany his wife."

Her response was not what Hajji expected to hear, yet he chose not to pursue the matter. He kindly handed the box of money to Sakineh and stepped back.

After only a glance at the box, Sakineh moved her attention to the spectators, looking at them carefully, one by one.

The initial attention she had drawn upon her arrival was dissipating quickly. The crowd was mostly looking down the road in anticipation of another car to arrive. It was clear that the villagers were not there to embrace her but to celebrate Ahrash's return.

"What the hell are all you spineless cowards looking for? Are you waiting for my son's murderer to arrive?" Sakineh shouted, boring into all the faces with repugnance.

"Do you have no shame? Has any one of you ever lost a son? Mine died in my arms – my beautiful Mahmood, bled to death with his head on my lap." Sakineh let out a wretched sigh and started pacing back and forth in the limited space the masses had allowed her. When she spoke again, her voice had risen even louder. "Do you know how my son appears in my dreams? I never see him standing tall and proud, the way he was in life; I can only see him buried underground, rats chewing away at his body."

A hush fell over the crowd. Ill at ease, many stepped back, unaware that the woman's madness was still in its infancy.

Sakineh went on and on, blaming and swearing at everyone for being there.

All of a sudden, she spotted Neloo amidst the throng, a sinful, dazzling goddess standing next to a worthless blind man. She rushed to her, a seething hatred exuding from her eyes, a murderous hatred.

Before Neloo was able to step back, two fists struck her chest sending her to the ground.

"Look everyone! Look at my shameless girl, my little whore, all dressed up, waiting for Ahrash!" Sakineh bellowed, pointing at her quivering daughter. "You and the blind and all these fucking traitors can stay here as long as you want. Autumn will arrive and winter will follow, but Ahrash will never be back," she continued.

Smiling wickedly, she then moved closer to Neloo, ready to enter the dagger deeper into her heart. "He is gone, my dear daughter. Ahrash is dead. Do you understand? Ahrash is dead. I killed that bastard. I killed him myself."

CHAPTER 75

Three days earlier at the Capital

With no trees around, the sun was in total control of the vicinity. Sakineh and Sharif stood in the heat, somberly waiting for the courthouse to open. They were both deep in thought but, neither was willing to say a word or share a sentiment.

About a half an hour later, the massive door before them turned on its hinges and they were carried inside by a wave of rushing bodies.

The husband and wife pushed down a long corridor to the security desk and from there were guided to a small courtroom.

At exactly 8am, Judge Kasra arrived and walked straight to the podium. He seemed content, probably looking forward to closing the last chapter of this heavily convoluted case.

"Mrs. Mansoor," Kasra started right away, "I have been informed that you are willing to sign for Ahrash's release."

Sakineh did not say a word. She sat there in silence, seemingly oblivious to Kasra and his statement.

Finding villainy in his wife's behavior, Sharif nervously spoke in her place. "Yes, your honor, we have decided to forgive Ahrash."

"Alright then. All we need is a signature now," the judge said, holding a piece of paper in the air.

One of the guards standing by the door rushed to retrieve the paper. He planted the form and a pen in front of Sakineh. "Here is where you should sign in," he said politely, pointing at a spot on the page with a stubby forefinger.

Sakineh read the entire page unhurriedly. She then placed the pen down, pushed the paper to the edge of the table. She sat back, not uttering a word.

Her strange action did not suit the irritable Kasra, "Do you have any questions, Mrs. Mansoor?" he asked rather crossly.

"This is the wrong form, your honor. I will sign the one agreeing to an execution, not a release," Sakineh answered in a clear voice.

Sharif jumped out of his seat. He had predicted a storm, a deluge, and was now drowning in fear.

"Your honor, my wife and I had already agreed on releasing Ahrash," he said, eyeing Sakineh with trepidation. "We have been on the road for two straight days; my wife must be tired and confused."

"Are you in agreement with your husband's statement, Mrs. Mansoor?"

"No. I have always wanted Ahrash dead. And I want permission to kill him myself."

"She is lying, your honor. I have several witnesses," Sharif interrupted Sakineh. "In fact, I no longer want my wife involved in this matter and would like to have permission to handle the situation myself."

"Go ahead, Mr. Mansoor. Tell the court your decision – loud and clear."

"I, Sharif Mansoor, the father of Mahmood Mansoor, request the release of Ahrash Bedel, who caused my son's death five years ago."

"Very well, Mr. Mansoor. The court requires your signature now," Kasra sent another sheet out.

Sharif signed the form hurriedly and sent it back to the judge, all along avoiding any eye contact with his wife.

Adding the release form to the folder, Judge Kasra started wrapping up. Something in the file however, stopped him in his tracks. Head buried in the binder, he read for a couple of minutes, his brow shooting higher and higher as he moved on.

"Mr. Mansoor," he finally spoke. "It has been recorded here that you have forfeited all your rights in this case, assigning your wife as the sole responsible party."

"That is true, your honor, but I am recanting my previous decision now."

"You had the opportunity to remove your wife from her duties before this court proceeding. Didn't you receive the information in the mail? It was sent out to you a couple of months ago," Kasra explained with his eyes still on the folder. "At this point, your wife is the only person who can decide on the punishment for your son's murderer."

"What letter? I never received one," Sharif protested angrily, the veins in his neck bulging out, ready to burst. He turned to Sakineh, staring at her with an intense disgust. "You! You destroyed the letter. You wicked traitor," he shouted, lunging at his wife, shaking her violently. "You were never going to release the boy!"

The guards rushed to him, trying to remove his hands from Sakineh, which were now around her neck and squeezing.

"I will not allow you to kill that child. I would rather both of us be dead. Do you understand?" He continued pressing on Sakineh's throat while kicking at and fighting the guards.

Eventually, Sharif was subdued.

"Take this man out of my courtroom immediately," Judge Kasra ordered with finality.

آرش

Endeavoring to get a grip on what had happened in the courtroom, Sharif remained in the corner of the hall where the guards had left him. He was in shock, helpless and defeated. "What will happen now?" he said aloud, unable to push away the grisliest of thoughts.

It was only a week ago that Khalil and Aziz had surprised Sharif in the field.

They had a wedding gift for Neloo, a gold bracelet that has been in

Aziz's family for generations. "Neloo is like a true daughter to me," Aziz expressed her feelings openly. "I would love for her to carry on the tradition."

At the end of their visit, the men, the two old friends, embraced tightly. Khalil then kissed Sharif's hand, before he could be stopped. "Thank you for giving our son back to us," he said, tears running down his face.

"I have to stop Sakineh. I have to stop her," Sharif ran back like a whirlwind. "I must convince the judge that I have been deceived by my wife. I will tell him that my son was evil and that he himself, not Ahrash, was responsible for his death."

In a flash, the distraught Sharif was back into the courtroom, ready to bring his grievances to the judge. With his first step in, however, he was stopped and handcuffed by the guards.

"Remove him from the building!" Kasra roared, not giving the man a chance to speak.

The guards dragged Sharif outside. They freed his hands and pushed him away from the courthouse. Sharif lost his footing and landed painfully on the hard concrete.

──────────── آرش ────────────

"The authorities can get unnecessarily rough here," a gentleman said, reaching out for Sharif's hand.

Sharif rose to his feet, the grave anguish in his face screaming for help.

"You look stressed, my friend. May I be of any assistance to you?" the stranger asked.

Mumbling raw and random words, Sharif tried to tell his story.

He did not have to say much as the man and his family had been following Ahrash's saga for months, praying for the boy to be set free.

"You must contact the warden right away," the stranger told Sharif while leading him to the nearest telephone booth. They hurriedly searched the phonebook for Ramzi's number.

Minutes later, he dialed the warden's office and handed the phone to Sharif.

The phone rang a few times and a message followed: *Warden Ramzi will be out of the office from September 4th through the 8th...*

The words hammered at Sharif's heart. His face turned pale, his body covered in an icy sweat.

He felt so weak, as if his organs were all bleeding inside unable to support his existence much longer. When his speech also became somewhat unclear, the benevolent stranger offered to take him to a nearby hospital. Sharif refused to go, instead, he managed to ask if he could be helped to locate Ahrash's parents.

آرش

After sending Sharif out of his courtroom, Judge Kasra immediately regretted his decision, recognizing that the man could have been an asset in controlling his stubborn wife.

"What will happen to my career when the boy is put to death?" Kasra pondered. "If I am scrutinized over only a jail sentence, his execution would certainly create much more noise and trouble for me."

"Your husband was seriously upset by your decision, Mrs. Mansoor. Are you aware that you have to live with him when you go back home? Wouldn't your safety be compromised by Ahrash's execution?" he asked Sakineh.

"I will be fine, your honor. My husband has never had any power over me."

Despite his tendency to get irritated quickly, Kasra continued lecturing Sakineh, encouraging her to forgive Ahrash. He tried beyond his normal abilities, using various avenues of logic and reasoning, even threatening to charge her with destroying court documentation.

Sakineh remained incorrigible.

"I can arrange another meeting for tomorrow. You had better sleep on your decision, Mrs. Mansoor," Kasra said knowing it would be his last attempt at challenging the headstrong and willful woman.

"Nothing can change my mind, your honor, no amount of time, money or convincing, Sakineh declared. "I am a scorned mother, unable to stop my grief until I put a noose around my son's murderer's neck."

Kasra sent out the form for Sakineh's signature without saying another word.

On death row

Dawood was chatting with a new inmate when the two guards from the hanging room entered death row. He knew the pair well and was surprised to see them in the hall at this time of day. Suspicious about the men in his domain, he kept his eyes on them, watching their movement closely.

The guards stopped at Ahrash's cell.

Dawood took off running toward them.

"Where are you taking my prisoner?" he confronted the guards who already had Ahrash out of his cell.

"The victim's mother has requested immediate execution. She carried out the court order herself."

"There must be a mistake. This prisoner was supposed to be released before noon, not executed. Where is the warden's signature?" Dawood demanded.

"Mr. Davar, the warden's assistant, is in charge today. We have his signature right here on this court order."

Amidst the three quarreling guards, Ahrash stood fearful, battling to comprehend the confusing situation. His face was washed of any blood; his hands were shaking and his legs rattled the shackles around them. A short glance at him was long enough for Dawood to understand the sheer terror his friend was experiencing.

"No, I cannot let you take him. You have to wait until I contact Warden Ramzi," Dawood protested again.

"The warden is in surgery at the moment. He is having his appendix removed," one guard explained.

Aware of the imminent danger that Ahrash was in and seething at the slight of his authority, Dawood puffed out his chest, bumping up against the bigger guard. "Still, I cannot let you."

The guard stepped back calmly and made a phone call.

An officer arrived quickly, followed by Mr. Davar himself.

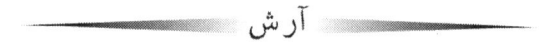

───── آرش ─────

The guards took Ahrash into a room where Sakineh, head to toe in black, was pacing. The grim reaper was poised and ready to take a young life away.

At the sight of Sakineh, Ahrash's horror reached its peak. His face became as white as funeral flowers, his legs like stacks of cotton wool, unable to keep him up right.

The guards carried him forward like a rag doll.

Once Ahrash was at the rope, Sakineh unexpectedly struck him across the face with unfathomable force.

"You are not allowed to do that Ma'am," one guard objected sternly, stepping between Ahrash and his executor. "The victim's parents can only put the noose around the prisoner's neck. You must agree to follow the rules otherwise you have to leave the room."

The guard continued blocking access to Ahrash until the mad woman agreed to cooperate.

Sakineh placed the rope around Ahrash's neck. With a push of a button by the guard, Ahrash was yanked from the ground.

Back in the village

Only a glimmer of hope kept the crowd in place. They wishfully believed that Sakineh was playing a cruel joke just to punish her daughter.

"Are you fools still waiting for Ahrash?" Sakineh shouted at the villagers who could not yet take their eyes off the road. "Believe me – he is dead. I killed him myself," she said, her mouth stretched wide into a depraved smile. "You should have seen me! I was all over his corpse, beating it with my fists, biting into its dirty flesh. Even two big guards couldn't pull me off of him."

Pride was oozing from every pore of Sakineh's skin, as she was reliving her savage act. Her sadistic mind however was not sufficiently appeased yet. She had to finish her narrative with one final blow; she had to cut slices through hearts.

She took a few steps and once again, stood in front of her daughter and Issa.

"The bastard's neck was so thin that he did not die easily. I kept pulling his leg until I saw his eyes bulged out and his blue tongue, as big as my hand, hang from the corner of his mouth," Sakineh described animatedly, letting out a boisterous laugh.

Neloo, folded her face into Issa's chest, bawling.
Issa stood silently, dissolving in a flood of tears.

Sakineh continued talking but the crowd could not bear hearing more. They stepped backward, slowly widening their distance from the monstrous, sinful woman.

Her audience lost, Sakineh slammed the box of money to the ground, where Hajji stood. She straightened her scarf and solidly walked toward her house – victorious.

AUTHOR'S NOTES

I have been to the Kultappa village once when the real-life Ahrash was probably about two years old. I do not remember meeting him or any other character depicted in my novel, except for Sakineh.

A few months after my visit to Kultappa, I permanently moved to the United States.

When I was pregnant with my son, my mother-in-law shared Ahrash's story with me. The boy's saga affected me tremendously. It resided in the deepest folds of my brain and never left me.

Upon retirement, I decided to put pen to paper.

With English as my second language, I traveled a challenging road to complete my novel. But I knew creating this work was the only way to broadly illuminate Ahrash's life experiences.

In the end, I am proud to be a voice for this innocent boy.

———— آرش ————

I made attempts to follow the lives of all the people who were a part of my book, with moderate success. I learned the following:

Sakineh remained married to Sharif. She lived well into her 80s, proudly professing her triumph to anyone who would listen.

(Incidentally, she is the only character I chose to identify by her real name.)

Ali received his paramedic certificate and successfully took over Hakim's position. He later married a local girl and started a family. When Hannah decided to seek a higher education abroad, Ali gladly supported his sister financially.

Issa and Aziz left the village and moved to the city of Tabriz where Issa attended a school for the blind. A couple of years later, he married Shereen. They had four boys; the eldest was named Ahrash.

Neloo became a nurse. She moved to a different region of the country and refused to see Sakineh again. Before the twins started high school, she invited them to live with her. The boys agreed. They successfully finished school and both entered college.

Neloo never married or had any children.

Khalil, unfortunately, was not able to meet any of his grandchildren. He died in his sleep before his family moved to Tabriz. He was only forty-eight years old.

DEATH ROW BOY

NASRIN SADRIAN

ACKNOWLEDGMENTS

I'd like to first acknowledge my late mother-in-law, Batoul, for giving me a window into Ahrash's life and igniting the desire to share his story with the world.

Secondly, tremendous gratitude goes to my husband, Hossein, for his unwavering love and support. Your patience through the long journey of writing my novel deserves admiration. You believed in me and my success and continuously gave me the confidence to reach my goal. I would be remiss if I did not mention your extensive contribution in sharing your knowledge about Kultappa and the customs and the history of its Turkish population – many of the stories in the book stem directly from your anecdotes.

A big thank you also goes to my son, Alex, who has been a constant source of encouragement, cheering me on throughout the process.

And finally, an enormous thank you to my daughter, Heather, my best friend, my writing buddy, and my editor. While I cannot list all the ways you supported me as I created *Death Row Boy,* I will note the amount of time you put into editing and re-editing my words.

Your ability to catch the subtle and not-so-subtle mistakes, to provide taboo-free solutions, and above all to deal with your stubborn mother never ceased to amaze me. You are a dedicated editor and selfless daughter; I am forever indebted to you. <u>Without you there would not exist a book named *Death Row Boy.*</u>

Special thanks must also go to my extended family members and friends who have shown an interest in and have been supportive of my writing – you know who you are!

NASRIN SADRIAN

ABOUT THE AUTHOR

Nasrin Sadrian was born in Tehran, Iran and moved to the United States in 1974. She is a retired educator who lives with her husband in Northern California.

Death Row Boy is her first novel.

Made in the USA
Middletown, DE
09 November 2024